# The Book of Wizzy

# The Book of Wizzy

Ann Chamberlin

**www.penmorepress.com**

The Book of Wizzy by Ann Chamberlin



ISBN-13: 978-1-942756-70-5(Paperback)
ISBN :-978-1-942756-71-2(e-book)

BISAC Subject Headings:
FIC022040 FICTION / Mystery & Detective / Women Sleuths

Editing: Chris Wozney
Cover Illustration by Christine Horner

Address all correspondence to:

Penmore Press LLC
920 N Javelina Pl
Tucson AZ 85748

For Helen

Illustration by Pat Bagley

# Acknowledgments

I would like to thank my critique group of nearly twenty years, The Wasatch Mountain Fiction Writers. My sister Helen, now a professor of microbiology, and Nick and Robbie Snow were my inspiration thirty years ago when the idea first entered my mind. Just living along the Wasatch Front presents daily sparks for plot, and I want to thank my fellow citizens for that.

My dear friends Teddi Kachi and Karen Porcher also deserve special thanks. Teddi, who loves mysteries, heard about this story at the very start and always pushed for it to be written, and Karen listened with helpful attention as I plotted the whole thing on the long drive up from Cedar City.

# Chapter 1

*"Ai, tengo frio."*

Consuela complained of the cold as their skis slid along the road that the snowplow had yet to clear in this outlying cul-de-sac. Cold throbbed off the white walls of ice, which were now packed higher than either woman's head from previous snowfalls.

Brittany knew this was only the second time her co-worker had been on skis, and only the third time she'd seen snow, as she'd spent all thirty-six previous years of her life in Guatemala. But Consuela had no car, no license, probably no green card, and Brittany, who was half her coworker's age, loved to ski. In fact, she had dropped out of the U. for the semester and taken this job cleaning condos in Park City, thinking it would be a step towards her dreams of making the Olympic team. She refused to drive her third-hand clunker when so much fresh powder had fallen during the night, so Consuela had to be a good sport and accept the loan of Brittany's second-best cross-countries, with her best ski skins clipped to the bottom to give excellent traction. Although she wasn't happy about it and had fallen twice, the older woman soldiered on. It wasn't as if they'd traveled the whole way on skis; the two of them had ridden the free city bus to the stop just a block down the hill from the Pine Enterprises-owned triplex at the end of this road.

Brittany's usual co-worker was her best friend since grade school, Sarah Drake, who had been the main spearhead of this Olympic-team scheme, but Sarah's family was wealthy enough to let her call in sick whenever new snow fell, even through their boss had threatened that Sarah might lose this job. That wouldn't bother Sarah, as long as she kept the small rental they shared right in the center of the old mining town. It would leave her more time to ski all day and hunt for rich ski bums each evening in the bars and restaurants that were out of Brittany's price range.

Consuela was a good sport. She needed to be, to keep the job and to send money back to her family. The prospect of the warmth of the condos they would be cleaning helped spur her along on the awkward slats of wood, poling about twenty yards behind Brittany until they reached the triplex.

"The supplies are in this closet here," Brittany showed her companion, after keying into the basement garage that had a space for each condo. "Here are hooks for our coats and spots for the skis and boots."

All three parking spaces were occupied: a full house. There were California plates on Unit C's battered sedan. None of the tenants were scheduled to check out until Monday morning. They were probably all out on the slopes on such a perfect day. Regretfully, Brittany shut the door on the brilliant snow and blue sky outside and, in the garage's funk of motor oil, antifreeze and Ajax, began to load up a carryall of rags and cleansers for each of them.

A door slammed and a commotion began at the far end of the echoing cement cave. Brittany glanced that way and saw what she called a Mormon-mobile: an SUV with space for a large family. Her own family of eight had always had such a conveyance, until she, the youngest, moved out and her parents sold it before they left for their new mission. Sure enough, five or six kids between three and fourteen, followed by their parents, were spilling down the stairwell from the apartment above and making their way to the gumball-blue vehicle. Skis, boots, and bags bumped walls and were slammed into the back of the SUV or into the streamlined carrier on top.

Brittany picked a few comments out of the cacophony of shouts, complaints and tears.

"Why do we have to go so soon?"

"Your sister's got the flu."

"She doesn't have to ski. Just let her stay here and throw up."

Brittany felt a little queasy, thinking of the bathroom upstairs she would have to clean. She could almost smell it from here.

"Evan, how many times do I have to tell you? You are not allowed to play World of Warcraft! It doesn't hold with our values."

"Peggy, I think—"

The eldest son interrupted the father. "Everybody *else* does!"

"You'll be grounded for a week when we get home."

"Aw, Mom, don't you want me to fit in socially?"

"Gretel's forgotten her bunny slippers. Evan, run back and get them."

"I don't know where they are!"

"Go and find them. Somewhere between the bed and the bathroom. That's the only place she went."

"Does this mean I can play World of Warcraft?"

"No!"

The father of this brood began giving directions on how

to pack so as to make use of every square inch.

"Mom, don't we even get to say good-bye to Uncle Boo?"

"Your uncle Boo is still asleep. He was up late last night. Oh. Hello."

This last word was meant for the housekeepers, Brittany and Consuela. Brittany came face to face with the X-ray, her term for women who were too thin for their own good and who managed to present the world a face without an eyelash out of place, even with six kids. Brittany didn't know how such women managed. This one had the leg muscles of a skier, a runner, or both. Her spangly pink ski pants had not seen the slopes on this outing, however.

"Hello, ma'am," Brittany replied. Usually housekeepers were invisible. "Are you leaving us so soon?"

A look of panic crossed the woman's face. The bathroom must really be awful. "Yes, my daughter's sick."

"I'm sorry to hear that. You can check out down the hill at the office—"

"Yes, I know the drill," the woman snapped.

"Have a good day," was the only way to answer such an attitude.

The father, a nondescript man with the fringe to his premature balding already grey, pressed a five on Brittany when they met around the other side of the car. The bathroom must be really, *really* bad.

Brittany tried to thank him, but he put a finger to his lips and nodded in his wife's direction.

"I will take this unit," Consuela offered, heading up the stairs.

"Are you sure? You understand about the, er ...?" She'd be sure to give Consuela the five.

The World of Warcraft aficionado barged his way down the stairwell past them, a pair of small bunny slippers in his hands. "Gross! Mom, they've got barf all over them." The boy dropped the slippers and continued down the stairs.

Brittany cringed.

"Oh, for ...!" The mother turned to one of the girls. "Hannah, would you please ...?"

Another crisis on the garage floor just beside the Mormon-mobile's back door interrupted her plea. Four pairs of stylish snow boots jumped out of the way to groans of "Eww! Gretel!" as their youngest sister threw up yet again. The little girl sputtered and sobbed her misery.

"Hannah!" the mom ordered.

"Why do I always have to?" The girl, too old for her ten or so years, wore ear buds tangled in dangling earrings.

Coming around the car, Brittany got a good look at the sick child. Perhaps it was just the energy-saving bare bulbs in the garage, but the poor thing looked blue. She flopped like a rag doll in her mother's arms as the X-ray hefted her into a car seat. Brittany felt sick herself. She hoped the family hadn't left this medical emergency too long.

Consuela had picked up the pair of pink slippers and returned with them. "Ma'am, here."

They were snatched from her hand. No word of thanks followed as the final doors slammed on "Frank, will you *hurry*?" The garage door slid open, and the Mormon-mobile rolled out onto the snow-covered street, barely missing the plow coming from the other direction.

Brittany's conscience compelled her. "Consuela, maybe we should do this unit together. The little girl was sick. Do you understand?" She did her best to mimic vomiting, and pointed to the mess they'd have to clean off the cement floor behind them before they left.

"Is good," Consuela assured her. "I like when they move out."

"Okay," Brittany let her voice rise with doubt, "but let me know if you need help."

She could hardly believe her luck! The day was looking up, even though it had started out so badly, with Sarah abandoning her for the slopes. Her substitute coworker was taking the worst unit. Brittany wouldn't mind doing both the other condos if it meant avoiding vomit.

And then there was that other thing: Dave Jaramillo in Unit B. He was one of the millionaire ski bums Sarah was always so keen to cultivate. They had met him several times, as he lived in the condo year round. Enough time for Sarah to get a good crush on him—and to claim Unit B as her own personal cleaning operation.

"Only I know how to do it the way he likes it," she'd say, ignoring, or perhaps oblivious to the double entendre.

Brittany was used to letting her friend take first dibs on the guys they met and contenting herself with the leftovers. An Olympic star didn't really have time for boyfriends, anyway. But Brittany had always nursed a 'Dave crush' of her own, one that she didn't dare express with Sarah around. Now the unit was hers—at least for the half hour or so that it would take to clean.

Her heart beat a little faster. She would have to make his bed. Her parents would turn right around from their mission in California if they knew what their baby was doing.

"Housekeeping," Brittany called, knocking on the door as she let herself in.

Dave wasn't there, of course. He'd be out skiing.

Brittany set down her carry-all and walked through the quiet apartment, just to take in the smell of Dave Jaramillo, the natural olive oil soap he liked, and ... and a strange smell of poached eggs. Burnt poached eggs.

She didn't want to face the bedroom just yet, so she just lingered over the computer, the electronic keyboard and headphones, the sink full of dishes, the lack of fast food wrappers in the trash, the rice cooker that she would have to clean. She didn't mind; a man who did his own cooking, brown rice and lentils, was a pleasure to clean up after.

Strangely, some of the lights were on. For a man who always complained about the coal-fired power plants making the air in the Salt Lake Valley below them unbreatheable, that was very odd. She walked toward the illuminated living room, with its wall of glass beyond which was the deck, and a magnificent view of the rising, snow-covered mountain that made the units so popular.

As she turned off the lights, she remembered a story that one of the other housekeepers had told. She had been working in the resort at Glacier National Park. In the half-light of an empty hotel bedroom, the woman had discovered a strange, baby-sized lump lying deathly still under the blankets, and a terrible odor. She'd had to call in reinforcements before they dared pull back the covers—to discover a bundle of off-smelling trout that the guests had left behind.

In the brief three weeks that she'd been working this job, Brittany had found her share of disgusting things, as bad as what Consuela must be facing next door. Things like used condoms in the bottom of the bed—another thing her parents would fly back from California to spare her from. They probably didn't even know she knew what condoms were.

Sarah's complaint on that occasion—"Don't these people have any sense of shame?"—Brittany had answered with a quiet, "In front of us? Their condo housekeepers?"

But Dave had strong morals, and not just about energy conservation. He'd told the housekeepers about them right off the bat. Brittany wasn't sure her parents would approve, but her dream world didn't contain that sort of conflict. Dave was a vegetarian and super eco-conscious. He provided his own organic cleaning supplies for them to use. In Brittany's dream world, he would never have had sex with someone other than her, protected or otherwise. Not even with Sarah.

She reached the tall glass doors that slid open onto the breathtaking view: tall, ermined pines and boulders wearing pointy hats of snow. She put her hand on the chilled pane, noting with curiosity that two pairs of ski tracks slid down through the night's fall of snow from the empty mountainside.

On the deck, steam rose from the hot tub. Somebody, she saw, had shoveled the snow from the redwood boards. The shovel, clotted with snow, stood by the door to Unit C. All three units shared the deck and the tub, but nobody was out there now, not today when the newly laden slopes beckoned—or an emergency appointment with a pediatrician compelled.

No beer bottles, no crumpled towels. It didn't look like the deck would require much work.

"*Ai, qué lío.*"

Consuela's complaint about the mess next door reminded Brittany she had a job to do. She was about to turn away when a dark shadow, half-glimpsed through the steam of the tub, caught her attention. She looked closer. Someone seemed to be floating in the water. She slid open the door and stepped out.

The smell like burnt poached eggs overwhelmed her nose, crowding out what should have been the fresh alpine fragrance.

The person in the hot tub seemed poised to climb out, hand on the metal rail. Brittany recognized the green Hawaiian-print swim trunks. She'd seen them hanging on the shower knob a couple of mornings before, and Sarah had gotten to move them before applying the organic cleansing spray Dave kept beneath the bathroom sink.

Brittany waited through two deep breaths of the stewy smell. The body did not rise. Nobody could hold his breath that long, not even Dave, who was in such good shape.

She screamed.

# Chapter 2

Helen Snow sat outside the bishop's office across from the regulation-issue Heinrich Hofmann print of Jesus hanging on the regulation-issue green-tint wall. Bishop Irvine, who was perhaps all of forty—ten years her junior—and who looked and behaved as if he were even younger, had ordered her to attend him at nine AM this wintry Saturday morning, and she had arrived early. The storm had blown the choking inversion out of the Salt Lake Valley, and Helen would have preferred to be out walking Jinx, the dog. Yet here she was.

Helen couldn't meet the Jesus eyes. The same picture, supposed to be glowing with compassion, had hung over a different bishop, backing him up, when Helen and her husband Mark had gone for counseling all those years ago. Helen remembered the bundle of their newborn daughter Elizabeth in her arms; they had spoken over the little one.

"We cannot always understand the ways of God," Helen remembered that bishop saying, "but it is quite clear there can only be two reasons for this. When a child dies before its parents, or when it is born with such a handicap as yours has, either it has done something wrong in the Pre-Existence or the parents have sinned. You need to search your souls and repent for what you have done. And I would counsel putting your daughter in some sort of facility for the rest of her days so you can concentrate on giving your boys a normal life."

He had been alluding to Elizabeth's Down syndrome.

Helen remembered her arms closing on that bundle in the bishop's office as if she would crush the tiny frame with her desire to protect Elizabeth—her Lizzy, or, as the child's older twin brothers soon christened her—Wizzy. All the while Helen had had to smile bravely back at the authority and the mass print of Jesus.

Mark hadn't touched her in the eighteen years since. As if the love that had created Wizzy were the sin. Helen knew her husband was hurting in a terrible way: hurting that his priesthood had not been strong enough to bless that pregnancy with perfection, hurting that he was not a man worthy of a better wife and child. She had tried to salve that hurt, putting on the faithful front, being the obedient wife, reaching out to him, even suggesting more counseling—not in the bishop's office. With someone who had actual training.

But Mark saw counseling as further proof of weakness, only for people whose faith wasn't strong enough. He had focused instead, as the bishop had advised, on the boys, especially on the strong, healthy bodies born of male sports. He was an excellent father—for the boys.

Divorce had been out of the question. No matter how painful the distance between them had become,

Helen was glad Mark's sense of faith forbade divorce. Dissolution of their temple marriage would bar Helen from the Celestial Kingdom for all eternity, from seeing Wizzy in the Afterlife.

Three years after Wizzy's birth, the same glowing, mass-produced Jesus had looked down on Helen in the chapel foyer as she had fled from the tiny casket smothered in the yellow roses that Wizzy had liked best. Fled from the funeral sermon where another, different bishop had said, "Such children are the blessed of God. Their proper minds restored, they have gone directly to the Celestial Kingdom where they wait for their parents. Their parents, if they live righteous lives, will be granted the privilege of raising these blessed spirits in the next life. If not, these little souls will be given to others, more righteous, to raise."

That's when Helen's sobs, even on those massive doses of drugs the M.D./bishop had prescribed, had become so violent that she'd lurched to her feet, crashing into the casket on its wheeled base and fleeing the scene.

The sermon's words had followed her up the aisle:

"Those who weep uncontrollably at the loss of a loved one are those who do not have a proper understanding of God's plan as I've just outlined it for you. O ye of little faith."

In the foyer had been that same Jesus, who was supposed to be Compassion incarnate. Helen had gone farther into the bowels of the ward house where the smell of funeral potatoes and ham nearly made her vomit, vomit up all those damned worthless mood enhancers. No one had come after her to preach more forbearance, thank God. They all acted as if her lack of faith might rub off on them, just as that antibacterial-immune bug in the hospital had rubbed off on Wizzy during a well-baby visit.

In that darkened corner of the building, away from the Hoffmann Christ, there had been a print of Mary by some artist whose name Helen still didn't know. Mormons weren't comfortable calling this woman "Virgin". You'd have to explain to your virgins what "virgin" meant, as if you had to be ashamed of it. You couldn't call her "Mother of God" either. Just plain Mary. But Mary, at least, understood what it was to be a mother. She knew what it was to have a child die. And nobody was accusing her of being less than perfect.

Helen knew this was heretical thinking. Worse, it was probably Catholic. But that had been the last time she had "Amen"ed "in the Name of Jesus Christ".

The only way she had been able to face the Hoffmann Christ since had been to set Wizzy's squinty, "deformed" eyes in that face. Those eyes had only looked up at her, never down on her, with perfect acceptance and love.

In all the fifteen years since Wizzy's death, the only church calling Helen had held was as Primary pianist. For all fifteen years. Some busybodies, meaning only the best, had suggested that being with the little kids wasn't good for Helen's healing. She felt just the opposite. At the piano, she could close her eyes and remember how Wizzy had loved to lean against the spinet at home while Helen played.

And yet, Helen had to admit she was ready for something, some change, some purpose in her life now that her sons were on their missions, her sister

Karen on a mission, her niece Brittany moved to Park City. Over the years, Helen's sense of the constant presence of her lost child had transformed her grief into a sort of trust that she had never found the words for, nor heard described by others. That trust had been making her, in recent months, feel poised to tackle something big, lest she risk heavenly condemnation for having buried her talents. What her talents were, however, she wasn't quite sure. Could a demanding calling possibly be the answer?

The Bishop had said, over the phone, that he had prayed over the task of finding a replacement Relief Society president, implying that, unlikely as it seemed, she was the answer to his prayers. Was this right, to accept a calling as Relief Society president? Today? To plunge in way up over her head?

"If it is right, I shall cause that your bosom shall burn," said *The Doctrine and Covenants*. The old joke about this verse crossed Helen's mind—that it referred to Sister Jones's chili and not to the promptings of the Holy Ghost.

Helen's bosom was not burning. Her stomach was churning with dread. Was this the nudging from the Holy Ghost? How did one tell? Especially—and here was the problem—when the divine whisperings she heard were in opposition to authority, the authority of her husband and of the bishop?

Was it a mistake in the theology that insisted an all-seeing God was compassionately guiding the lives of his children? Helen had seen all too often that what the deluded called the Holy Ghost had led them to polygamy, to abuse, to purchase the snowmobile that led to bankruptcy, to shooting rampages. These were the "inspirations" that manifested themselves;

everything else manifested as blind obedience.

In most Mormons' books, obedience trumped personal revelation every time.

Helen didn't speak in church. She never stood to bear her testimony. Pianists didn't have to deal in words.

"In the beginning was the Word, and the Word was with God, and the Word was God." So begins the Gospel of John.

But Wizzy had never learned words. The whole three years of the child's existence on earth, Helen had found music the best way to communicate with her daughter. The music they shared—piano music, church hymns, songs sung and songs on the radio— had seemed primal, less subject to misinterpretation, to exploitation, than words. Like breathing.

And for the past fifteen years, providing the incidental music in Primary, Helen could play what she liked. As long as she shoved tempo and harmony in Bach's direction, she could play her favorites, Wizzy's favorites: African-American spirituals like "Sometimes I Feel Like a Motherless Child" and "A Man of Constant Sorrow". She always gave "O My Father" four verses instead of the three it had been reduced to in her lifetime to avoid the verse that said, "Truth eternal tells me I've a Mother there."

Church leaders had been content to leave her at that for many years ... just grateful, she supposed, that she wasn't more trouble. But now, as the Scripture said, "There arose up a new king in Egypt, which knew not Joseph."

Shouldn't that be "who"? The Bible was "The word of God" only as far as it was translated correctly.

Wasn't that the rub? Translated—or edited ... or censored.

* * * * *

Last week had been the Farewell for Helen's sister Karen and her husband LeMar. They'd been called to preside over the California Anaheim mission. Leave it to Karen to get the Disneyland precinct.

Walt Disney himself had converted to Mormonism shortly before his death—or shortly thereafter, according to faith-promoting revelation, which Karen had repeated in her farewell sermon. Disney had liked to hire Mormons to upper management, and they would have known how to manage a happy ending.

For the past three years, Karen had been Relief Society president of the ward in the East Millcreek neighborhood of Salt Lake City where both their families lived. Relief Society president was the highest church calling a woman could hold at the local level. Helen had been quite content to sit in her sister's shadow.

Sometimes Helen thought sitting in the shadow of the perfect faith that blessed Karen with her perfect husband and six perfect children was as close as she herself could come to the righteousness she'd been told she lacked.

Helen had never refused a calling in her life, but if the words "Relief Society president" came out of Bishop Irvine's mouth, she would have to suspect this new bishop's gift of revelation was tainted by faith-based science; he must have figured the skills for the job were genetic. Living in the same ward as an over-achieving sibling did have its drawbacks.

# THE BOOK OF WIZZY

Relief Society president was a massive undertaking, since it was well known in the church that men held the power and women did the work. Bishop Irvine, *new* Bishop Irvine, had requested that Helen's husband Mark attend this meeting, as was regulation. The head of a household had to give his approval if his wife was going to be gone running compassionate service eighteen hours a day. Having parked the car after dropping her off at the door, Mark now sat obediently beside her. He was smaller than she was, which Helen knew always made people uncomfortable to look at them. They sat in silence. After twenty-five years of marriage, since Wizzy's death—since her birth—they had nothing to say to each other. Especially not now, when his burning bosom conflicted with hers.

The inspiration Helen had come to believe in for solving life's problems was something she called *The Book of Wizzy*. It had gotten her through the last fifteen years. It worked in the same way that she used to know just what song Wizzy wanted to hear on the piano: she just *knew*. Now, when she wasn't being assigned to play other people's choices, the song that came into Helen's head at any given time seemed to be the best possible guide, clearing away any stupor of thought. She was beginning to trust them more and more, these communications from her daughter beyond the grave.

Now this. She fought against the panic in her heart and listened to the tune playing in her head as she sat under the Hoffmann Jesus. Unusual for Wizzy, it was in fact a hymn. Number 193: "I Stand All Amazed". A hymn couldn't be too off base for the priesthood, could it? She could have been hearing "Amazing

Grace" channeled from her daughter, which, yes, the Mormon Tabernacle Choir did sing, but which was not in the hymn book. Too much "grace over works". Mormons were nothing if not believers in "faith without works is dead."

Being Relief Society president would be work. Karen had demonstrated that. Helen's mind wandered to consideration of what would Karen do if she were sitting in this same place. Helen knew what Karen would do. She wouldn't hesitate a moment before saying piously, "Thy will be done."

Right now, Karen was probably hearing "It's a Small World". The world from Anaheim to Zimbabwe was full of happy little people who only needed to be wound up on Mormonism to get them goose-stepping to the same beat.

Oh, great. Now "It's a Small World" had taken over in Helen's mind. But Wizzy's world, contrary to what so many thought, had been anything but small.

No, here was "I Stand All Amazed" back again. What did it mean? And how would authority think of the way she'd always replaced the name Wizzy for Jesus in the opening line, "I stand all amazed at the love Wizzy offers me"? How would they feel about how Wizzy had helped Helen remove the guilt from the verses? Not pleased. Not pleased at all.

The bishop's door opened. Barney, the ward clerk, invited them in, but Bishop Irvine came barging out past the clerk and caught Mark by the hand. "Mark, come in, come in." For her, a nod and a more distant, "Sister Snow."

If she was going to take on such a huge task, Helen did not like to receive second billing. Fortunately, her cell phone rang just then. *Saved by the bell*, she thought. The tune was Christmasy: "Winter Wonderland". Just right for a kid who was crazy about skiing. It was Brittany.

"After you, Sister Snow," the bishop invited her in to his office.

"Turn the phone off, Helen," Mark told her.

Both men stood aside to let her enter. So did wardens when they ushered a prisoner into lock-up.

The phone stopped ringing. The regulation-issue wooden bishop's desk yawned before her, amazingly uncluttered for such a task as running a ward. Remembering Karen's work load, Helen realized that much of the clutter ended up on the Relief Society president's kitchen table. More than once she had thought that Karen had jumped at the chance to be "mother of the mission" in California so she could enjoy a table unburdened by visiting teaching lists, faith-promoting Strawberry Shortcake stickers, dill pickle recipes and empty funeral potato dishes waiting to be returned to their originating homes.

Helen did not look forward to her own kitchen turning into that.

Hoffmann's Jesus looked down on her. Wizzy's eyes.

The word "confused" starting hymn 193's second line leapt out at her.

Her phone started ringing again.

*The Book of Wizzy* sang, "Oh, it is wonderful."

"Winter Wonderland" was wonderful. Like when Helen had been on the mood enhancers and suddenly went cold turkey. Stupor gone.

"Excuse me. I'd really better take this call."

Helen stepped back from the bishop's door. She knew without a doubt that she should listen to Wizzy's spirit. Only then could Helen be of service as she craved to be. Only then.

"Helen, this is the bishop," Mark urged.

"And this is Brittany. You know my niece," she explained to the church authority. "Karen's daughter, who just graduated from high school last year?"

"What I've noticed," the bishop said, "when the attendance rolls have been presented to me, is that the girl has not been coming to her meetings. You will have to fellowship her."

His first order, based on ignorance.

"Brittany has moved up to Park City," Helen explained, reining in her impatience. "She attends up there."

The bishop's well-scrubbed face darkened, and Helen knew she had to play to his ego to make him think he was competent in his calling. That was part of her calling as a woman in the Mormon Church ... a calling that Karen would not have failed in.

"I've been charged to keep a particular eye on her while her parents are on their mission," she said—and answered the phone.

Brittany. In all Helen's attempts to emulate her sister, she would not have named a daughter that. Who could see the name Brittany Bingham on a dissertation in microbiology? Helen would have chosen a name like—well, like Elizabeth. But Brittany it was. Shortly after Wizzy's death, when preparing to lead the Young Women on a week's retreat to St. George (Young Women's president, such a plum calling), Karen had tentatively asked if she could leave three-year-old Brittany in Helen's care.

"I could always ask the Relief Society president instead," she'd suggested.

"No. No, I'd be happy to," Helen had been surprised to hear herself say. She had still felt numb from loss. But that was the last mood enhancer she'd taken. She'd wanted her best wits about her with the new gift she'd been granted. Just for a week.

Of course, it wasn't just that week. Over the years, with five older brothers and sisters, and all of Karen and LeMar's church responsibilities, Brittany often turned to her aunt for the support and attention she was unlikely to get at home. Helen secretly came to think she had raised her niece.

Karen and LeMar, as Helen's departed father had liked to say, "aren't just active members of the Church; they're hyperactive." But he never said that in their hearing. Punning could be seen as heresy, twisting words to mean something other than what God intended. But that hyperactivity had left room for Helen and Brittany.

Brittany didn't replace Wizzy. Nothing could replace angelic, sinless Wizzy. Nevertheless, Helen had attended Brittany's every ballet recital, accompanied every performance on the flute. There had been a hundred batches of home-baked cookies after school, a hundred walks around the neighborhood on cooling summer evenings, arm in arm, smelling the barbecues, running through the sprinklers that infringed on the sidewalks, talking. Girl talk. Stuff Brittany couldn't bring up with her parents because it wasn't "in the program". Like what it meant to be a virgin.

But Brittany was almost grown now, and so into this skiing. *She doesn't get that from me,* Helen knew.

Brittany was a name for a skier, a name to run on that little bar at the bottom of the TV screen when the news was full of sports, so Karen and LeMar had had more influence on the girl after all, just by naming her. And they had never asked Helen to drive her niece to any ski meet; they liked the slopes, too.

But it wasn't her mother Brittany turned to now.

The men in the bishop's office shrugged at each other helplessly. Still, they seemed content to engage in men's small talk with the clerk, slapping each other on the back and congratulating each other for being at the center of God's plan. The plan at the moment seemed to be heavy into potlatch, like the ceremonies of the Northwest native tribes where chieftains tried to outdo each other in gift-giving and conspicuous consumption. These men were vying in what they would give the "little woman" or "my lovely bride" for Christmas: jewelry mostly, to make her an even more valuable object to hang on his arm, an advertisement of his own success.

Mark said nothing. Of course he couldn't, not with her within earshot and disobediently answering the phone.

"Brittany!" Helen moved further out into the darkened hall. The *thunk-thunk-thunk* of a basketball game in progress came to her from the cultural hall's open door. "How are you, dear?"

Helen strained to listen over the game. The poor girl was choking with tears, rattling confusedly of vomit in the garage, Sarah being missing. A dead man.

"Where? What? No. No, that can't be. And you found him? Baby, it's okay. It's going to be okay. Are the police there? Okay, sorry, it's a sheriff in Summit County. You haven't called them? You called me first?"

In spite of the girl's panic and her own, Helen couldn't suppress a bit of gratification that her niece thought of her before she thought of male authority figures.

"Well, call them now," she said, the moment the thought had passed. "Now. You hear me? And you've watched enough *CSI*. Don't touch anything."

Helen listened patiently. "You're right. Probably just an unfortunate accident. Drowned in his own hot-tub. But we have to be sure."

She listened again, then said, "Baby, I'll be there as fast as I can. Twenty minutes. Maybe thirty with the snow, but as fast as I can. Call the police—the sheriff. Get Consuela to be with you and just sit tight. First right turn after the resort sign on 224. Gotcha. I should be able to see the emergency vehicles after that. It'll be all right. I love you, Baby. God loves you."

Helen straightened her spine and turned to face the brethren. "Mark," she said. "The keys."

"What?"

"The car keys. You can walk home."

"But the bishop! Your calling!"

"Now, Lorenzo Mark Snow."

At the mention of his dreaded first name—fifth prophet, seer and revelator of the Church and Mark's sixth-great-grandfather—Mark forgot all about the show of who was boss for the bishop. He dropped the keys into her open palm.

"I'm going to Park City," Helen explained. "Emergency. I'll call and fill you in on my way up Parley's Canyon."

A dumbfounded silence from the men made her think she ought to say something ... "I'll pray for you." And she shoved out the ward house door.

Michael Monarch's driving guitar from "Born to Be Wild" thrummed in her head. *Get your motor running* followed Helen to her staid Ford Flex.

# Chapter 3

The drive took longer than half an hour. Just past the summit, a semi with two refrigerator trailers barreling down from Wyoming like arctic air had jack-knifed in the snow, closing all but one lane. That one lane, barely plowed, was clogged with cars sporting California plates and no snow tires. By the time Helen turned off Route 224, all of Summit County's finest—those not attending to frozen holiday turkeys or LA film stars playing bumper cars on the freeway—had firmly established themselves around Pine Enterprises' trio of condominiums at the end of the cul-de-sac.

As she stepped out of the warm car, Helen realized that she was still dressed in her Sunday best for an interview with the bishop for the calling of Relief Society president. She felt like a movie star herself, foolishly unprepared for a set that hadn't been tailored for her comfort and safety.

On heels, albeit sensible ones, Helen teetered across new snow pounded to ice by many emergency vehicles. She made the trek to the first cop car and string of yellow tape, under the silent glare of law enforcement eyes blackened of all emotion by mirror sunglasses.

"Excuse me," Helen said politely, "I think my niece is the person who found the body, and she's a little—"

Probably the eyes behind those glasses narrowed with suspicion.

"Body?" The black jacket cinched in at the waist, and the belt holding a gun, holster, night stick, cuffs and who-knew-what else, did nothing at all for the figure of the female sheriff's deputy who strode to meet her. Or rather, it did a little too much. "How do you know there's a body?"

"The phone." Helen produced the evidence from her pocket. "My niece ... she's only seventeen. A minor. I think she needs—"

"That's a good one. Never heard that excuse from a snoopy reporter before."

"I'm not a reporter." Helen bristled with indignation and eyed the official patch, just at breast height. The name "Moody" seemed all too fitting. She groped for her next line, then found: "I'm a Relief Society president."

"Even better."

In dire need of gloss, the female law enforcer's chapped lips were struggling to suppress a guffaw. Well, it assured Helen that her little lie would be overlooked. Besides, who in her family had ever said "No" to any calling? It wasn't a lie, just jumping the gun a little, she told herself. Karen, of course, would never lie.

"Jumping the gun" seemed a bad turn of phrase under the circumstances. Even more so when the gun-weighted hips swung at her threateningly and Deputy Moody added, "I'll give this to you, you're the first of your kind on the scene. What are you? *The Deseret News*? They tell their reporters to gain access with that Relief Society line now? Every other reporter seems to be finding the jack-knifed semi at the summit a better photo op."

Standing with hands on those hips was not a good fashion statement, either, Helen reflected. Being defensive made her judgmental in a way that felt uncomfortable. She had already noticed the officer's ringless left hand. If Helen really cared about this woman as a child of God, as Karen would, she would win her way by offering helpful hints. She would know the latest diets, have a gym recommendation, even know how to suggest such things tactfully, intimately. Karen would make it clear that no marriage prospects would be forthcoming without a complete makeover. Probably even a change of career. What man wanted the mother of his children putting her safety on the line every day?

Something in Deputy Moody's voice, glib though the words were, made Helen very glad she had come up the canyon. Something serious was indeed going on behind that tape. The Spanish "Cuidado", black on yellow twisting against the pristine snow in the cold wind, was the only word she saw between the police cruiser—correction, Sheriff's cruiser—and the "Incident Management" van. Besides, Helen had actually had a job at the *Salt Lake Tribune* for a while, straight out of college with her journalism degree. She'd only ever written obits, hoping to work her way up out of the cemeteries, but children had intervened. Still, she thought she would have made a good reporter, always asking the probing question.

Or maybe, alas, all she was good for was Relief

Society president.

"Lord, I Can't Stay Here by Myself" was the tune in Helen's head.

The phone still lay in her hand and she used it. She explained the situation to a tearful Brittany, said she'd pray for her, then stood looking over the fences poking out of snow-covered farm fields and wondering what to do next. Helen knew she'd never hear the end of it if she returned the car keys to Mark without even having seen their niece.

Back at the tapeline, she watched two deputies come and go from the incident van, then a third undertook an exchange with Deputy Moody, who pointed in Helen's direction. The two nodded at each other, then Moody passed under the tape—they must practice how to do that without getting those gun belts caught on the plastic—and strode toward her.

"Helen Snow?"

For a moment, Helen was too stunned to answer.

"*Sister* Snow?"

How the deputy said it suggested that, although familiar with the ways of the tribe among which she lived, she herself was not "hyperactive". No doubt in her line of work, she had seen plenty to convince her that living right did not always keep bad things from happening to you.

Helen stopped being stunned and worked for compassion instead. "Yes?"

"Come on in. The sergeant needs your niece to give the best evidence she can, and she seems too distraught at the moment."

Helen wanted to feel relief, but it didn't rise. She was too worried about Brittany.

"And just so you know," Deputy Moody advised as she lifted the tape for Helen to pass under, "her license says your niece has had her birthday. She's eighteen. You can't claim her as a minor anymore."

Belatedly, Helen realized her mistake. They'd celebrated the event early because of Brittany's parents leaving for the mission field, and Helen still had it in her mind that the big milestone was in the future. This did not bode well for a calling that included making sure that every woman in the ward got a faith-promoting card on her special day. At this rate, what other lies would Helen tell before the day was out?

"Here." Helen handed Deputy Moody the spare tube of lip-gloss—medicated, cherry flavored—that she always carried in her purse. She still toted a bag almost as big as the one she'd had for Wizzy. The things she carried now were different from the diapers, change of little-girl clothes, and monkey-faced Tupperware tub of Cheerios: all those things, which, in the end, had failed to save her daughter. But Helen still wanted to be prepared for any situation, hoping each time that something she carried would be just what was needed to ease a life, if not save it.

The deputy stopped chewing her lip. "Gee. Thanks."
Helen would mention the hands-on-hips stance another time. With that thought, she entered the scene of the accident. Or had it been a crime?

*****

A strangely conflicted wet smell of burned flesh

29

permeated the air as Helen Snow sat holding her niece's hand in the dead young man's living room. They sat side by side on a very comfortable leather couch.

"Only it isn't leather, Aunt Helen," Brittany assured her, when she commented. "Dave was a vegetarian. He wouldn't have leather. It's too cruel to animals." Brittany was babbling with fear and nerves.

Dave? Helen studied her niece. That was not what a girl called the average young man she cleaned house for. Just what was going on here? Something that Karen didn't know about, Helen was suddenly sure of that.

A vegetarian.

Helen threw off the thought that such a life choice might have deserved a death sentence. She had heard LeMar call anyone who refused a slab of roast at Chuck o' Rama an apostate. Her brother-in-law also held that the scriptural Word of Wisdom's "meat in moderation" meant "in moderation at lunch and dinner and only four slices of bacon at a weekday breakfast." One had to consider, said this same self-confident authority, the context in which that section of the canon was revealed. In those days, when people had to kill their own meat, moderation was a necessity born of scarcity and the labor-intensive nature of hunting under the primitive conditions of the times. Now the only time men had to stalk and shoot their prey was the annual deer hunt, and then of course you got others to butcher and pack your trophies for the freezer.

This young man would never have fit in at Fourth of July grills. Or at a Mormon funeral—all that ham. Helen remembered the smell of ham and yellow roses that had pursued her to the dark corner of the ward house where she'd gone to cry the tears no good Mormon ever cries at a funeral, not even for a three-year-old daughter. The old Gospel song "Death, O Death" hummed tremblingly from *The Book of Wizzy.*

This wet ashes, burnt flesh smell... like the end of a camp-out when the fire had been drowned. It was a the sort of smell that made vegetarianism seem appealing. Helen sympathized with the young man—and with her niece, who sat beside her, shuddering and taking gasping breaths.

The sheriff sergeant had told them to "hang on a few minutes" while he and his deputies continued their investigation. Out on the deck, a sheet-shrouded gurney bore the body of the young man Helen had never met. The wind had tugged a corner of the sheet loose. A hand extended from the cover, clutching at air.

The Oscar Meyer wiener song. The thought was terrible, but it had been one of Wizzy's favorites.

> ... 'Cause if I were an Oscar Meyer wiener
> Everyone would be in love with me.

The dead man's fingers, Helen thought, looked as if they were hot dogs that had been too long on Mark's summer grill. Sheriff's deputies were draining the hot tub. Looking for clues, she supposed.

Brittany wore snug jeans and an attractive turtleneck. Such a pretty girl, every bit as pretty as Karen had been at that age. Too bad Brittany had to take such a job, exposed to such unpleasantness. The bright pink smock and the Pine Enterprises logo that included a snow-dusted Christmas tree embroidered on the shirt was at odds with the girl's obvious distress. Karen would urge her daughter to get another job, just to get out of that unflattering uniform. But Karen hadn't bothered to learn enough about this job to know that it entailed pink smocks.

Helen looked around. "Didn't you say you have a friend, a co-worker? Where is—?"

"Hush, Aunt Helen!"

"What?"

"Consuela is undocumented."

"You mean illegal?" Helen couldn't hide her surprise.

"The minute I mentioned the police, she left. She didn't even take the skis. She doesn't like them anyway." Brittany dropped her voice. "How will I get two pairs of skis home?" Then even lower, "I hope Consuela's okay."

Helen was touched that her niece, who'd just had the shock of her young life, could feel compassion for another. Then sudden alarm made her ask, "You don't think she might be responsible for—?" Helen bent her head slightly in the direction of the shrouded figure on the deck, and the hot tub still steaming against the snowy mountainside.

"Consuela? Sweet Consuela?" Brittany was indignant. "Never. She'd never even been to this condominium before this morning. She just didn't want to meet the sheriff, that's all."

"And now her ski marks are pretty well obscured by the sheriff's vehicles."

Brittany shrugged, settling back into the couch in an attempt to project calm.

Helen noticed a row of photos on the mantel showing a handsome young man with gentle eyes in different clusters of friends and family: on the slopes, best man at a wedding, with an older man and a pudgy older girl buried in life vests for a river run. So full of life, so happy. Nothing at all to do with the shrouded figure out on the deck. Still, at some point Helen would have to remind her niece that he had not been the returned missionary type every Mormon girl was supposed to be waiting for. Karen would probably pronounce it good that he was ... out of the picture, so to speak.

Helen also noticed that the digital clock on the fancy sound system was blinking on and off, a red "12:00".

"Did the young man ... Dave, I think you said?"

Brittany nodded.

"Did Dave have anything wrong with his hands? A congenital disfiguration or something?"

"No. Dave was ... Dave was perfect."

Helen handed her niece a tissue from the depths of her handbag. Such a youthful word, that "perfect".

To change the subject, Helen pointed out the wall of glass sliding doors that the couch faced, to take in the view. A steep, breath-taking mountainside of boulders and pines blocked out any glimpse of the sky from Helen's angle. Across that landscape ran two pairs of parallel lines, the tracks of skis leading directly to and from the deck. "What about those marks? Ski marks, I suppose they are?"

Brittany avoided looking directly in that direction. "I don't know. They were there when we came. We came in from the road."

"That's last night's snow. That finished falling ... what? About ten o'clock? Eleven up here?"

"I don't know. I was home, fast asleep after cleaning all day."

"I'd say this makes a perfect closed manor house case," Helen mused. "You said yours was the first trail on the road. The plow hadn't even been by yet. You said there was a family with lots of kids in the first unit. Who's in the other one?"

"Aunt Helen, it doesn't matter."

"I think it does matter. The culprit must have been overnight in one of these units."

"Aunt Helen, there is no culprit."

"What about those marks?"

Helen's pointing arm nearly swiped the pistol off Deputy Moody's ample hip. The law enforcer had been relieved of her cold post at the barricade tape and had come in to take Brittany's statement. She had moved so silently over the thick carpet that Helen had not heard her approach.

"Your niece is right, Sister Snow," the deputy said. "There is no culprit. We're treating this as an unfortunate accident."

Helen wondered how much else the deputy had heard. She did notice with gratification that the woman's appearance was improved by the cherry lip-gloss; one good deed done here, anyway.

Deputy Moody joined them on the faux leather couch, sitting uncomfortably with her over-burdened hips. As part of the change in the guard, two EMTs went out on the deck to claim the gurney and its grim burden for their ambulance. The older technician adjusted the sheet so the dreadful, blackened hand was no longer visible.

"What about that hand?" Helen challenged the woman deputy.

All three of them paused to watch the burden being wheeled through the living room, incongruous in surroundings that spoke of such vibrant, young life.

Deputy Moody swallowed, then nodded. "It looks like electrocution. Accidental. It happens—especially when people mix drinking with home entertainment."

"Not drowning, then."

That explained the terrible smell, and the strangely blackened hand. Helen felt somehow vindicated for her observation. At the same time, she was finding this a quandary that cut to her soul. Why had she been so set on discovering that this young man's death was a murder, anyway?

Was she in thrall to a conspiracy theory? It had been her secret belief, ever since Wizzy's death, that she could detect and dismiss anything that smacked of trumped-up conspiracy theory. Allegations and accusations thick with paranoia came fast and furious over the pulpit, spoken in tones which assured that damnation waited for anyone who disbelieved. Fluoride in the water was a control scheme of big government. Health care was a communist plot. School shootings were caused not by people exercising their right to bear arms but by gay rights advocates. Evil groups from al-Qaeda to Black Panthers were known to have maps showing the home of every Mormon, so that when they took over the country, they would know exactly where to go to steal the year's supply of food and leave the faithful to starve. Had Helen, by throwing stones at such believers, even if only in her mind, condemned herself to the same sin?

She certainly felt for this young man's mother, whomever she might be, who must soon learn the worst and get hit with the thought that it was somehow her fault, something she had done. Helen clung to compassion to exorcise the other thoughts.

"He reached for the metal handrail," the deputy was saying, "and the electric current that was in the water suddenly leapt, making his body a ground wire. It probably stopped his heart instantly. He couldn't have pulled his hand away from the rail if he'd wanted to."

"Yes, that's what it looked like ... when I ... when I saw him," Brittany said, growing pale again at the description of her young man's struggle in the last seconds of life. Helen squeezed her hand, but her niece quickly pulled herself together. "But ... 'current in the water'?"

"You know you need to be careful when cleaning bathrooms," Deputy Moody said. "No blow driers in the shower, that sort of thing. Water and electricity, a deadly combination."

Brittany nodded, but frowned.

"We suspect faulty wiring. The lights, the pump, the jets: lots of things to go wrong in a hot tub."

Helen had never been in such a frivolous device as a hot tub and now was certain she never would. Its unnerving similarity to a Mormon baptismal font did not help.

Beside her, Brittany shivered. "But the building is so new—so easy to clean—"

"That man's the electrician." Deputy Moody pointed out the only person in the crowded room whose dark jump-suit uniform did not have *Summit Sheriff* printed on it. "We've called him in to check. That's why the fellows had to empty the tub."

It all made perfect sense. With Deputy Moody's encouragement, Brittany began to make her statement, reciting all that she'd already told Helen over the phone and while they waited. She left out only her co-worker, the illegal Consuela.

Helen felt that her presence was hardly needed, Brittany showed so much composure. Helen was proud of her.

But ... Helen did want the authorities to know the whole truth. (How many times had she heard LeMar holding forth on "illegals"?) She didn't feel good about ratting the poor woman out, however. Just then, in silent confirmation of her reservations, Hymn 29 entered her mind: "A Poor Wayfaring Man of Grief".

Nonetheless, she opened her mouth. "Brittany, dear, don't you think you ought to tell the deputy about...?"

Deputy Moody rebuffed her. "Please, Sister Snow. It's her story,"

And Brittany added, "Yes, please, Aunt Helen. I am telling the deputy everything. *Everything*," she added keenly.

Helen got up from the faux leather, grateful to be saved, or excused, from something she hadn't felt good about. Only then did she think of all the reasons that tattling about Consuela wouldn't have been a good idea. The undocumented woman had probably suffered much, maybe even the death of loved ones, to get where she was. Scripture didn't say, "Tell the truth, the whole truth and nothing but the truth." It said, "I was a stranger and you took me in."

It also said, "Thou shalt not bear false witness."

"A Poor Wayfaring Man of Grief" said:

> I heard his voice abroad and flew
> To bid him welcome to my roof.

Wizzy saved her, overriding the conflict. This case was plain to law enforcement as it was, in its simple accident form.

Worst of all, had she spoken up, she would have lost Brittany's trust.

Feeling herself useless, and knowing the view through the plate glass was no longer so distressing, Helen strolled over and allowed her attention to wander. *What is wrong with this picture?* she found herself wondering. But hadn't Wizzy's death taught her not to question the end when it came to anyone, no matter how hale or saintly? Sometimes there was no reason humans could discern, no cause they could prevent.

But sometimes death, like Wizzy's, was caused by people with the very best intentions, trying to rid the world of deadly bacteria with antibiotics, but in the process creating bugs that nothing could stop.

Wizzy hummed, "To Everything There is a Season".

# Chapter 4

Dark-uniformed and busy authorities were swarming around the condo deck, clustered around the yawning hot tub of death. A young man with a thick head of tousled red curls appeared, framed by the glass doors of unit C. He wore grey sweats and had his leg in a cast. Supported by crutches, he stood watching the proceedings.

Helen felt a pull, as if a door had opened. Something clicked, a tune began. "The Dawning of the Age of Aquarius," of all songs. She had been looking for an opportunity to expand her world. Was this it?

She looked back at the two women on the couch. As the interview progressed, Deputy Moody reapplied lip-gloss. Helen got a nod of acknowledgement from her niece that she was all right, heard "Aquarius" modulate into a setting of Robert Frost's "I Took the Road Less Travelled By". She slipped out into the cold air of the deck, to meet the young man on crutches.

He smiled a weak, crooked smile at her approach. "Jeez. Just imagine. If it hadn't been for this leg, I'd have been in that tub last night."

"Skiing accident?" Helen asked, nodding at the leg.

"Snowboard. But yeah, first day on the slopes. Saturday morning. First run, even. Just my luck. A little out of shape, I guess. Just didn't make that turn. Busted in three places. Hurt like hell. Still hurts like hell. Without these." He patted the pocket of his sweats. The sound of pills in a plastic bottle issued from the depths.

"I'm sorry to hear that."

The young man must have caught the distaste in her tone at his profane language. She hadn't meant to be judgmental. It was just that, in the world she inhabited, "hell" did not exist. Mormons didn't even believe in hell as an option for the afterlife. Supposedly, there were simply realms where those less than perfect would feel more comfortable, more at home. But how could she learn anything if she stayed within the careful walls of the world she knew? "Judge not that ye be not judged" would have to take precedence over avoiding the "mere appearance of evil."

"Sorry, ma'am."

The kid had some consciousness of manners after all. He quickly changed the subject. "Me and a couple buddies came up from Southern California. Took a week off from USC—and this happens. The first day."

Southern California. Where Karen and her husband were serving their mission. "I'm sorry to hear that. My name's Helen Snow. I'm ... I'm connected to the unit next door."

Helen wondered if that would count as a lie. It was always so hard to know where to draw the line. What was falsehood and what just polite conversation? The strange young man didn't need to know all the details. Especially when Brittany had probably cleaned a bathtub draped with his wet underwear, and made his bed, too.

"Family?" the young man asked. "I'm so sorry."

"Family ... family friend."

Was that two lies in as many seconds? *Had* Brittany been friends with the young man?

"Still. I'm sorry."

The young man again brought out his manners. Injuries tend to encourage that in the otherwise oblivious young, she'd noticed: teaching them that life isn't just a video game you can reboot whenever you please.

He extended a hand. "Quinn. Quinn Rhodes."

"How do you do?"

"Just think. All I got was a broken leg. Could have been me. And Dave—Dave was such a great guy."

"You knew him?"

"Yeah. Quiet. Serious. But still, we had some good times this past week. Sitting out here on the deck together. Shooting the breeze. Talking slopes and bars and chicks—excuse me, ma'am. Young ladies."

*Not my niece, I hope.* "A couple of friends, you say?"

"Well, three. Four of us drove up all together." He gestured vaguely in the direction of the garage. "Hammy's car, 'cause it's the biggest. Can hold all the gear and everything. We're supposed to leave Monday morning. Drive straight through, if all goes well." His eyes on the proceedings around the hot tub suggested this might not be the case. The young man spoke,

Helen thought, in sentences each no longer than a single Tweet.

"And they did fiddle with it," Quinn added.

"Fiddled? With what?"

"The mechanics of the tub. At one point."

"They *what?*"

"They wanted the jets to come on stronger."

"Have you told this to the sheriff?"

Quinn dismissed it with a wave of his hand. "Hammy didn't know what he was doing. He was pretty drunk."

That didn't make Helen feel any better. "Are your friends here now?"

"Oh, no, of course not. They're not klutzes like me. They hit the slopes early. They'll be gone all day."

"And yet, I'm told there was no sign of any exit from the cul-de-sac this morning." Helen pointed out the ski marks on the slope just before them. It could be not one path in and one out but two, side by side. And a third, carefully inside the trail of the skiers before him? "They didn't ski out?"

"Not today." With signs of pain and weariness, Quinn settled himself and his crutches on the nearest lounge chair. "They weren't even here. My buddies called last night. They picked up some chicks—er, young ladies. At a bar. One for each of them. Or rather, the ch—er, ladies picked them up."

Helen wondered if this was a good missionary moment: tell Quinn about the blessings of purity and keeping oneself for Temple Marriage. Could she prime this young man before sending him back to Southern California and to Karen, who would clinch the deal? But if Helen did that, she wouldn't learn anything more.

She knew from experience that once Karen took center stage, even in the abstract as a role model, she herself would fade from all awareness. And Helen had an odd foreboding that Karen would regard the conversion of one outsider more important than investigating the circumstances of another outsider's death to get at the truth. She must leave Karen out of this.

"So you were alone here last night?" she asked.

"Yeah. Damn it. Excuse me, ma'am."

"Did you ...?"

"Hear or see anything? Like the cops already asked me?"

"Did you?"

Quinn pulled the amber pharmacist's bottle out of his pocket and studied it gratefully. Helen understood that some redheads were much more susceptible to pain and less able to find relief from drugs than the rest of the population.

"I take a couple of these and I'm dead to the ... er. Anyway, the answer's no," Quinn said. "Only when I did get up—to use the facilities—there was no power."

"Had you heard something? Is that what woke you?"

"Yeah, maybe. I remember thinking, 'Oh, they're blasting for avalanche control.' You know, like they do. Set the slides off before people get under them and there's a danger. But I didn't hear anything once I was awake. Or see anything. That was a pain."

"Had your drugs worn off?"

"No. Finding the john. In the dark, in a strange place. On crutches. I had to take another couple of these babies afterward."

Helen made sounds of sympathy. "But the power's on now."

Quinn shrugged. "Yeah."

"You didn't throw the switch?"

"Nope. Not with this leg. Less I moved, the better."

"Or maybe the lines just got blown down in the storm and the power company fixed it. Although all that power surging through the hot tub...."

"That would do it, yeah."

That thought seemed to cause the young man fresh pain. He spilled two horse-sized pills from his bottle and tossed them back, swallowing them without water.

"Those can give you constipation." Helen felt it was her Christian duty to advise the young man.

He glared at her.

So much for her Christian duty. *Ah, the stamina of youth,* she mused.

"Was no one else around?"

"Family with a bunch of noisy kids. Came in about supper time last night. I was glad for these babies then." He stowed the pills close at hand, back in his sweats.

"Did they interact at all with the dead man?"

"With Dave? The kids played in the hot tub. Screaming, jumping in, running around. Dave was pretty patient with them."

A chill ran down Helen's spine, and it wasn't just the wind blowing off the nearby slope. Kids in bathing suits playing in water that turned so quickly deadly. She remembered that Brittany had said the one little girl was sick. But vomiting had nothing to do with high voltage.

She said the words out loud. "High voltage."

"Yeah. A little freaky, I guess. I didn't think of that until now. Last night I was just cursing the parents for being so hands-off. Guess you don't notice after you've got four or five of them."

Helen thought of her sister Karen, whose sixth child was talking to a deputy sheriff in the condo. Karen never let things get out of hand. That's why she'd made such a good Relief Society president, mother of the ward, and now mother of a mission.

"Well, I hope you heal well," she said to the young man.

"Thanks."

"I'll pray for you," she said automatically—and got no thanks for that. Discomfort fell like a wet blanket through the freezing air upon them.

Okay, Wizzy had had nothing to do with that statement; that had been all her. Desperate to make things right again, turning, her gaze fell on the ski tracks heading up and down the slope again. "You couldn't venture a guess as to who might have made those tracks, then? If it wasn't your friends."

"I haven't even been here a week," Quinn reminded her. "But on a guess, I'd say it might have been Ben."

"Who's Ben?"

"Gentle Ben. Like the bear. All big and hairy. Friend of Dave's. Something of a mountain man, if you know what I mean."

"I'm sorry, I don't."

"Dave introduced us once or twice. Seems Ben

lives up there."

"On the *mountain*?" Helen stared and craned her neck. She couldn't imagine it.

"Not exactly sure where, but yeah. In a cave, wouldn't surprise me. He'd come down for a shower sometimes, sometimes just for the company, though he didn't like folks much, only Dave. I got the impression that Dave's the one who lets him live up there."

"And how would Dave ...?"

"Well, his family owns the mountain, the whole resort, don't you know." Helen almost heard the "duh" in the young man's tone. "That's how he could live here, no job, no rent."

"Oh, yes. Of course." If she was playing friend of the family, she would know that, wouldn't she? Lying was so hard. You had to remember so much. Unlike going through the motions of attending church, where there were plenty of folks there to remember for you. And remind you.

"I got the impression Ben's on the payroll, too. Although some of the family don't like that, apparently."

"Which family?"

"Dave mentioned a sister."

"Oh, yes." Helen tried to make it sound like, of course, she knew which sister that would be.

"There were differences, but Dave and Ben are—were—on the same side."

Helen was about to ask another question, but two sheriff's deputies slid back the glass door on Quinn's condo, stepped onto the deck, and approached. "Excuse me, Mr. Rhodes," the bigger one said.

"Yes?" The young man looked up. The morphine was probably just kicking in. His blue eyes appeared a little bleary under that mop of red hair, the pupils constricted.

"We have a few more questions to ask."

The two deputies helped him to his crutches and, taking him none-too-gently by the elbow, ushered him inside.

"Gentlemen," Helen began protectively, "this young man has a broken—"

They ignored her. A moment later, she was glad they had. Seeing Brittany alone on the faux couch, she moved to join her. Over her niece's head, Helen saw that the attention of every law officer in the condo was focused on a baggie held in the latex-gloved hands of one officer standing triumphant in the doorway to the young man's bedroom. "In the sock drawer," he said. Printed across the packet, plump with it dusty-looking green contents, were the words "For Medical Use Only."

Helen shot a look of compassion at her niece. This young man had drugs in his sock drawer. Perhaps Brittany had been naively ignorant of this possession, but there was nothing like drugs to bring down the wrath of God. Brittany should consider herself lucky that their acquaintance had gone no further. Perhaps the death was the mercy of God and a reward bestowed on Karen—and Brittany—for having lived so righteously.

"David Sebastiano Jaramillo had marijuana in his sock drawer."

Lead dropped in Helen's stomach. All three names, like the announcers say on TV. Like it says in the police docket. One more reason to conclude the death an accident—a deserved one for using drugs that made a young person clumsy and stupid.

Brittany rose to her feet. She plucked a dusting cloth out of her cleaning carryall and used it as if out of nervous habit, as if hoping to make herself one with the furniture so everyone would overlook her.

Just as the glass doors slid open to the scene on the deck, Helen heard the electrician say, "Really, fellas. I can't tell you what caused the arc. Everything looks good to me."

So, no short in the jets, none in the filter; Quinn and his friends next door were not responsible. What, then?

"Thank you, ladies," Moody told Helen and the busy Brittany. "You're free to go. We have your contact information. We'll let you know if we have any more questions concerning this unfortunate accident."

Brittany turned from dusting a sideboard with a thin screen 32-inch television on its tiny stand, its cord dangling, perched incongruously among a haphazard collection of New Age self-help books, like a stork in a pond of frogs.

"I don't know what your boss will tell you," Deputy Moody was saying to the girl, by way of dismissal. "I think we've finally contacted him."

"Tom?" Brittany asked, dazed.

"He's on his way up now. I can't imagine he'd insist you do any more cleaning today. Not here. You've had quite enough for one day."

Helen thought of the vomit in Unit A, the death and dope in Unit B, the medical morphine in C. No, her niece should definitely not be expected to clean up any more today. Deputy Moody had already turned away, paying no more attention to the invisible activity of keeping dust at bay. She was done here.

"But, why ...?" The officer stopped in the doorway. "Why do you have two carryalls? Isn't this work hard enough without doubling the load?"

There sat Consuela's yellow plastic carryall, just in front of the entryway, right where she'd abandoned it at the first sound of the word "police".

# Chapter 5

"That was your boss?" Helen asked her niece as they made their way under the yellow tape and past the silent, closed doors of the ambulance to her waiting car. Going down the slope of the hill was harder than going up when every step threatened to send them sliding down to the valley.

Brittany nodded silently. She was intent on her footing.

"He seems like a very nice man. And he arrived just in the nick of time to cover for the two carryalls."

Brittany shrugged.

"'All my cleaners carry two when they work alone,'" Helen echoed the man's words. "'In case they run out of any supplies.'" Helen would have disbelieved that anyone could accept such a thing as true. But the deputies had. Maybe because they'd seen the vomit mess in the garage.

"He doesn't want to get in trouble for hiring an undocumented worker," Brittany said, having checked over her shoulder that they were beyond earshot of any first responders.

Such contortions in the world had not occurred to Helen. She considered them now as she and her niece performed more physical contortions to get two pairs of skis and poles in Helen's small SUV that had no rack on the roof.

Helen did not envy the Hispanic woman, so far from home, struggling down this path in tennis shoes, trying to hurry before the police arrived. But that had left a problem—two pairs of skis. Brittany had neatly explained them to Deputy Moody by saying, "I'm such an idiot. I left this other pair here yesterday and forgot all about them until I tried to set out this morning." Both pairs were her skis, after all.

The skis only fit into the car diagonally with Brittany scrunched over in the back seat and the rear window open.

"Who do you suppose made those tracks up behind the hot tub?" Helen wondered as she drove, trying to keep her teeth from chattering. The double pairs of skis jutting by her right shoulder made her consider this odd detail.

"Don't know," Brittany said, her fingers now warm enough to type out messages on her phone.

*Ah, youth.* The resiliency of youth: it was as if Brittany had put all the strangeness and horror of the morning behind her.

So why was Helen continuing to stew over what authority had told her was an accident? Just some poor mother's child dead before her. The guilt, the loss ... oh, Wizzy ...

Could Helen ease that unknown mother's sorrow in any way? And didn't that wish make Helen the perfect fodder for the calling of Relief Society president? For the first time, she seriously considered that she might actually be well suited to the work, even if it were in a different way from her efficient, perfect sister.

"Somebody came and went last night. After the snow," Helen mused.

"Could have been someone went and returned."

"You're right." Helen had to give her niece credit. Brittany was not so wound up, neither with her grief nor with those eleven-and-a-half square inches of glowing electronics, that she couldn't reach logical conclusions.

"Dave always said ..." Here Brittany lowered the phone to sniffle again. "Dave liked living there, with his back to the mountain. He told us ..." Sniffle. "He told us how, on nights with a full moon, he liked to buckle on his skis and head out cross country." Another sniffle. "How Sarah wanted to live with him! For just such midnight roams."

More sniffles, which Helen was grateful for. They covered her gasp. Her niece lived with a young woman who had such fancies? Unmarried?

"*I* wanted to live with him." Brittany gave in so completely to her grief that Helen forgot to feel shock and only wished she wasn't still driving on icy roads. She wanted to put her arms around those young shoulders again. Helen swallowed her virtuous concerns.

"Was there a full moon last night?" she wondered.

"There wouldn't have been any moon last night. Not until after the storm blew over."

"Of course. And that probably wasn't until after ... after the ... electrical malfunction."

Helen passed the box of tissues from the glove

compartment back to her niece and let her use them for a while before she asked, "What about this Ben?"

"Ben?"

"Gentle Ben. Something of a mountain man. The young man in Unit C told me about him. Seems he lives somewhere up on that mountain and came to visit Dave Jaramillo sometimes."

"Oh, yes. Gentle Ben. Everyone in Park City knows Gentle Ben."

Helen raised an eyebrow at her niece by way of the rearview mirror. At this point, she wouldn't be shocked at anything her niece told her.

"Knows *of* him," Brittany amended. "I've never seen him. Or maybe I just didn't know him from all the other characters in this town who match his hairy description."

By this time they had reached the low trailer that served as Pine Enterprises' office. Helen had decided to join her niece inside, although Brittany said her business would "only take a minute". Even wearing gloves, with the car window open to accommodate the long skis, Helen's hands had stopped feeling the steering wheel, and whether or not her feet hit the brake she had to take on faith alone. Brittany took a moment to wipe her tears and blow her nose, then led the way.

With the boss still up at the hot-tub accident site, a substitute from the back room had taken his place at the reception desk, a very pregnant young woman with missing teeth and tufts of dry, dirty hair escaping out of a short, purple pony-tail. Helen wondered if the family in Unit A would have even rented from Pine Enterprises if this woman had been the regular receptionist. Almost certainly not. But she was probably essential tech support, kept hidden away in the back room like a goblin spinning straw into gold. In any case, this young woman seemed to know her business. She gave Brittany the rest of the day off to get over her trauma, *if* Brittany promised to come in on Sunday and clean the units at the end of the cul-de-sac—vomit and all—to get the condos ready for their new renters by Monday evening. If the sheriff let them, they would even try to clear Dave Jaramillo's residence to squeeze in one more rental at this busiest time of the year.

"Isn't that rather sudden?" Helen had to step in and ask. "For a police crime scene?"

"It's not a crime scene, Aunt Helen," Brittany insisted. "It's only an accidental death."

"And word has come from the owner to go ahead," the woman behind the desk said. "That's why it took Tom so long to get up there and take over, he was on the phone. Tom is authorized to speed up the investigation in any way possible."

"You mean, to bribe the police so he can get the room rented out sooner?" Helen asked.

"Sheriff, Aunt Helen," Brittany hissed.

"But you didn't correct me on the bribe part." Helen's suspicions were out of character, but a few bars of the old tune "I've Got a Feeling You're Fooling" had entered her mind. Where would that have come from, if not from Wizzy? Helen didn't think she even had the music for that tune at home, but she saw no reason why her daughter might not have met the Dorsey Brothers in heaven.

Some members of the Church probably thought

speakeasy-era musicians unlikely candidates for any heaven, but she had often entertained a wildly giggling Wizzy with wide arm enactments of Tommy Dorsey's tromboning on "The Music Goes Round and Round". God knew what He was doing with her precious angel.

Did He let big band musicians into the heavenly choir? That would take some mental readjustment.

"No one's even thinking bribes," the woman behind the computer said coolly.

Was this just business as usual in Summit County? Fooling or not, Helen hated to see such callousness over the death of some other woman's child. But when hadn't bribes been business as usual in Salt Lake County, under the very shadows of the capitol dome and the temple? The owner wouldn't want it getting out that his hot tub was unsafe, after all.

"Now, about that Sarah friend of yours ..." The expectant mother stretched her back with a groan.

Brittany and the woman, who was leaning forward over the counter as far as her belly allowed, had it out over Sarah. Brittany told so many lies in defense of her friend and roommate that Helen couldn't listen any more.

"The music goes round and round, oh-oh-oh-oh." Wizzy seemed to be playing a child who puts her fingers—her stubby little fingers—in her ears and sings "La, la, la, la" at the top of her celestially fortified lungs. "I can't hear you."

Brittany was trying to negotiate out of the Sunday clean up, pleading that Sunday was her only day to ski. Karen and LaMar, Helen reflected with a pang of guilt, never allowed skiing on the Sabbath. And Helen had told a lie to the bishop then, when she said her niece was attending regular services in Park City. Did that count as a lie? She had thought it was the truth when she'd said that.

La, la, la, la.

Helen liked the idea that, rather than becoming too worldly wise with the Dorsey Brothers, her Wizzy was playing with this woman-at-the-computer's unborn child in the spirit world, where the afterlife bumped up against the preexistence. Wizzy would be giving this child the wisdom and strength he or she would need to make the compromises that being this purple-haired woman's child would entail.

Now the lies in defense of Consuela began. At least, Helen mused, those were on behalf of someone who wanted to work, not play hooky to go skiing with young men.

La, la, la, la.

In a desperate search for distraction, Helen looked at the computer screen. She had just figured out that it was open to the block of condos that would not get cleaned today when Brittany, cowed and subdued, promised that, to keep her job, she would be there —"with Sarah"—bright and early tomorrow morning, and tugged on her aunt's arm to effect her escape.

Back in the car, Helen asked her niece, "What does Code 5 mean?"

Brittany didn't answer. She blank-screened her phone, frustrated, after a futile call to her friend.

"Well," Helen said, "if your boss wants to keep Consuela under wraps and this death in his hot tub a secret from further rentals, I hope that's not what you're twitting all over the world."

"That's tweeting, Aunt Helen. And no. I do have more sense than that. I'm just trying to find Sarah. Sarah at least should be told. She's the one who usually cleaned the condo. Heck—" the tone of that mild Mormon expletive, as close as a good Mormon would ever come to swearing, told Helen that Brittany was using it for her benefit. Had her expressions morphed into something stronger with her parents gone? "—I don't want to have to clean that unit alone. I need Sarah! But nobody seems to have seen her."

The hymn playing in Helen's head now was number 194. She didn't want anything in her head right now, nothing but her concern for Brittany. And a song that began with "There is a green hill far away" was absurd as they drove through snow-covered mountains. All Helen could do was to hope that Wizzy was warm and happy somewhere. Maybe she was making the soul of that poor electrocuted young man welcome.

"I don't understand it," Brittany went on. "Sarah *lives* on that phone of hers. She hasn't picked up since last night when she told me to call in sick for her. Just about the time the snow began to fall. The rat."

Helen could hardly begin to think through all the worrisome things this revelation might mean. She forgot about the computer screen and asked, "Gentle Ben? Does Sarah know Gentle Ben?"

"Sarah knows everyone. She would certainly know him by sight. She was the one who told me about him."

"Well, we shall have to ask her if she knows whether the ski tracks up the hillside are his."

"She won't be at home," Brittany said. Helen could see the young hands twisting a Kleenex in the rearview. "Not with the snow perfect like it is."

Then they had to concentrate, Brittany giving directions and Helen following them through the steep and narrow streets of historic Park City to Brittany's apartment.

"You can tell Mormons didn't settle this place," Helen remarked, hoping to lighten the mood.

"Didn't have the smarts—excuse me, the 'inspiration'—to get the gold out of these hills," Brittany scoffed.

"They would have built wider streets."

Wizzy begged to differ: "Strait is the Way" she hummed.

"There's no place for wider streets in this narrow valley." Brittany was not thinking scripture, but civil engineering. "City Hall should close the roads to all but foot and ski traffic. That's how it most was when the Gentile Welsh and Greeks came to work the mines. I think City Hall gets too much pressure from the Californians today. Yep, there's another. Careful, Aunt Helen, don't hit—"

Helen barely missed the car that came out of nowhere at thirty-five MPH. She also barely missed the one parked in a "No Parking" zone.

"Two BMWs with one blow. That would have given you a lot of points, Aunt Helen."

When her heartbeat returned to normal, Helen sought the comfort of traditional values. "The Prophet Brigham Young knew cars would be coming, that they would need three lanes going each way. 'Wide enough to turn a wagon and four around,' he said."

"Wide enough so his spies could see how everyone came and went."

Helen listened hard to Wizzy's giggle so as not to say something that would alienate her niece.

"If old Brigham had really been inspired," Brittany added, "he should have considered parking spots for all those cars. "

"Parking can now take up the middle two lanes," Helen pointed out.

"Here. That's our place," Brittany called out.

Helen didn't get a good look at more than a wooden porch. She had to start trying to find a parking place, and there weren't any. "I don't know why on earth they called this place 'Park City'," she wondered aloud. "Clearly, you can't."

"No, not during ski season when the piled-up snow takes up half of the road."

Brittany offered suggestions. Helen tried to follow them, but things only got worse. There was no parking *anywhere*. Exhausted, she finally got to turn off the ignition in the lot adjacent to a mall, miles out of town. They had even passed the entry to Pine Enterprises, where sheriff lights still swirled up on the white hillside.

"There's a bus," Brittany promised. "A free bus. It stops right in front of our house. The release of air brakes wakes me early every morning."

But a bus meant they had to drag the skis with them. And in her heels, Helen didn't dare brave the mound of snow to reach the bus shelter to ease the long cold wait until the bus came. She stood in cold misery near the curb, clutching her purse and one pair of skis, while Brittany renewed her attempts to reach Sarah. At last, when Helen's feet and hands had gone from numb to immobilized, a bus lumbered up and settled to a stop with a pneumatic wheeze. A swirl of "Clean, Natural Gas" exhaust—as advertised on the beast's great flank—hit the frigid air.

Once on board, Brittany gave her aunt the only free seat while she loaded the skis into the bins provided for them. Everyone onboard was bulky with winter coats and hats. Drying wool and many breaths steamed the windows, so Helen had no idea where they were going. She'd have to trust the standing Brittany with that. How far could she trust the girl, after all she'd learned about Brittany-without-parents today?

Helen tried to relax into that trust, the lack of ultimate responsibility for another person's child. And they wanted her for Relief Society president? She appreciated the warmth, but to relax on a bus was simply beyond her.

She tried to get Wizzy to hum "The Wheels on the Bus Go Round and Round," an old favorite. Helen realized with regret that she'd never taken her daughter on a bus. She supposed that if her little girl had lived, she would have had to learn to take a bus. Helen would have had to teach her, as Brittany was teaching Helen now.

Slush built up in the aisles of the bus, sending passengers sliding into one another. No one seemed to mind. This was a resort. They had come here to slip and slide around. People were on vacation. From big cities, where they rode buses.

Bus riding evoked a sense of a different world, the world of big Gentile cities, of Europe, even. Of creeping socialism.

"I've a feeling that we're not in Kansas anymore," came to her mind as she parsed what had been a touch of panic. Her thoughts heralded the strains of Wizzy's "Somewhere Over the Rainbow", a switch from black-and-white to Technicolor. Could Helen perceive this strange, terrible city as a sort of Oz?

Having a car was part of the Mormon believers' mandate to be "self-reliant", the good mother making sure her children were driven to every opportunity of middle class consumption. Just look at the acres of asphalt that surrounded every chapel in town, empty all week, full on Sunday, even though no one had to travel more than three blocks to their meetings. Mormons drove *everywhere*, so they wouldn't have to walk among the unjust. The hub of Mormondom in the valley below was only just getting light rail and public transportation service. Residents had resisted for years, claiming it would lower property values, which was a polite way of saying they didn't want neighbors who couldn't afford multiple cars. Public transportation was for those not living to the full God's capitalistic commandments. Murmurs of offended morality edged Helen's claustrophobia, a feeling of uncleanliness, of brushing too much with unbelievers.

"Code 5?" It took Helen a moment to register that this was her niece talking, not Wizzy. Talking to her, not to the handsome—albeit tattooed—young man hanging onto the bus strap beside her. And the girl was repeating Helen's own words to her, calm enough in such surroundings to return to a previous train of thought.

"Yes," Helen said, starting as if suddenly

awakened.

Yes, perhaps the jiggle of the bus and the warmth had lulled her almost to sleep. It was also possible that the press of so many strangers in such a tight space had made her numb in another way as the cold numbness wore off. Or induced hypoxia.

"Yes, Code 5." Helen repeated. She had to speak loudly. Did everyone on the bus have to know their business? Oh, for the privacy of a car!

But Helen had to know. "I happened to see it on the computer screen in the Pine Enterprises office," she shouted to her niece. "It was in conjunction with what I took to be the records for the triplex of condos where you ... you had to clean today."

"It would be up, wouldn't it, since Marge and I had just been discussing my work schedule."

Marge must be the pregnant woman whose unborn child Wizzy had been playing with. "Unit B had Code 5 in one column, while Unit C had a bunch of numbers," Helen went on. "Looked like room charges, although I can't imagine who would pay $450 a night for a hotel room." Suddenly "There is a Green Hill Far Away" made sense, at least as much sense as anything out of *The Book of Wizzy* made sense. The line "to pay the price of sin" was featured in the third verse.

"Aunt Helen, $450 is a good price. For Park City. During the season."

Two or three people standing between Helen and her niece nodded emphatically. One asked, "Where's this great deal?" with a Brooklyn accent.

Helen blinked, trying to process this pronouncement. $450 a *night*? A good price?

After sending the Brooklynite to her employer—without mentioning the hot tub—Brittany returned to her aunt. "I bet Unit A cost more per night. All those kids and extra cots …."

"But that's the thing," Helen said. "Unit A was also Code 5." She wasn't sure her niece even heard over the noise and jostling around them.

Brittany's reply got lost in her neighbor's effort to reach the bus's bell cord. Helen had to reach it for the young 'boarder, stretching awkwardly over a huge man who, at the same time, was trying to make his way to the exit. Womanly modesty was difficult to maintain in a crowded bus. Just one more reason to use cars. Helen sighed. *Oz*, she firmly reminded herself.

Something dreadful in traffic happened ahead. The driver tapped his horn and slammed the brakes, hurling the people standing on slush into one another again.

People laughed. Wizzy giggled. "The horn on the bus goes beep, beep, beep..." Helen could hear her daughter sing that verse, watch her pump an air horn all twelve times with her stubby little hand. Helen took a deep breath; the near miss on these narrow Park City streets was not her fault.

Helen thought of Sister Janet Olsen, the woman in the ward who always walked down the hill to the bus stop. Janet was an object of curiosity, of pity, if not condemnation for heresy. She must lack faith that God created the world for man to subdue. Or did Janet Olsen not trust that Christ would return to "reward the just and punish the sinner" before the entitled made the air too unbreathable? She was the sister who used the time on the emptier buses down in the valley to read her scriptures. Helen would reach out to her now, after this ride. Not to offer her a ride, but to congratulate her.

*Now, if I were Relief Society president,* Helen found herself musing further, *I could get Janet Olsen to teach the sisters the bus schedules.* It could fit into even the most straitened Sunday lesson. "Provident Living", perhaps, or "Finding Time to Read the Scriptures Every Day." The Utah Transit Authority ran extra trains for Church Conference, didn't they? And for BYU-Utah games.

Could anyone accustomed to the impersonal shelter of a car ever make the adjustment to this jumble of damp limbs and brief smiles, of "Excuse me"s and "Wonderful storm last night"s exchanged by complete strangers?

"The wipers on the bus go swish, swish, swish." Wizzy would have loved the bus.

Helen pulled the cord for Brittany. She hefted her share of the burden—now just the poles—and slipped and slid after her niece to solid ground once more, where filthy slush splashed up her nylons to the hem of her Sunday skirt. No wonder everyone drove half a block to meetings.

Wizzy stopped singing.

Helen couldn't wait to reach Brittany's house.

# Chapter 6

Her niece's residence offered none of the comfort Helen longed for.

It had no doubt once served as home to a miner and his seven or eight dependents, within walking distance of the mine shaft. Apparently nothing had been fixed or modernized since the man had died of black—or silver—lung. Brittany's present landlords must just be waiting for the market to be right before tearing it down and replacing it with skiers' condos.

"They own the place next door, too," Brittany explained as they stood on the porch and she juggled skis and groped in her backpack for her keys.

Helen didn't like the thought of this happening when her niece was alone in the dark. The narrow doorframe had probably once held a very insecure single pane of glass. The insecurity must have been breached once upon a time; the pane had been replaced with a thin sheet of heavily knotted plywood.

"I don't think they'll tear that place down, though," Brittany continued, still looking for the keys. One ski clattered to the porch. "It's a historic site."

Helen bent to pick up the ski. Under the slush and wind-blown snow she saw warped boards and peeling paint. How long before the porch collapsed and injured a young renter?

"Let me deal with the lock," she suggested. Brittany had just found the key, but with her hands full couldn't get it turned around in the right direction.

The building next door, of the same vintage as the house but better maintained, sported a neon sign that read "The Happy Miner", flashing even at this hour of the day. A hairy old-time miner with a leering grin danced in blue and red: pickax in, pickax out, pickax in, pickax out. Every "pickax in", the mechanism squeaked. "Live music. Line dancing" were advertised, and the names of twenty beer brands filled the rest of the front window like the lights of a secular Christmas tree.

Helen turned the key the other way because the usual way didn't want to go.

The space between the apartment and the bar was so narrow that the larger patrons would get stuck if they tried to take a short cut, but obviously it was a thoroughfare for others. Plenty of empty bottles and broken glass and—Helen had never seen such a thing before, but were those slugs, ugh, spent condoms?—proved that bar patrons did use this route—directly under what must be Brittany or Sarah's bedroom window.

"Let me," Brittany said, and relieved Helen of the nonfunctioning key. "It is temperamental, even after a full can of WD-40."

"I hope they don't keep you awake too often,"

Helen attempted, just to keep herself from saying, "I hope you've never been any closer to that place than this." Or, "Move out, child. Now."

"You get used to it," Brittany said. She added as she swung the door open, "I've been next door a couple times with Sarah. Line dancing's fun. And Sarah says that a lot of rich ski bums hang out there, although I haven't met any."

Neither of the girls was twenty-one.

Karen and LeMar must have been focused on getting ready for the mission. *What could go wrong,* must have been their thinking, *while we are doing the Lord's work?* They certainly could have no idea of the condition of the "digs"—Helen couldn't escape the word; the house certainly seemed like a dank burrow —their youngest daughter had found.

I've been given this child to care for, Helen thought. If I'm not worthy, she'll be given to someone else.

Helen dove through the now-open house door to escape the ugliness outside, only to encounter new offences to her frayed sensibilities. The smell of mildew, so rare in dry Utah, was overpowering, and—

*Bang!* Something fired like a gun. Helen flinched.

"Just turned up the heat," Brittany, behind her, apologized. "The furnace is an old clunker, converted from coal. There's no insulation, and I like to keep it as low as possible, just enough so the pipes don't freeze, when no one's home. We have to pay for the gas."

This meant Sarah wasn't here. Had not returned. Brittany didn't say anything, but concern showed on her face.

Something rustled and scrabbled behind the closed door across the sparse living room.

Rats? Helen shuddered.

Fearlessly, Brittany crossed the room and opened the door.

A brown, rat-like creature shot out of the other room, aiming directly for Helen's unprotected ankles.

Even after she realized it was only a toy-sized dog, not a plague-bearing rat, Helen's near heart attack subsided only slowly. Snapping and snarling, the creature must be smelling Jinx on Helen's clothes. Helen tried not to be afraid. The resident dog was no more than a foot high, a brown-and-white pug, but ugly—pug-ugly! Helen tried not to judge creatures by their appearance, but this grimacing, wrinkled face seemed incapable of anything resembling joy. Like one of those plural wives in the old photos.

"That's Taffy," Brittany said over her shoulder as she dragged the two pairs of skis to their corner in the tiny living room. Dripping snow was not helping the bare floorboards.

Taffy? Helen thought immediately not of the soft pulled candy but of a cough remedy masquerading as candy. Visits to Brigham Young's residence in downtown Salt Lake—the Lion House with its row of dormer windows, one window for each wife—used to conclude with the handout of a lump of the hard, brown stuff to each visitor to demonstrate just how tough those ancestors were. See, kids? This is what candy used to be like; this used to be a special treat! There was always a small mound of the stuff in the garden patch just outside the Lion House door, abandoned by Primary children with groans and gags of "Ew! Ick!" That other, herbal name popped into her head and seemed to suit the creature better— horehound—but Helen would never say it aloud.

"Sarah's dog," Brittany added. "Isn't she cute?"

"Cute" was not the word Helen was thinking of as she fended off the little teeth, glad she hadn't yet given up the ski poles. And there was an under-smell to the mildew—dog unmentionable. Helen would have to take care where she stepped. And sat. But then she realized that for seating, the living room only offered two cheap plastic patio chairs, probably bought at discount when the season changed.

The dog continued to yap and snarl and growl at the intruder.

"Come, Taff. Leave Auntie Helen alone." Unburdened of skis, Brittany undertook the next chore. "Come. Want to go out?"

Helen wanted to go out, but she didn't know if she could find her car again on her own.

Taffy indeed wanted to go out, and did her business in the yard, where her leavings joined those of every other dog in the neighborhood on the new layer of snow.

Taffy soon came back in—it was cold, and the archaic furnace was slowly coming to life. Coming in meant she wanted to enter the dogfight-by-proxy again.

Dog snarling at her ankles, Helen viewed the house and saw it had only one bedroom. The two girls shared it, in rickety bunk beds. No doubt the happy miner had raised his eight kids in this space, but the kids had all left at fourteen.

Maybe twelve.

Helen asked to use the restroom, hoping for a respite from the assaults to her senses. Brittany pointed the way through the kitchen with its crooked counters and paint—probably leaded—peeling from the cabinets. The stove and fridge would have been at home in the kitchen where Helen's mother had grown up.

"Go ahead, Aunt Helen," Brittany said, striving to be the perfect hostess. "I'll see if I can't rustle us up some lunch by the time you're finished."

The bathroom offered no reprieve. Its lock was broken, but Helen wouldn't have dared use it had there been one. She didn't want to spend any more time than strictest necessity dictated within these walls. What if the lock stuck, in sympathy with the one on the front door?

The shower curtain and tub must have been the major source of the mildew smell. Rust stains bled out from the faucet and drain, and a thin crack ran the whole length of the tub. This seemed to be the last room in the house that the heat reached. Helen recognized the towels as the worn set her sister Karen had tossed out during her last remodel. Helen had thought they'd gone to Deseret Industries. A wire stand that must have been rejected by that same thrift store was stuffed with magazines—all of the questionable tabloid sort—that must have cost more than the entire room's furnishings combined.

Helen checked the much-painted medicine cabinet with its cracked mirror. No birth control pills. That was a relief.

Or was it?

Then she sat on the toilet ...

and felt herself and the toilet sink a good four inches into the floor. Helen screamed.

Brittany burst into the room from the kitchen.

"Sorry, Aunt Helen! I should have warned you. The floor boards around the toilet have rotted away from leak after leak. It's best to plant your feet wide and hold yourself off the seat as much as you can. You've only got the old pipe holding you up."

That explained the collapse, but Helen wondered how anyone could read a magazine in the awkward position she was forced to adopt to use the toilet. Maybe they were for bath time. But why anyone would spend any more time in that ghastly place than they absolutely had to?

"I'm surprised the landlords don't rent only to young men," Helen said as she ventured back into the kitchen and closed the door on that unpleasant experience.

"For two thousand a month, we think we're really lucky, for Park City during the ski season." Brittany would defend her choices to the end.

She steered Helen to the chipped Formica table (also reminiscent of Helen's grandmother's kitchen) and the two rickety aluminum café chairs with torn vinyl cushion seats. Lunch awaited.

"We get the leftovers when we clean out the condos," Brittany said, to explain the spread. She must have seen the look on Helen's face, for she added, "Yeah, lots of chips and dip. Lucky Charms. Coco Puffs. Open cold cuts and shriveled carrots on veggie plates if we're lucky. If *I'm* lucky, I guess I should say. Sarah eats out a lot. I usually can't afford it."

Chips bristled in clam dip. They could easily have belonged to that sick little girl from Unit A. Popcorn and the dregs of roasted nuts, the cashews all picked out, were also arranged as neatly as Brittany could manage. The prospect turned Helen's stomach. This was only one step up from dumpster diving.

Brittany looked directly into Helen's eye, judging her reaction, before adding, "And beer. There's always lots of beer left in the fridges. Those out-of-staters don't know what they're getting when they buy the watered-down Utah beer in the grocery stores. They buy a case, and then leave most of it when they discover it's not worth drinking."

To prove it, Brittany opened the fridge. Amber stalagmites of 3.2 percent beer filled at least two shelves.

For a full sixty seconds, Helen didn't know how to respond. How *could* her sister have run off to Disneyland, leaving a daughter who knew all this about beer? So much for the utility of Utah's Church-sponsored liquor laws protecting the youth. Within the space of twenty minutes, her niece, under twenty-one, had just confessed to 1) having gone dancing in the bar next door and 2) to cleaning out Californians' refrigerators of rejected beer on a regular basis.

"It's okay, Aunt Helen," Brittany said. "I've discovered I don't like beer. But I've become real good at beer-batter tempura. I cook a lot of vegetables that way. When I can afford vegetables. The alcohol cooks off, you know."

Ah, reprieve. Helen had been too mentally paralyzed to come to the inescapable conclusion that she *had* to notify her sister of Brittany's dire circumstances, but it had been looming before her, like the Mormon Temple outside of Washington DC, visible from the beltway. For years the words "Surrender Dorothy" had been spray-painted onto a bridge; it had been a famous—or infamous—sight.

Still, even if that was the only way Brittany consumed alcohol, livid debates were waged in Relief Society about the "cooking off" theory. Few staunch Mormons were takers.

Helen took a deep breath. Beer in the fridge was beer not yet drunk. But ... what about Sarah? It worried Helen that Brittany had not vouched for Sarah's abstinence from all but cook-off alcohol.

Brittany was using the chips to scoop up dip. "And sometimes we trade bottles to guys to come and fix stuff around the house."

Certainly the more guys who came to fix up, the better. Only not the kind of guys a young woman could buy with beer.

"Come." Helen pushed away the Formica. "Let me take you out to lunch." "I'd Like to Teach the World to Sing" played loud and clear in Helen's head. A nice song, nice harmony, nice sentiment. But it was, after all, only a Coke advertisement. Corporate-fabricated sentiment and calories, not the real thing. "We passed plenty of restaurants along Main Street." Walking distance even in heels. Helen would make it walking distance.

"They're all so expensive, Aunt Helen. And I'd like to wait around in case Sarah—"

"Brittany, come." Helen was on her feet, and since it had never gotten really warm, she hadn't taken off her coat. "Brittany Jane, that is an order."

Helen heard herself sounding just like her sister

Karen, echoing the cadences of Karen's perfect motherhood. Perhaps she was Relief Society president material after all!

# Chapter 7

The restaurant *was* expensive. Every person in it—these starlets who wanted to be seen where the action was—wore ten grand worth of ski togs, even though the closest they wanted to get to the slopes was this: looking out the café window during lunchtime. And, Helen supposed, sitting by a lodge fire at night.

But every time Helen wanted to ask how they could charge twenty dollars for nothing more than ground round with a bun and a pickle—a sandwich that she could make herself for under five dollars—she remembered the leftover clam dip on the Formica in Brittany's kitchen. That kept her mouth shut on the topic. It was worth the price just to see that her niece got some decent food in her.

And then there was the matter of blessing. Helen hadn't eaten unblessed food since—well, she couldn't remember when. Not since her rebellious youth, perhaps. But the minute she folded her arms and bowed her head, Brittany gave her a glare and hissed, "Please! I'd be too embarrassed. Not in front of Simon."

Simon? Simon who? Paul Simon? Surely not. Wrong generation. Wizzy offered no helpful musical hint. Helen took a surreptitious look around.

The beautiful people all looked alike. Wait staff clad in black scurried among them, as invisible as nighttime shadows.

No one who could possibly fit the description, "Blessed art thou, Simon bar Jonah ..." A name from the Gospels, then. With blessing attached. Was that a sign? She fervently hoped so. Maybe that was sufficient blessing.

Still: unblessed food, the first step to apostasy.

The agonized look on Brittany's face reminded Helen of another passage from the New Testament, the one about it was not what went into a man's mouth, but what came out of it, that mattered. Maybe a mental blessing would count.

Helen unclasped her hands and said with forced brightness, "Let's call this your birthday lunch. I forgot, with your mom gone and all ..."

Brittany clearly wasn't listening. Busy checking her phone, she was ignoring her food.

"You know, I didn't really start worrying about Sarah until ... until I found Dave and saw those ski tracks and began to think," she said.

"Have you called her parents? Maybe they've heard from her."

"I don't want to tattle. But I've been checking the avalanche report for the back country."

Helen had not considered avalanches. She had only been thinking of murders in hot tubs ... only they had told her it was just an accident. She considered avalanches now. She remembered the young man Quinn in Unit C explaining how a sound had wakened him in the night. He had taken it for the booming discharges of avalanche control. Helen grew even more certain that the Drakes should be called and said so.

"The site assures me there's no avalanche problem," Brittany argued.

Wizzy added her voice by humming "I Wanna Be Free", but maybe Helen shouldn't listen to anyone under thirty in a case like this. She could feel another hair turning gray.

She pressed her niece. "Last night was the last time you saw Sarah?"

"Yes." Brittany's voice had an edge of teenaged impatience with adults-who-don't-get-it. "I realize you're trying to help, Aunt Helen—" She interrupted herself to take a bite, which was good, wasn't it? Real food must promote maturity, even if slowly. It seemed to foster common sense now. "Maybe it would be useful just to go over it with you."

Relieved by this permission, Helen picked up her questioning. "Sarah took her skis?"

"Yes. The storm had started, but she said not to worry. She would stay with a friend and 'be right there on the mountain to start skiing first thing in the morning', she said. She was really looking forward to that."

"What friend?"

"I don't know. She didn't say."

"But what friend would it be? 'On the mountain'— closer than your ... er, home?"

"I didn't like to ask. In case it was a boy, you know. She talks such a lot about boys, always trying to impress me. I didn't want her to think I was judging her."

After a bite of pickle, Brittany added, "Ha. *Me* judge *her*? Sarah, who always gets everything right?"

Helen knew what that was like. Furthermore, she'd just spent the morning worrying that Brittany thought she was judging her.

"Well, I don't think she's got this right," Helen judged. "Not letting her roommate know where she was. Going out skiing in a storm."

Brittany chewed with a glare.

Helen sighed and asked, "Had she stayed out before?"

"No. Not really. 'Til the bars closed, yeah. But she always came home, and mostly she got up in time to go to work."

"Did she ever mention any names?"

"Dave. Just Dave. But that was kind of a joke. He was friendly. But it wasn't like we met in the bar or anything. We cleaned his condo. I don't think he thought of us, either of us, as marriage material."

*Marriage material?* Now Wizzy was chanting "I've Got a Feeling You're Fooling" again. Or was that merely a mundane earworm?

Brittany was talking Karen-speak, which she rarely did when they were alone together, aunt and niece. This was Helen's cue to back off from trying to get this young adult to do other than make the mistakes she had to make at this age. Different from the sorts of mistakes women Helen's age had got to make.

But why was the girl hedging? Was her own commitment to putting marriage first flagging? If Brittany had changed her views about that, it was a change from the young woman Helen had sounded out on their last walk around the neighborhood together. But that had been before the snow fell and the seasonal tourists arrived.

Helen could look around and see that with the competition in this eatery, in this town, her niece would be branded as the girl from the wrong side of the bank vault. Sarah Drake perhaps not so much, but still, they were working their way to the slopes in Park City. They were not here as their due.

Helen knew the Drakes, Sarah's family. They lived in the stake, in the next ward over. She had their phone number, but only in the book at home. She wanted to drive back down into the Valley to alert these unsuspecting parents. Instead, she stuck with her niece, helping her think this through, listening to her. Sarah had left with a plan, after all, and plenty of confidence, apparently. She was a good skier, Brittany assured her, with good equipment. A headlamp, even.

"But you haven't been able to get her on the phone?" Helen asked.

Brittany shook her head and poked at the phone again.

"Everything all right with you ladies?" a waiter stopped by to ask.

"Yes, thank you." Helen wondered how these guys always knew the very worst time to come and interrupt with a question.

Brittany stopped poking her phone and actually set it down. She pushed her mousy hair behind her ears and looked up anxiously.

"Oh, hi, Simon. I didn't realize you worked here. I thought you worked ..."

Helen realized this wasn't the same fellow who'd

taken their order, although every young man on the staff wore a tight black T-shirt painted on to well-developed pecs. Beefcake. She blushed to think of the word, to admit she even knew it. He was obviously not a returned missionary, unless he'd committed the sin of taking his temple garments off to get the job. Helen instantly categorized him: *not for my niece.*

But that was how Karen would categorize him. Wizzy was humming the *Superman* theme. Which voice would Helen listen to?

This fellow, unlike the first waiter, had an English accent. That helped distinguish him from the rest; otherwise they all looked pretty much the same to Helen. Young. Handsome. Dangerous for her niece.

In Karen-speak.

Helen decided to go with Wizzy on this.

He now used his accented voice to say, very charmingly, "I work at the library, yes, during the week."

Okay, so maybe that had been a rash judgment—to think the young man, because of physique alone, could not be the sharpest tool in the shed.

"A bloke has to work two jobs just to eat in this town," Simon continued. "Forget about the skiing, which is what I came for. Olympic team, all of that. Where was I to ski in England? But when do I have time here?"

Brittany nodded sympathetically. "I know what you mean."

"I saw you come in and asked to trade tables," he concluded his explanation.

Helen looked at her niece, watched that nervous habit: Brittany shoving the hair behind her ears yet again. Her prominent ears were better left covered. Karen was always bringing up the option of plastic surgery.

But Simon, with that body, had English teeth. They didn't keep him from flashing a winning smile.

Brittany looked down at her plate. "Good to see you."

The young man had to dash off then to take an order at the next table. Brittany seemed to deflate.

He returned as soon as he could, and when he did, Brittany introduced them. "Aunt Helen, this is Simon. This is my aunt, Helen Snow."

Helen noticed Brittany didn't touch her phone during the whole time that the young man hovered. Helen was also glad that her niece had taken time at home to change out of the awful pink cleaning smock.

"How-do-you-do?"s and a handshake were exchanged.

"It's Brittany's birthday lunch," Helen tried for small talk.

Brittany gave an "I want to die" groan. "Now you've done it, Aunt Helen. Now the restaurant will have to do one of those awful, embarrassing singing things with a sparkler in the cake and ...." Brittany hid her face in her hands in Drama Queen mode.

"Your birthday? Really?" Simon said.

Finished with her meal, having saved half of it to go home with her niece, Helen put up her napkin and watched the young people.

"It was. Not today. Last week."

"Many happy returns."

"Thank you" came out muffled.

"No embarrassing singing thing, I promise,"

Simon assured her.

Brittany unburied her face.

"May I ask how old?"

"Eighteen." The blush ran clear to Brittany's roots.

"So you're legal now, eh?" That "eh?" was so charming.

"Legal for some things. Not bars."

"Right. I forget. This isn't England, where you can drink in a pub at eighteen. You can drink in private at five." This Simon was also trying to impress in the sweetest way. Too bad this was Utah, not England. "But you can vote," he attempted to recover himself. "Well, I hope you'll get in there and change local government. Make Main Street off-limits to cars."

Brittany nodded as if cars on Main Street had been the first thought on her mind for the past eighteen years.

Simon had an order up and left them.

Brittany turned to Helen with a sheepish explanation. "Simon works at the library."

So Brittany was a little flustered. This young man was important to her. And it was important to her that he made a good impression on her relations.

"So I understand." Helen hoped that was encouraging enough. It was certainly encouraging that her niece had entered the library even once since dropping out of college in her first semester and coming up to Park City.

"Oh, Sarah and I get plenty of reading material when we clean out the apartments. Or, I do. Sarah's not much of a reader. Except for the magazines. She likes her magazines. There are always plenty of them in the condos, too. *Vogue, People.*" Ah, that explained the magazine rack back in the mildewed bathroom.

Helen's heart dropped as it had when the toilet in that wreck of a house her niece rented had given way under her. Here was her niece turning the talk away from herself and to the always-popular Sarah instead. Helen decided she ought to do her auntly duty and see to it that this conversation with the young man didn't become all about the absent roommate.

Simon returned, with another "How are you ladies doing?"

Helen picked up the conversation from where it had left off. "Brittany always was a great reader," she offered. This brought another blush to her niece's face. "She could read before she started kindergarten."

"And people who stay a week in a condo think leaving a paperback or two will do instead of a tip." Brittany turned the praise as quickly as she could to something more grown up.

Simon smiled in sympathy, then had to hurry off to collect a not-so-great-tip of his own and answer a complaint from a gaunt woman with faux fur frothing around her neck who wouldn't possibly eat more than two bites of her order. While the young man's back was turned, Brittany dug into her burger, even though it was cold by now. She kept a watchful eye over Simon's movements among the tables and made frequent use of her napkin. When she saw him returning, the size of the lump of food she quickly swallowed made her briefly resemble a boa constrictor, but she was able to continue the conversation without her mouth full.

"I think I'm the only one on the cleaning crew who

reads. All the books come to me. The latest bestsellers, mostly. People finish them, don't want to pack them to take home on the plane. They just leave them. If they're not something I'm interested in, I cart them over to the library. My good deed for the day."

"And selling them in the book sale pays my pitiful wage. Less and less with all the e-readers these days." Simon grinned at the bizarre ways of the world as if he were a septuagenarian. "And how is your roommate, the lovely Sarah Drake?"

Helen scanned her niece's face for signs of jealousy. Hmmm. Perhaps.

Brittany recovered by stealing a glance at the phone lying at her right elbow.

"Fine."

"You know, I saw her in the library last night. I was working the late shift."

"Sarah...?"

"I know. No one was more surprised than I to see her without you, the bookworm. Not carrying a box of paperbacks to donate or anything."

"What did she ...?"

"I think it was already snowing. She parked her skis at the door and ... yes, drops of melting snow did shed off her when she came up to the help desk. I noticed a pretty big pack on her back, too."

"What did she want?"

"She wanted to look at the local maps. At the trails and such. Up behind those lower mountains, you know. The Back Wasatch."

"Just above Pine Enterprises. Where we work." Brittany beamed with relief and interest.

"Exactly. Must be great powder up there this afternoon."

Brittany turned her gaze to meet Helen's. As clearly as if they'd sent each other a photo on the iPhone, the image of the two parallel tracks rising above the condo's hot tub passed between aunt and niece.

"Here, let me clear your plates." Simon put on the waiter manner again and left them.

Helen and Brittany hardly needed words between them to formulate a plan.

"I'd go with you," Helen offered. "I'd almost insist, for your mother's sake. Except that I can't ski, and you'd spend all your time hauling me out of drifts."

Helen had the credit card between her two fingers when Simon returned, and Brittany had shoved back her chair, but Simon bore a chocolate lava cake, two plates and two forks.

"On me," he said with a lowered voice. "For the birthday girl. But I promise, no singing."

Brittany sat back down. "Thanks," she said after the first bite. Then, "And thanks, too, for telling me about Sarah and the maps last night. I wanted to join her skiing this afternoon when I got off work." That was carefully worded to reveal nothing about of her worry over Sarah or about Dave, Helen noticed. "But she didn't say where she was going."

"It must be glorious up there," Simon agreed. "Hey, I'm off in half an hour. I can't tell you how long it's been since I got in some cross-country. Might be a little crowded on the Saturday, but how about we both get our skis, and I'll meet you at the last bus stop before the trails begin? We'll find her together and … if not, we'll just have a jolly good time, as we say in the Merry Olde—"

Before he had time to say "England", Brittany was already nodding emphatically. The date was set. And then….

"Hello. My name's Simon and I'll be your server today," he was saying in that wonderful British at the next table before Brittany got "That'd be great" out. It was as if he hoped to make that last half hour go by faster by working harder.

# Chapter 8

"You don't want me to call Sarah's parents when I get down the hill?" Helen asked her niece as they stepped out onto Main Street's busy sidewalk.

Brittany turned from waving at Simon through the restaurant window. Helen might have been mistaken, because sun on snow on plate glass made a heavy glare, but she thought he might have blown a kiss. Helen had to repeat her question.

"No. No, don't call them. Don't worry them. Simon and I will find her."

"Do you want me to stay here until you get back? At your house?" The thought turned the twenty-dollar burger in Helen's stomach to lead. Alone for hours with the mildew and the Horehound? An opportunity to scrub, but ....

"No. I'll call you and tell you everything when we get back this evening. You just drive down to Salt Lake. Well, I guess the first thing is to get you back to your car. There's a bus stop right across—"

"I don't think I can manage the bus without you," Helen was not ashamed to admit. To herself she had to admit that perhaps she was worrying too much about her niece. The girl had a job, had found a dead body and reported it to the proper authorities, and could manage the hazards of bus rides on a regular basis; she managed better than Helen sometimes did herself.

No. Helen remembered the smell of the house her niece rented and knew she probably didn't worry enough. For sure, Karen wasn't worrying enough down there in Disneyland. But it wasn't an aunt's duty to micromanage, only to support. If Karen wanted things to be different, she shouldn't have gone on that mission. If you didn't do it right, other people got to raise your kids.

"I could hail you a cab."

Brittany even knew how to manage cabs. But the cab would cost another fortune to take Helen clear out to the mall. The burger had turned out to be worth it, though, meeting this Simon.

"The people on the bus go up and down ..."

Wizzy wanted to ride the bus again, so Helen would let her. Gathering her resolve, she said, "No, thank you, dear. I think I can manage after all. Which bus stop do I need?"

What a pity they had only *sung* about buses while Wizzy was alive.

Helen took care of her phone messages on the way.

*****

Bishop Irvine had found time to squeeze in a second appointment for her in the afternoon. That was the message that he—and Mark, in a second voice mail—had left on her phone while Helen had been occupied with her niece. Back in her car once more, with the heat turned to the highest setting, Helen set off down the canyon.

The sun lowering early on this winter's day—less than three weeks to the solstice—caught some of the lower hills with pink. It was the same color pink Wizzy wore in Helen's favorite picture of her: that crooked smile of widely spaced teeth, those narrow but completely accepting eyes, pink crinkles of a Sunday dress as she sat upon the floor and listened to the piano. Wizzy's smile seemed to spread over the hillsides.

And a song. All the way down the canyon, under Wizzy's eyes and with a song from *The Book of Wizzy* sounding in her ears, the car sped on its own momentum. Helen had to ride the brake to keep from driving into the back of the liberated semis.

The song, "The Good Old Way", with no such brakes, rolled through her brain. This old hymn, attributed to the Manx Primitive Methodists, was definitely not in the Mormon book, not with its jubilant, dissident, primitive, every-man-for-himself opportunities for improvisation and ecstasy. And for the women, sopranos soaring in descant unchained from the ground. The words were only slightly changed in *The Book of Wizzy*:

> Lift up your hearts, Emanuel's friends,
> And taste the joy that Wizzy sends.
> Let nothing cause you to delay
> But hasten in the good old way.
> For I have a sweet hope ...

Helen didn't know all the verses, but with this song it didn't matter. You could make them up, as God inspired you. Primitive. You could work and love and worship with abandon. Just like the early days of the Mormon Church when people had danced before the altar and spoken in tongues, when women were priestesses and goddesses and received their own revelation and blessed their loved ones with their own power. Before so much material wealth got connected to the organization that it had to be protected at any cost—at the cost of the souls it was meant to save.

> Our conflicts here, though great they be,
> Shall not prevent our victory
> If we but work and watch and pray ...

You could hum tunelessly like Wizzy in the good old tradition, just as long as you did it with joy and enthusiasm. Like the things that Helen had done today since the phone call in the bishop's office.

She couldn't quite give what she had done a name. And had she done it? It felt like a gift. It felt like having received a new calling, one that took precedence over being Relief Society president. But Mark wouldn't like that explanation. The bishop certainly wouldn't.

"Calling" was just a word, when it came down to it. "Song" was a word. And so was "feeling". You were supposed to put your feelings into words, prescribed words, the same as everyone else. The bishops wanted words so they could make sure that everyone's feeling was the same, all the time.

Miracle. Mystery. Sacred secret.

So what had she done?

She had tried to help a dead young man. A dead

child of God.

And help others who had lost a child. Help children whose parents had flown. Not helping so much as ... investigating? Letting them tell their own stories while she listened. Private investigator. Only nobody was going to pay her for this, or put her on TV. Maybe not even put her in heaven. But Wizzy would, in her heaven.

Maybe a RS prez used some of these same skills; maybe the two callings wouldn't conflict; maybe they'd even complement each other. Helen could take the church calling, but be clear to herself as to what would take precedence.

The words of commandment?

Or a song of Wizzy.

Helen knew that Wizzy had given her this song, knew she loved it. She knew it was what Wizzy had been preparing her to do all those years of mourning. Helen knew that her mourning had been in part because she didn't know how to do such different things, had no church-sanctioned role model for them, so she hadn't dared. She'd feared she would lose Wizzy more than she already had. Mormon families were forever—but only if those families lived righteously. A mother not righteous enough would have to watch another more celestial family take over her failed duties; she would lose her daughter not only in this life but in the life to come.

What she had found in the Wasatch Back, in a room smelling of burnt water, in the company of a young man with red hair like a clown wig, and then with her niece, was something new, something more helpful to those who had cause to mourn than platitudes, than proscribed words. Something maybe even a little dangerous, things she'd never find in the normal round of suburban life with Relief Society. She'd never felt so exhilarated. She wanted to "endure" this case to its end. She wanted to do this for the rest of her life. Did that necessitate more untimely deaths? She certainly hoped not, but if she didn't pursue this search for answers to the unfathomable ways of God in the case of David Jaramillo, she would go mad. She would, in fact and contrary to authority, be sinning. She would be lying to herself, pretending she did not have "eyes to see, ears to hear".

And far beyond this mortal shore
We'll meet with those who have gone before ...

*Wizzy, Wizzy, thank you.*

And shout to think we've gained the day
When we have run in the good old way ...

How bizarre. Bishop Irvine would no doubt condemn this as wild heresy, the wild singing, the glowing face on the hillside, listening instead of preaching. All of it, all "The Good Old Way". His latter-day cleansing did away with "the primitive church," as primitive, as innocent as a child with Downs. Yet it was the layering of "The Good Old Way" on top of the bishop's order that made Helen decide, as she turned west off the freeway onto Thirty-Third, that she could undertake the latter-day form of Relief Society president. When she had been trying to fit into the model vacated by her sister Karen, she hadn't felt up to the job. She couldn't be the perfect Karen, but Wizzy would help her fill those shoes as the best Helen she could be. And now she had something else, this death of a young man in his hot tub, to puzzle out; that suited her personality better. She would fit Relief Society around this new thing, this life as new as Easter morning, that she had stumbled into.

The music sang in her heart, so she sang, shouted to the lonely car,

"For I have a sweet hope of glory in my soul,
"I have a sweet hope ..."

Her voice soared.

"For I know I have and I feel I have ..."

A thump on the steering wheel on "know", another on "feel".

"A sweet hope of glory in my soul!"

And on that refrain, girding her loins to accept limits only as they suited this rich, new feeling, she pulled into the church parking lot. She strode past the Hoffmann Jesus—with Wizzy's eyes—and into the bishop's office.

# Chapter 9

Helen agreed to the calling, declared herself worthy and got set apart. The priesthood bearers' hands were heavy on her head, but each of their forty wiggling fingers was like a thought niggling her brain throughout the rite. Few of those niggles had anything to do with her sisters, her new charges in the ward. In fact, the feel of the fingers reminded her mostly of the burnt-sausage fingers of the dead young man under his gurney sheet. She had a vision while under this influence of the power of God—a vision of those burnt fingers wiggling, beckoning her.

*The Book of Wizzy* turned the page to "The Worms Crawl In, the Worms Crawl Out". The scene in Helen's brain flashed to the day she'd first sung that song to her daughter. Wizzy, who'd never learned to walk without holding a hand, had gone out for a stroll on a rainy fall day and found worms by the score flushed out onto the sidewalk. Wizzy had had to bend and look and touch—and even eat. At first, Helen had been revolted. But then she came to share in her daughter's delight at the wonders of the world— although she did draw the line at eating. The worms playing pinochle on Wizzy's cute little snout. Helen wished she had a picture ... still, she would never forget.

God, too, must delight in worms on rainy days. He made so many of them.

The memory almost made Helen guffaw out loud in the middle of the rite. This shiny new, old doctrine saw no difference between worms and the glory of God that shouted out "Glo-ory, Glo-ory in the good old way."

At home—which seemed a stranger's house for a moment, and sterile without sagging pipes and the smell of mildew—Helen made dinner. She called Brittany just before she and Mark sat down to baked chicken and peas.

No answer.

After dinner and the dishes, Helen called her new councilors and made a few calls to visiting teachers. She hung a wreath on the door and strung some lights around the mantel. Along with all the rest, a Relief Society president had to set the ward standard for home decorating, especially around the holidays. Once Helen would have gone all out, to delight Wizzy. But Wizzy had all the stars in heaven now. No point in setting the bar too high, not in this new, post-Karen dispensation.

Helen wrote a few cards; she'd have so many more to do now. She checked over her gift list and hoped Mark would help her make a few purchases online. That seemed like cheating, completely out of the spirit of the season, but something would have to give somewhere.

A frustratingly tedious surf of the web did eventually land her on a site full of suggestions for

Relief Society craft projects. One was a scrapbook of family photos. Helen had wanted to do such a thing of the pictures she had of Wizzy in an old shoe box and hadn't been able to look at in fifteen years. Somehow she felt strong enough now, as if she would actually enjoy such a journey. Perhaps she could make another one for Mark of the boys growing up for his Christmas present. She looked over at Mark, who, having delivered her into this new Relief Society responsibility, was watching a game he "couldn't miss".

A priesthood holder could make his eternal companion do all sorts of things: spend holiday meals with his family, sit through the deadliest Sunday evening fireside meeting, iron his priesthood session shirts. But he could not command her to root for BYU, his alma mater, God's own university, not even for her eternal salvation.

Instead, she called Brittany again. Still no answer.

She fed Jinx and the cat. She began letters to her twins, the two boys serving missions in different parts of the country, Nathan in San Francisco—Mandarin—and Ethan in New York City—Spanish. She always tried to write different letters, but not a single word more to the one than to the other. She didn't get very far with that.

Twenty minutes after her latest attempt to get through to her niece, just as she picked up the phone to try again, a call came in: the "Winter Wonderland" ring tone. "Brittany" flashed in the phone's little window, the photo of the young woman with her mousey hair pushed back behind her ears.

Helen answered on the first ring.

"Are you okay?"

"Fine, Aunt Helen. Fine."

Helen heard Horehound yapping in the background and heavy thuds in a Western beat; Saturday night at The Happy Miner. Pick-ax in, pick-ax out, tush-push, cowboy cha-cha-cha and 4.5 percent beer on tap.

Good. The girl had made it home safe. If being in that house could be called safe.

"And Sarah?

The phone sat quiet just a beat too long.

"Brittany? Did you find Sarah?"

"We didn't actually see her, no. But we think we know where she is."

"I'm calling her parents."

"No, Aunt Helen. We're pretty sure she's safe."

"This 'we' would be?"

"Simon and me."

"And Simon ...?"

"He's here with me."

A rumble of British that Helen couldn't make out confirmed that. A *thunk* of cheap plastic dish ware meant that he was serving her a second meal of the day.

Brittany went on. "He's going to spend the night. I got home to the cold, dark house, and after Dave and all, I just ... I've made up Sarah's bed, and he'll spend the night on top ..."

Helen had the car keys in her hand.

"... of Sarah's top bunk."

Her niece must be pretty sure Sarah was not going to come home again that night. "Brittany, my hand is on the garage door opener. I'm coming up there."

"Aunt Helen, just relax. It's going to be okay. Sit down, relax. Take a few deep breaths."

Why did taking a few deep breaths seem so un-Mormon?

"I'll tell you all that happened this afternoon," Brittany continued, "and then you'll know it's okay."

Helen found her phone's power cord and plugged it in so the thing wouldn't run out of juice before the end of the tale. She meant to keep her niece on the phone—and out of that bed—as long as possible.

"Okay, Brittany. I'm listening."

Brittany began the tale of her afternoon's skiing adventure.

*****

Brittany had been right. The backcountry, with its fresh, new snow, was crowded with Saturday afternoon trekkers. If Sarah had come this way, you'd never know it with all the ruts worn by ski after ski running over her tracks. A lot of the people were returning by the time she and Simon set out; the tourists were out of trail mix, and the après ski hot cider beckoned. Although the sky was bright and clear, it was still cold, especially when the lowering sun slid behind trees and high rises, casting shadows. Then the snow turned to ice.

Simon let her set the pace. She was a little proud when sometimes she turned around and saw he was struggling to keep up. Of course, he always politely slid off the path to let those coming down pass.

Once when she paused to allow him catch up, he apologized. "I guess working in the library hasn't been all that great for my Olympic hopes. I'm really out of shape. Besides, there's the altitude here."

She didn't say anything to Simon—or her aunt—about how good those pecs still looked in the black restaurant T-shirt. And she was glad that making beds and washing tubs all day hadn't put her too far down from Olympic hopes. She'd been at such a peak her senior year in high school: captain of the team. It would be really bad if moving to the mountain had caused a drop in her strength.

Instead, she said, "It's okay. I've been pushing it. I needed to stop."

The next time she waited for him, she slid to a stop and adjusted her goggles against the glare, panting, poles dangling from her wrists. "Do you know where a trail turns east again?"

Simon was breathing harder. He shook his head.

"There must be one."

"It looks to me like it'd be pretty steep. I don't suppose too many people would use it, even on a crowded day like today."

"But I bet Pine Enterprises is just on the other side of that hill."

"Where I'm from," said the BBC voice, "we'd call that a mountain."

Brittany set off again. She didn't want to spend too much time listening to that voice, or she'd give up on the quest altogether, turn right around and head back to the library.

But Sarah had gone to the library, just last night. Sarah probably had a crush on Simon, too, and Brittany would have to back down when they found her. If they found her.

They would find her. Sarah had gone to the library with a plan. She'd looked at the map. On the bus,

Simon said she'd even copied as much of the map as would fit in one scan on the copier.

Simon says. Like the old game. Brittany would do whatever Simon said. If she didn't ask "Mother, may I?" would she lose the game?

"Do you think this was the part she copied?" Brittany asked.

"Could have been. The larger map did contain this part of the Back Wasatch."

"There!"

Brittany pointed. Two stalwart souls were pushing down the hill.

"I don't think that's Sarah," Simon said. A moment later, "Yeah, they're two guys."

"Okay, but let's see where they've been."

Brittany led the way to meet the pair.

They turned out to be two men with Asian features. They responded to Brittany's "How was it up there?" with bows and "Good. Very good."

"Japanese Olympic team," she told Simon as they kept going, following their ski marks, "enjoying the best snow on earth."

Then those marks gave out where the Japanese pair had called it a day and turned back. Brittany and Simon were alone, climbing—often resorting to herringboning their skis sideways at the steepest points—through pristine snow. If Sarah had come this way, she'd come before most of the snow had fallen. The trees on this face of the hill weren't the pines Brittany had seen out of Dave's window, but the rocks were familiar. She kept going, even when the snow stopped being the greatest on earth and turned into the enemy instead. Sarah would have done the same.

Brittany stopped waiting for Simon. Far below, she heard him call her name. "Brittany. It's getting dark."

It was. Dark and cold. They hadn't seen anyone else since the Japanese skiers, at least an hour before. If she had any sense, she would turn back. Come on her next free day. When would that be? Sunday, tomorrow, she had to work to make up for today.

Would Sarah have done this trek? When it was colder? Darker? For a man?

Brittany decided her roommate would indeed do such a thing for Dave Jaramillo and pushed on.

The next voice she heard came from in front of her, and it had no hint of England's "scepter'd isle" in it at all. "Hold it right there."

She looked up. Up and up. High on a ledge stood a man. The shotgun he held in his hands pointed right at her head.

Brittany took a deep breath. It turned out not to be her last. Of course, she was breathing hard from the climb. She took a lot of deep breaths while she waited for her head to stop spinning. She had never been so scared in all her life. If her head didn't spin her backwards off this mountainside, a bullet might. But an edge of triumph tempered the fear.

When she could, she spoke. "Mr. Gentle Ben, I presume?"

The bear-man looked at her. "Says who?"

*Simon says.* She was just light-headed enough to think that, and almost to burst out laughing. She remained serious instead. "My name is Brittany and ..."

"Well, *Brittany*,"—he said it as if only dogs might

get named that, whereas half a dozen girls in her class had had that name, two in her own ward—"you'd better just turn right around and git yerself outa here."

"Or what? You'll add my body count to Dave Jaramillo's?"

The firearm drooped. "What do you know about Dave Jaramillo?"

"Only that he was found dead this morning."

"Dead?" The man really seemed surprised. Pained. And Brittany imagined that it would take a lot to surprise Gentle Ben.

The gun was raised again. "You lying to me?"

"No, sir. I'm the one who found him."

"Well, now, that's enough to put a man right off humans altogether, that is."

"They think it was an accident."

"If Dave Jaramillo's dead, you can bet it weren't no accident." He looked angry, sad and angry.

Just how crazy was this man? Brittany thought maybe not so much.

"Those ski tracks down to his condo from your place up here on the hill look mighty fishy," she said.

Even through all the hair on that face, this detail registered. He stopped to think about that, what danger it might pose.

"If you didn't kill him," Brittany pressed, "who did?"

"I ain't saying." The bear-man seemed about to turn away, back to his lair. Or to turn that gun on whomever his bear-nose made him suspect.

"Wait, please, Mr. Gentle Ben."

Ben turned back to the ledge. "Dave never

mentioned no Brittany."

No, he wouldn't would he? "But what about Sarah? Did he mention a Sarah?"

"Sarah," the man repeated. "This Sarah, she a friend of yours?"

"Yes, sir. My best friend since grade school. We live together, down in town."

"This death of Dave's, that's going to hurt her real bad."

"I'm sure it is. Is Sarah okay?"

"Better than I found her last night, wandering around this mountain in that storm."

"You took her in, Ben?"

"Wouldn't leave my worst enemy out like that. Then I said she should stay warm by my fire while I skied down to tell Dave she was with me. He was just fine when I got to his place. Sitting in the hot tub, steam all around him. He said he had company and couldn't take her in just then."

Brittany breathed a sigh of relief. Sarah was fine, and less traumatized than she would have been had she made it to the condo and found Dave with ... someone else. "I ... I'd like to see my friend. Be with her. When she hears. About Dave."

"That's what all them cop cars were then? This morning? Down at the condos?"

"That's right. About Dave."

"They weren't come after Sarah? They weren't looking for her? Looking for her to be with David? That's what we was thinking, so we laid real low."

"Can I see Sarah?"

"Laying real low; that's what we gotta do. Don't let those as did for Dave do for her." Gentle Ben turned then and disappeared in the deepening twilight just as Simon reached Brittany.

She had fallen into the security of his arms through a tangle of skis and poles and goggles and hats. But Brittany didn't tell her aunt that part.

*****

At this point in the tale, Helen stopped listening to her niece on the phone.

"Brittany, I'm calling Brother and Sister Drake this moment."

"Aunt Helen, don't do that. Sarah's okay, I'm sure of it. This may not be the smartest thing she ever did, but it was her choice."

"We live in the state where Elizabeth Smart was abducted by a deranged mountain man, and you tell me she's *okay*?"

"Ben is—was—Dave's friend. The guy in Unit C told you so. If you'd seen his face on that ledge when I told him, you'd know."

"Honey, you don't know how these crazy men are, talking to God. Luring young ladies away—"

"Ben will tell Sarah, as gently as he can, that Dave is dead. She'll realize then that her infatuation is really, finally hopeless, and she'll come home."

"This is a serious situation that you're in the middle of, Brittany. This Ben is armed and not in his right mind. He lives in a *cave*."

"In an abandoned mine, actually. That part of the Wasatch Back doesn't have any caves, but everybody and their brother dug a mine near Park City during the silver rush."

*Don't get smart with me, young lady,* Helen

wanted to shout. She felt blessed to keep her words to "Am I going to have to come up there and save Sarah Drake myself?" *I'll bring you back, too.*

*The Book of Wizzy* was pleading, "Leave it there, leave it there." Not a Mormon hymn.

"Forget it, Aunt Helen, just forget it. Forget I ever told you anything!"

"But I can't, honey—"

Brittany hung up. Helen stared at the phone. She couldn't believe that dear, sweet Brittany had done that to her.

Helen had to make a choice. She couldn't "Leave It There". Brittany with Simon? Or Sarah with the crazed mountain man?

She chose to try to rescue Sarah from Gentle Ben.

Wizzy did not sing "Choose the Right".

# Chapter 10

Early Sunday morning, ironing Mark's priesthood shirt, Helen was gratified to see the report on the local news program.

"Late last night, the Summit County Sheriff's Department made a daring helicopter raid on the mountain cave inhabited by a local Park City homeless man, Benjamin T. Ursule, alias Gentle Ben. A young Salt Lake woman was rescued from his hideout where, authorities say, she had been kept since disappearing from her home Friday night."

Helen saw the scruffy man in cuffs. Deputy Moody was ushering him away, her hips leading. Helen caught a glimpse of Sarah Drake. The newsroom had pixelated her face out. The young woman seemed unharmed, if distressed. Helen thanked her Heavenly Father for inspiring her to do the obviously right thing—alert the Drakes of their daughter's absence.

Wizzy seemed to sulk behind a chorus of "Have I Done Any Good in the World Today?"

"Wake up and do something more
Than dream of your mansions above."

Probably all Relief Society presidents got that earworm, especially when they were running on four hours of sleep.

Helen did not set the iron on its heel to turn off the television. She changed the channel. Some families forbade Sunday TV. The sports channel kept that from being a rule in her house, however much Mark suggested that women had other Sunday duties that must take precedence. Women who watched the news instead of getting it filtered through the priesthood probably were more likely to apostatize. Some sociologist could do a study of this, producing data which would be reported somewhere, but which the woman who took no control over her own remote would never get to see.

Footage on the next channel showed a different shot of Sarah. And what was this? The young woman's stance showed resistance, a lunge to try to save her captor. Her host, as Brittany said? Did she yell something at the camera? Helen couldn't tell what. Could this even be Sarah? These thoughts brought up Wizzy's chorus again, "Have I helped anyone in need?"

This newscast closed with an interior shot of the mine, its ancient beams and trusses solid with the old world care some immigrant had brought with him, used to shelter his fellow exploited workers. The cavern actually seemed quite snug, considering all the snow that had fallen during the night. Deputy Moody's hips also put in an anonymous appearance here. Cameras did not flatter the woman.

No mention of Dave Jaramillo at all. The sheriff's office must be continuing to treat the hot tub incident as an unfortunate accident. Perhaps they had found evidence of electrical malfunction after all.

Helen shoved the starched shoulders of her husband's shirt onto a hanger. Wizzy drifted beyond sulking to silence, which stung. But her silence had sometimes gone on for weeks, before this current flurry.

Helen found herself in need of justification for her action of calling Sarah's parents. "Have I done any good?" There was no answer from Wizzy, from anyone. Silence.

She put on a pair of heels and walked up the hill to church to assume her new duties as Relief Society president, trudging through the mounds of snow that the plows had pushed up at every intersection. Mark, who did not have a new calling, would come later. Their various duties meant they would scarcely ever sit together on the same pew in the course of a Sunday morning.

On the way, pausing before a lake of slush, Helen checked that she had everything in her bag. She found her cell phone had registered a message. The ID read Eve Drake, Sarah's mother, so Helen thought she'd better take it. She stepped into the thin shade of a naked tree to get out of the glare.

"Eve, how's Sarah?" Helen asked.

"Well, she's still in her room and not speaking to us," Eve replied.

"She'll come around. She'll be grateful someday." Helen hoped what she said was true.

"Well, she ate the pancakes I made especially for her and left near her door. This adventure didn't affect her appetite any. The monster probably starved her. She's got to watch it if we keep her grounded.

She packs on the pounds too easily if she doesn't ski."

Helen thought this seemed like a low priority concern, but she'd never raised a daughter to adulthood. Maybe it mattered a great deal.

"She's like me," Eve Drake continued, "unless she exercises food goes right to her hips. And then who would want her? I have to make sure she stays attractive."

Wizzy's death had left Helen with only the boys, and a haunting feeling that she wasn't a very good mother. And now they'd made her Mother of the Ward? Shouldn't having experience with a daughter be a prerequisite? Did the Lord even know what He was doing?

"You're in my prayers," she told Eve. Sometimes praying was all a mother could do, and often as not those petitions didn't get answered.

Helen didn't add that she hadn't heard anything from Brittany, and it worried her. At least the Drakes now knew behind which door Sarah was fuming. Where was Brittany?

"Thanks. The deal is," Eve went on, "why I called is, I was assigned to provide a casserole for a family in our ward, the Vaughns? Do you know them?"

Helen did not.

"Their three-year-old daughter is in the LDS hospital."

*Three-year-old daughter* wrenched Helen's heart in a way she had hoped she was past, but maybe never would be. "What does the child have?"

"From what I hear, she's become very dehydrated and seems ..." Eve had to pause a moment to find the proper words. They didn't really exist in her world.

"... at death's door. The thing is, I can make the casserole, but Xavier has a priesthood meeting, and I hate to leave Sarah for a minute in the state she's in. Who knows when she might come out, and I want to be here for her. Our own Relief Society president is out of town with a new grandbaby. Could you possibly just run the dish over?"

Eve didn't know the calling Helen had just accepted. Surely there were counselors in the Drake's ward who could fit this task into their Sunday runs.

But Eve Drake would want to keep the ward gossip about Sarah's "kidnapping" to a minimum, never mind that it had been on the morning news. They hadn't given out Sarah's name and had pixelated her face. Many families outlawed Sunday TV. There was a very good chance that most of them would never know of Sarah's rescue.

This was supposed to be a day of rest.

But "Of course," Helen said. "Right after I preside over my first meeting."

She would have to learn to delegate. At the moment, however, she did not have numbers of many women in her own ward in her speed dial.

She climbed up the ward house stairs to the side door she always entered because it faced her house and pulled open the door. She took a deep breath before opening the door to the Relief Society room and flipping down the foot lock. There was power.

Brother Sparks had turned on the furnace early. This end of the building, the end subject to the most hot flashes, always got cooked as the cavern of the soaring chapel slowly warmed to welcome those who would fill it. Helen threw open the windows and looked out over the snow-mounded viburnum. Elderly sisters would have to be ushered away from this frigid air, but surely the back reaches of the room would stay warm enough. Except then they probably couldn't hear.

Helen began to reset the cushioned chairs. Most other meeting rooms in the building had metal folding chairs.

*"Have I done any good ...?"*

Helen stopped and stared. She remembered how once Wizzy had lost a little pink sandal at church. Searching everywhere, Helen had found it at last right on that chair nearest the piano. Kicked off by her daughter, found by some tidying sister and left there for her to find. Helen froze, staring at the empty seat.

Two younger sisters came in and offered to take the chore of arranging seats off her hands. Helen moved on to that most emblematic of her duties: the spreading of a faux lace tablecloth across the laminate table at the head of the space between the two open windows.

More power.

The gesture was supposed to make the room look less like an institution, more like a cozy living room, for this meeting. It would not be spread for any meeting over which the priesthood would preside. *The Book of Mormon* said nothing about such rituals. It was an unwritten rule, but a constant, like hot air blasting through the furnace vents.

So it began.

More sisters entered, in twos and threes, according to age cohorts. Time for socializing, the most important part of the society. The pleasantries included a lot of what Helen secretly called "special talk" done to the tune of "Pick a Little, Talk a Little" from *The Music Man*. Gushing "You look so trim," "You did a good job." "Your son is so special," in a case where a southern lady might say "Bless his heart."

"Thanks," "thanks" and more "thanks," confirming Helen's belief that a little gratitude was the glue that held her congregation together. She would not try to curb this socializing, not hustle these women into their seats and impose an air of respectful, attentive silence, not even if it meant being called derelict in her duties.

Besides, the pianist was late.

"Remind me who the pianist is," Helen whispered to Nan, her also-newly-appointed second counselor. If Helen couldn't make even the music run smoothly, what hope was there for her?

"Allred." Nan's handbook of members was also a jumble. "Something Allred."

Not one of the inner circle, then. Pianists seldom were. Artists. *Think charitably*. Helen herself had hidden in the outer reaches of Primary piano for fifteen years.

She scanned the gathering women as they unburdened themselves of winter wraps they hadn't hung in the coat closet. Who looked like an Allred? It was a common Mormon name. Helen thought she might even recognize Allred features when she saw them, certainly if Wizzy gave a nudge.

*"Have I done any good—?"* Wizzy was now trying to get a word in edgewise, but it wasn't happening.

Not in the Relief Society room on a Sunday morning.

As she continued to greet the sisters, Helen noted four showing pregnancies. Each happy event would bring work to the Relief Society. She also noted three sisters either using canes or in those heavy boots podiatrists gave out. In snow! Did they get the necessary rides from the priesthood?

*"Have I done any good...?"*

Even more worrisome were those who did not appear. At least ten of the elderly had stayed home, either on account of the snow or from more permanent handicaps. Helen felt her memory getting swamped and resorted to making notes in the chaotic notebook she'd been handed.

The sister missionaries arrived, one from Anaheim, the other from New Jersey. The second sister had selected unfortunate horizontal stripes for her missionary wardrobe; was that a failure of Young Women's instruction in Atlantic City?

The sister missionaries would need dinner invitations. Helen, having lost the page on which she'd made her previous notes, made a new note on a new page.

*"Have I done any good—?"*

"We are so glad to have you take this position." Helen found herself surrounded by the bony arms of Cynthia Irvine, the bishop's wife.

Hugging was a new thing. Mormons in Helen's youth had been more reserved, less attuned to national emotional trends. This would take some getting used to.

Stepping back to look Cynthia in the eye, Helen barely stifled a gasp.

Under troweled-on makeup, the woman's face was bruised. Helen fumbled with how to discretely add a new heading, "Investigate for domestic violence"—and put the bishop's name at the head of that list. Fortunately, another look solved the mystery. Cynthia's bright red, newly puffy lips looked like a sneering beak from Angry Birds. Did plastic surgery warrant charity casseroles? Helen decided no. Not on her watch. Not unless she got orders from the priesthood—who might have ordered Cynthia's medical experience in the first place.

*"Have I done any good—?"*

The priesthood had made three hospital blessing visits during the week. Helen made her tally. More calls, more casseroles, more knocks on doors.

A sudden pound on the piano made Helen think her first fifteen minutes as Relief Society president must have qualified her for immediate divine translation.

Something Allred—*Sister* Allred—had arrived. Time to call the meeting to order.

It was after Thanksgiving. They could have sung Christmas carols. Instead, the hymns were "Battle Hymn of the Republic" and "Onward Christian Soldiers" to send the sisters out into world again. Not what Helen would have chosen that day, but she'd given up her job in the music department, hadn't she? She could only pray that "marching as to war" was helping Sister Allred—who looked like no Allred Helen knew, it must be a married name—work some of her demons out of her purple-tinted fingertips. The young—very young—woman's tattooed calf pressed the pedals as if she were in the high school marching band at the opening of the big game. Her hair was a tangle of mismatched braids and felted ropes. What were those called?

Wizzy helped out with a line from hymn number 285, "God Moves in a Mysterious Way":

> The clouds ye so much dread
> Are big with mercy...

A good Relief Society president would contact Sister Allred's visiting teachers to see what was up. Or perhaps make a personal visit.

The announcements included "a beautiful opportunity to bless" an unfortunate family in the next ward. Helen remembered Eve Drake's casserole with a flush of panic; it had all but slipped her mind, shoved out by everything else.

Michelle Banks patted her swelling, exhausted belly, announced with pleasure, with relief, that she was not having a sixth girl, and if anyone knew anyone who was expecting a daughter, they should come and clean out her closets.

"The Robinsons are looking to rent their home for six months. Does anybody know a worthy family?"

Helen fretted about Sister Allred all through that sweet spirit Sister Crockett's lesson on "Righteous Living in Perilous Times: The Teachings of President George Albert Smith".

"Sweet spirit" was Mormon code for someone, usually a woman, who didn't have much else going for her, neither looks nor money nor family connections, not even, Heaven forbid, brains.

Would they never quote a woman to a room full of women?

Another item for her unwritten list.

*"Have I done any good—?"*

Helen's mind was in a whirl by the time the Relief Society meeting was over. The pianist dashed out the door before Helen could introduce herself as the new president, and the rest of the ladies exited in a slow-moving, multi-colored wave. Then the tide turned and the Sunday School took over the room. Helen and her counselors used that portion of the three-hour Sunday marathon to go over the tally of who needed what help and to make a plan for the week. They had to sit together on a bench in the hall; all the rooms were taken, the offices going to the priesthood. The lack of a desk made planning and writing difficult. Now Helen understood why the president's notebook was such a disorganized jumble, too much even for Karen.

Then it was sacrament meeting, the final stretch of the marathon. She took her place beside Mark.

Eve Drake's phone call had reminded Helen that she had heard nothing from Brittany since the girl had hung up on her the night before. The one time Helen had tried to call her, there had been no answer. Her niece must be at church. No ... now Helen remembered. Brittany had to work, cleaning up the condos she'd missed the day before. Breaking the Sabbath.

Helen tried to sneak a look at her cell phone. Such devices were frowned upon when the Word of God was being preached over the pulpit, but surely there was a dispensation for Relief Society presidents.

A nudge from Mark told her there was not.

Another nudge told her she had just been called

upon to stand and receive the sustaining raised hands of every member of the congregation in recognition of her new calling as Relief Society president.

"Sister Snow?" The bishop called, his tone an admonishment against woolgathering, or worse. "Do you sustain yourself?"

Sheepishly, Helen raised her right arm "to the square" lest she seem unwilling to accept the honor. Odd how that old Masonic phrase and gesture had been incorporated into the ritual; but then, several of the earliest Brethren had been Masons.

With a touch of cynicism—Brittany was rubbing off on her—she wondered how many of those right hands would really sustain her when she needed assistance. Or would she have to depend mostly upon her own right arm?

And Wizzy. Of course, Wizzy.

> Then pealed the bells more loud and deep
> God is not dead nor does he sleep...

Well, Helen would try Brittany again in the evening. After delivering the casserole. Maybe by then the girl would have realized how good it was that her friend had been rescued from a fate worse than death. Before Helen had to go and rescue *her*.

# Chapter 11

"Hello?"

Brittany paused by the only car in the condo garage: a new Ford Escape, white, but quickly becoming the seasonal slush-gray, the hood still warm. The little girl's yellowish vomit was still there, frozen solid.

Brittany called again up the cement stairwell to no answer. When she'd left him at the bus stop, she'd assured Simon she'd be fine alone. Now, however, she wasn't so sure. Sarah had been released into the "protective custody" of her parents—hadn't even been allowed to call her best friend, roommate and dog sitter, and Consuela was nowhere to be found. The only good thing about Brittany's fear was that it shoved her fury at her aunt to the back burner. This was all Aunt Helen's fault.

"Hello?" Brittany called again.

This was creepy.

At the top of the stairs, she tried the door to Unit B—might as well get the hard part over first—and found it open.

"Hello?"

She stepped in with more confidence. The woman standing by the sliding doors had Latina features: high cheekbones and deep, sad, dark eyes. Was she Consuela's replacement, come to help with the housekeeping? This woman was older than Consuela, with gray streaks at her temples that she didn't bother to dye. Brittany had always hoped that she—that any woman—would have found other options than the hard work of housekeeping by the time her hair was turning grey. Or at least she'd dye it. "Salt and pepper belongs on the table," her Young Women's instructor had told the Sunday class, "not on your head."

The same instructor had also said, "Never date a non-Mormon." And Simon—Brittany would sort out those contradictions later.

The only thing that didn't match the notion that this woman might be squeegeeing the deck doors was the new car down below, not the kind a housekeeper could afford. Besides no squeegee in her hand. And the clothes. No pink cleaning smock. Tight jeans, a fashionable knit turtleneck with a cowl, and jewelry.

"Are you a friend of Consuela?" Brittany asked hesitantly.

"Who?"

"Consuela Martinez. She works here. Or worked here. She might have—I just wondered how she's doing."

"Sorry. Don't know a Consuela." The woman's voice held no hint of accent.

"I'm Brittany. Nice to meet you. I'm here to clean up...."

"I'm Diana Jaramillo. David's mother."

With a shock, Brittany recognized her as the woman in one of the photos she had dusted on Dave's end table. Seeing the woman as a replacement cleaner had been a bit of unintended racism on her part. Her "Oh, I am so sorry" had a double meaning.

Contrition opened her heart, and she saw the hopeless, helpless look that crossed the other woman's face. With a sob, Brittany crossed the room and flung her arms around the stranger.

A good cry in another woman's arms is a binding event, one Brittany was just learning to appreciate. She found herself crying for Dave, for his mother, for Sarah—and, yes, even for Aunt Helen, whose benighted morals had just cast a shadow on what had been, until that point, their close, eighteen-year relationship.

After the cry, and more "I'm so, so sorry"s, "I don't know what to say"s and "He was such a wonderful man," Brittany began to hear what Mrs. Jaramillo was saying through her fresh tears.

First, "Please, I'm not *Mrs.* Jaramillo." Then, with a fresh sob, "You call him a man. It is your age. I was only just beginning to call him that myself. I still called him *m'ijo.*"

After another embrace, Brittany fetched fresh tissues. The two women sat on the couch holding hands as the older woman continued to unburden herself. Brittany learned that Dave's mother wished she had insisted that she come and live with him up here. "In my culture, he would not have lived alone. I knew it was a mistake, but his father—"

"You mustn't blame yourself," Brittany said. But Diana Jaramillo might be right. What might happen to her, Brittany wondered for the first time, with her parents out of the picture?

"He wanted his independence," Dave's mother said, "all this health food and so on. Health food, to die so young like this." She smiled bitterly. "And he thought he'd have a better relationship with his father if I wasn't in the way." She shook her head. "This is so hard, knowing that I have to go through this alone. I have no one else in the world but him."

Brittany struggled to keep her surprise from sounding in her voice. "But Dave's father—? After your divorce, didn't he still...?"

"We never married."

Brittany had to smother a gasp as Diana Jaramillo seethed, "He's still married to the same woman: the 'eternal companion' that he was married to when I first met him twenty-six years ago."

So the man was a Mormon. Probably in good standing. But such things didn't happen in Mormondom!

Looks like they did. That *wasn't* okay.

Brittany thought of Simon. He'd spent the night. They hadn't "done" anything. Well, not much. He'd just said she needed the company after the distresses with Sarah and with Aunt Helen, and she realized it was true. He'd slept in Sarah's empty bunk.

Brittany had been supportive of Sarah's pursuit of Dave. Sarah was more daring than Brittany would have been, but the example of her friend's daring was helping her with Simon, giving Brittany the courage she needed to question her parent's injunctions as to what to look for in an eternal mate.

"I used to clean their house," the older woman

said.

That was *really* not okay, thought Brittany the housekeeper, seeing herself in that position. Seeing Sarah in that position. It seems that Dave was more ethical than his father, whoever he was, had been.

Brittany considered. "How is Dave's sister doing? Is she going to be okay?"

"David has no sister."

Brittany was quite sure Aunt Helen had said that the young man on crutches in Unit C had spoken of a sister. And weren't there photos of Dave with a sisterly girl in the apartment? Brittany had dusted them. She looked to the sideboard. The photos were gone.

Well, that young man wasn't in Unit C any more, so she couldn't ask him. It had looked like he was going to jail last time Brittany had seen him: jail, while the sheriff tried to pin drugs on him and his friends. Maybe malicious destruction of condo property, too. Maybe the neighbor hadn't been a reliable source of information. And after spilling the beans about Sarah's whereabouts, Brittany wasn't in the mood to trust Aunt Helen. Let her stay in Salt Lake and mind her own business for a change.

But... weren't missing her own mother and worse Aunt Helen's betrayal part of why she felt herself bonding with Diana Jaramillo so suddenly and completely?

For the first time since she'd fallen into the grieving woman's arms, Brittany remembered where she was. She was not sitting in the modest but pleasant home this woman described struggling to provide for her beloved only child. They sat together in the expensive condo Brittany had to clean, the expensive condo where Dave had lived—and died—alone.

"David's father helped from time to time. More to keep us quiet, I think, than from any real concern. David rarely saw his father; maybe twice in his life."

"That's awful."

For one moment, Brittany wondered if that "help" had ever been in response to blackmail. Had the woman she was sitting beside turned predator among predators for the sake of her child? Brittany had to admit, were she in this woman's position—a powerless position, with an abuser for a boss and a small son to raise—she probably wouldn't call it blackmail, either.

"Yes," Diana Jaramillo said. "In many respects, I think his father's family will be only too glad he's ... he's gone."

Brittany was appalled. Unable to think of anything to say, she looked around the room once again. Yes, the end table and the mantel were empty and bare, where only yesterday the photographs had sat. The photos were definitely gone.

Of course Dave's mother would take the photos.

"Would you like me to help you clean up?" Brittany asked. "That must be a horrible job when you've lost someone you love. Besides, they are paying me to do it."

Diana Jaramillo must have noticed the direction of Brittany's gaze. "I've only come to take a few mementos. The rest can go to Goodwill. It would only hurt to have them around."

Brittany nodded. Well, she'd take some to her run-down house on Main Street first, then Goodwill. Or rather, Deseret Industries, the Church thrift store. No, Diana Jaramillo had specified Goodwill. What if the father recognized any of the furniture as things that had belonged to his dead, illegitimate son? She would call Goodwill.

"I have to clean the other units, too," Brittany said, "so I'll let you be alone here until you're ready for me to take over."

Diana Jaramillo nodded her thanks, and Brittany went off to deal with the mess next door.

Just about the time that Brittany had finished the other two apartments—around noon—the grieving woman came and said that she had packed David's mementos into the car and she was leaving.

"David's TV's broken," Diana said as an afterthought. "The wiring burned out or something. I don't think Goodwill will take it."

Brittany remembered dusting the television on the sideboard the day before. She also remembered that Dave had told her and Sarah that he never watched TV. When they'd cleaned, they'd seen the set stashed in the storage closet out on the deck.

"We were strangers this morning," Diana Jaramillo said as they embraced once again in good-bye. "Now I feel we are friends."

Brittany brushed away fresh tears.

By mid afternoon, snacking on the leftovers of three fridges, Brittany had finished Unit B, too. Dave's things were sorted into two piles, one for Desert Industries—Goodwill, actually—and one for herself and Sarah. She felt opulent as she considered her newly-gained riches, all of which would have special meaning because they had belonged to such a nice young man, as well as adding much needed comfort to the miserable rental. A great deal of good food, for starters. Dozens, maybe hundreds of books, many of which would go to the library, which meant visiting Simon; a wonderfully warm blanket that Dave must have bought at a crafts market, brighter than the mass-produced blankets purchased in volume by Pine Enterprises; a framed poster of artistically arranged grains; and two smaller prints, one of horses, and one of a courtyard, fountain, and arched doorway; even some furniture: a sturdy stool and an extra bookshelf made of polished, solid, fine-grained dark wood. Brittany would need a car to carry it all, however. Maybe Simon could help?

She took the last of the trash out to the dumpster and prepared to call it a day. A jumble of papers, food wrappers and empty beer bottles slid from the wastebasket into the dumpster. She should take the time to recycle what she could, but she was tired.

The very last things to slide out caught her eye. They were the missing photographs, torn from their frames. Diana Jaramillo had not taken them, but rather had hoped never to see them again. Brittany fished them out and studied them.

She added the photos to her backpack, to the things she would carry out herself right now. A photo of the young man for whom Sarah had sacrificed so much might cheer her, when they could get together again. Oh, why had Aunt Helen done that stupid, old-lady-snitching thing? Missing her best friend, and missing her aunt more than she would admit to herself, Brittany got out her phone and called Simon.

# Chapter 12

The house was new. Helen, casserole in mitted hands, remembered the empty lot and the old brick bungalow with lace curtains that an elderly widow had inhabited until her removal to a nursing home four or five years previous. Then, as was the fate of many an old house in East Millcreek, down had come the red brick to be replaced by this McMansion, bulging at the seams of the lot with faux Tuscan balconies and faux tile roof. It all looked particularly faux in winter, with mere twigs of trees sticking out here and there, replacing the tall old cottonwoods. A vegetable garden had once spread where that circle of faux battlement tower with heavy glazing now loomed.

So much for a culture that put such verbal emphasis on "tradition".

Wizzy seemed to be excited about this first compassionate service delivery of Helen's tenure, even though it was out of the ward over which she had stewardship. Standing on this porch got "Standing on the Promises of God" for an accompaniment.

A boy who looked to be thirteen years old

answered the door. He was not at church. He was not even in Sunday suit and tie, but in gray sweats with a logo that Helen didn't look at too closely. Its dark colors indicated something violent.

The music drifting through the house sounded vaguely religious, but it was not the Mormon Tabernacle Choir. It was dark, medieval, Gregorian, Gothic: World of Warcraft theme music, as Helen knew from her own boys. From an upstairs corner of the house came the sound of two other, younger children screaming at each other.

"I've brought your family a yam and sausage casserole from Sister Drake down the street," Helen explained, presenting the covered dish as her bona fides.

"I hate yams," said the sweats-clad warrior with a furtive look over his shoulder. The game was proceeding without him.

"Well, one of your brothers or sisters might like it."

Helen continued to stand in the doorway, holding the casserole in the mitts she'd brought along with her, so as not to have to borrow Eve Drake's. Helen would have to buy new pads if she was going to be delivering meals in the days and months ahead. These old ones were—as Brittany might say—"grody". They were thin, too; Helen was feeling the dish's heat through the fabric.

The boy shrugged.

"May I take it to the kitchen?"

The boy shrugged again and stepped out of her way. She made it to a beautiful granite counter without, she hoped, burns bad enough to require hospitalization after this errand of mercy.

"I'm Sister Snow," she smiled, extending a hand only slightly reddened. "What's your name?"

"Evan." The boy retreated to hover in the arched doorway of the kitchen. The game beckoned, but good manners compelled him to be the host.

"I'm so sorry to hear about your little sister. I hope she's doing better." And when he still offered nothing, she asked, "What have you heard?"

"Not much. But Mom and Dad are up at the hospital."

And would turn off the orcs and dwarves when they got home. Right.

"These flu bugs that go around can be dangerous for little ones," Helen ventured, although she wasn't sure if the kid heard a word she said over the siren song of the game.

Strangely, he did. "Wasn't the flu. She drank kom ... can't remember the name. Sort of like toad food."

"Toad food? Oh, you mean tofu? Toad food. That's clever. Kom? ... Kombucha?"

Kombucha was tea, wasn't it? Helen herself had never drunk kombucha. Frankly, a drink with mold floating through it didn't seem—well, it didn't seem very *Mormon*. Probably it should be prohibited in the Word of Wisdom along with "hot drinks". The Brethren of the Liquor Commission in their beneficence had certainly thought so; Helen remembered the kerfuffle when they'd refused to allow the drink in natural food store coolers. In fact, that was where she'd learned the word, curious about the card with the official Utah logo on it dangling above an empty space next to other things she didn't drink: almond milk and suja and spinach chai with lemon grass.

The sign had since come down and the case refilled, perhaps with a watered-down product, the way Utah beer was watered down. Helen wasn't sure. She just knew that kombucha was fermented tea, so strong tasting that it could cover any other flavor. The poor little three-year-old. No wonder she had gotten sick.

Helen thought of the stuff fermenting in her niece's fridge and did not feel well. The *Book of Wizzy* shuddered with the old black spiritual "Follow the Drinking Gourd," the song of instruction for reaching freedom that would run beneath the white masters' understanding.

A girl who looked to be about ten years old with earbuds in her ears strode by the arched kitchen doorway, sending her half-hearted yells upstairs as a commentary on the scrap going on elsewhere.

"Can you put the casserole in the fridge in about an hour?" Helen asked her reluctant host. To demonstrate—sometimes, she knew, boys needed such physical demonstrations—she opened the fridge. At present, no kombucha graced the fridge. "The dish is too hot to go in now, but it should go in. Sausage spoils quickly."

This actually caught the boy's attention. "Don't want the rest of us in the hospital," he agreed, "from eating stuff that's gone bad."

"Like kombucha."

"Yeah," he agreed. "Kom-barf-ya. Well, I gotta go."

"I'll see my way out." Then, to his back, she said,

"We're all praying for your little sister."

Just at the door, the girl with the earbuds walked by again. The fight upstairs was still going on. Helen wondered if she should try to settle it.

"I see your mother got rid of all the kombucha in the fridge," Helen attempted. "Probably wise."

The girl pulled out one bud and made a gagging sound. "Kombucha. Disgusting. I would never drink Kombucha. Nobody but stupid little girls drink the stuff."

Helen hoped it wasn't dead little girls. *Oh, Wizzy ....*

Wizzy herself was not grieving over the little Vaughn girl's condition. Was that because the little girl would soon come to join Wizzy as a playmate in heaven? But Wizzy had never had a selfish bone in her body and was singing "Gird up your loins, fresh courage take," from "Come, Come Ye Saints", so Helen took heart.

Which shifted Helen's attention to the hot pads on her hands. The reason she hadn't bought new ones in over fifteen years was that she and Wizzy had used them as sock puppets. They even had names. The Christmas-y one was Santa—the comic straight man— with the batting falling out around his cuff in a very Brigham Young sort of beard. The mischievous one with fall colors and button eyes she'd sewn back on a dozen times was Brownie. Santa and Brownie went everywhere together and often sang together, even though they didn't match. Right now the puppets had joined Wizzy in singing Number 30. Brownie, as usual, was getting the lyrics wrong, but the "All is swell, all is swell" chorus helped answer the prayer of concern Helen had held in her heart for the hospitalized little girl who belonged in this house.

Less reverent were the lines that went,

"Come, come ye Saints,

No toilet paper here ..."

instead of the "no toil nor labor fear." What did "no toilet paper" say about the Vaughn home? Helen was sure the McMansion did have toilet paper—always. The softest, highest-priced kind that little Mormon Relief Society cartoon sister elves held quilting bees for. The commodes never missed a flush here, Helen would be willing to bear her testimony to that, even though her stay hadn't been long enough for personal witness.

Was Brownie underlining, to put a clean face upon it, that "there was something rotten in the state of Vaughn"? Something even toilet paper couldn't clean up? Something you'd need moist towelettes for? Naughty Brownie. Right there in the pristine Vaughn entry hall, Santa gave him a smack.

Wizzy's giggle resounded off the white marble.

Helen had moist towelettes in her bag, left over from Wizzy days. But Helen had to take care of what she could. "Sufficient unto the day" and all that. She couldn't stop the Vaughn kids fighting. She couldn't be an MD fighting to save a little three-year-old in the hospital. Not in this life—and Mormons didn't believe in reincarnation.

But she could buy new hot pads, ones that matched, in quiet colors. No eyes. The recipients of well-intentioned generosity would approve. Monday morning. And she'd retire Santa and Brownie to their proper places as mitt puppets in Wizzy's old room.

Only ... was she never to hear their lively banter again? Never to hear Wizzy's delighted giggle?

*****

As the door to the Vaughn home closed behind her, the automatic door to the garage on Helen's right came down, giving her a start. Just before the panels slipped into place, she saw that one of two spaces sat empty. A black BMW filled the other, fresh white tracks from the street leading to its tires across a spotless driveway that could only have been cleaned by a high-powered snow blower after the last snowfall.

And a man, haggard and gray with worry, stepped out of the garage through a side door. His hair was precise in a priesthood haircut, although he was not in a Sunday suit but in togs more suited to the ski slope. Of course, this must be Brother Vaughn. And who could blame him for his worry, with a small daughter in the hospital? Helen was predisposed to like him at once.

An examination of the plow job distracted him from actually seeing her. He kicked at the snow banks and at stray lumps. He obviously had not done the job himself and was inspecting someone else's work, hoping not to pay for more than he got. He was also talking on the phone.

He stood at the end of the walk. She couldn't very well march through the snow to avoid him, but Helen wondered at herself when she stepped behind a potted juniper topiaried into a spiral. She was The Relief Society. She had a right to be there; she didn't need to sneak around. Surely she didn't want to snoop, to hear any more of this phone conversation?

But she did. Wizzy, in fact, seemed to want to play Hide and Seek.

"You heard what the doctor said—" Brother Vaughn got cut off by the voice on the other end.

As soon as he could get a word in edgewise he attempted: "No, I didn't want to have this discussion face to face in the hospital! I knew it would turn into an argument, and I didn't want poor Gretel to—" This time the interruption seemed to come from Brother Vaughn himself, choking back sobs he wouldn't show in public. But it allowed the other end to chatter on in what sounded like, through the speaker, to be self-defense.

"Peggy, shut up for one minute and listen to me. The doctor said it wasn't the flu. It was Diazepam.

"No, I didn't know, but I had the sense to ask. Diazepam. Valium. And where would our daughter get an overdose of Valium? Don't let your addiction to mood enhancers make you deny that it must be your bottle, left lying around while we were in your hurry to pack and get out of the condo ... must be where Gretel—"

Brother Vaughn stood frozen on his own walkway, not seeing anything before him, just focusing on the voice at the other end. "Peggy, remember where you are. I know you're under stress—"

The one-sided conversation continued. "I know it's not your fault that you have to take—" Once again, he was interrupted by a voice so loud Helen could hear the tone, if not the words.

"We will get more. Go to Dr. Wilson—"

"I know—"

"But priesthood blessings can only do so much—"

"It's all my fault—"

"I know it's been stressful for you, I know you've been upset—"

"Peggy, just let it go. It may not be fair, but it's—"

The voice at the other end raised in what sounded like real fury.

"Peggy, we don't need—"

Helen's own phone rang. Not "Winter Wonderland", not Brittany. But her cover was blown.

She decided the most merciful act she could perform at that moment was to reveal herself, to give the poor man an out.

"Good day, Brother Vaughn. I'm the Relief Society." She strode toward him, hand outstretched. "I am so sorry to hear about your daughter."

And the kombucha story was just a teenaged boy's dislike of rotten tea and tofu. What was a Mormon family doing drinking tea anyway? Fermented tea? That should have been a red flag to her that the boy had got it wrong.

Massive doses of Valium? In Utah, with the highest anti-depressant use in the country? Particularly among Mormon women who could never be good enough, but whose busy lives sometimes precluded even enough time for exercise? Who got a new list of "be ye therefore perfects" every Sunday but who could not self-medicate with even a glass of wine or a cup of chamomile tea? Or kombucha? Where Helen herself had been offered such drugs to keep her from suffering her natural grief over the death of a child? Where she had seen it prescribed by a medical doctor moonlighting as a bishop to a woman who had born a daughter instead of the hoped-for son, even though the baby could become addicted via mother's milk? Where "man is that he might have joy" but women—?

How was Helen supposed to act as the president of an organization that worked in such a dissonant world? No wonder she clung to Wizzy's disparate but usually harmonious songs.

# Chapter 13

Helen didn't answer her own cell phone. The ring tone told her it wasn't Brittany, and that was the one person she wanted to hear from.

Wizzy had fallen still in sympathetic silence. Helen might almost say the silence was judgmental, as angry as Brittany's lack of communication was, except that Wizzy was never like that. That was clear from the Wizzy eyes in the Hoffmann Jesus face that floated above Brother Vaughn's body.

"Be ye therefore perfect" jostled with "Judge not that ye be not judged." *Do not judge me, Lord, unworthy of my child.*

This tension between *The Book of Wizzy* and *LDS Handbook 2* was almost more than Helen could bear. Would access to *Handbook 1*, only available to administering men and blocked behind priesthood-only firewalls that would make Apple proud, help soothe the worry this man endured? Three points made a plane, she remembered from geometry, and a plane allowed more freedom of movement than a line, narrow and strait. If one had to walk a rope, however, between *The Book of Wizzy* and *LDS Handbook 2*, no doubt it was better if it were tight.

*Pull tighter,* Helen begged of her celestial daughter. *More holiness give me.*

Wizzy did not take up the hint for a new hymn. Helen stood in the here and now, talking to Brother Vaughn, alone.

Her cell message went over to voicemail and made another *bing* as she stood in front of the Vaughn's, where an old Mormon widow's bungalow once stood, and heard that the youngest Vaughn seemed to be improving.

Helen put on her Relief Society smile. "Excellent news."

Bad things couldn't possibly happen to a family who lived in such a fabulous house, who went to church every Sunday. She told Brother Vaughn that she and the whole stake were behind him and had him in their prayers, that his children needed him, needed him to be strong, that she trusted in the power of the priesthood that he held. He had blessed his daughter, hadn't he? She would come and fetch the casserole dish in a few days.

The message on her phone, which she checked as she slid into her car, was from Sister Drake, Sarah's mom. The message seemed a little hysterical, which was not how Helen had left her when she had headed out with the casserole for the Vaughns'. Helen thought it best to stop by, since she was in the ward anyway.

Two cars and a TV van seemed incongruous parked in front of the house, all idling, the visible smoke from their tail pipes adding to the sinking inversion but keeping their occupants warm while they waited. They hadn't been there when she'd picked up the casserole. Didn't the press also get Sunday morning off?

As Helen approached, people jumped out of all three cars. Dressed for the camera was a step up from dressed for church, but dressed for church was what Helen was and it would have to do. She counted five cameras of different sizes. Each wielder rushed to be the first to accost her.

"Are you a friend of the Drake family?"

"A relative?"

"Do you know Sarah?"

"Was she raped?"

The press. Of course they would be interested in a case that seemed an echo of Elizabeth Smart's ordeal. That there weren't more cameras maybe meant the good news that it wasn't like the Smart case.

The "r" word. Who had said anything about the "r" word?

After taking a few steps back and almost landing in a snow bank, Helen justified herself by saying "Relief Society." She was amazed how well that worked, even without a casserole dish in her hands. The news people climbed back in their vehicles.

At her knock, the Drake's door opened a crack and let her in.

The Drake's McMansion was older than the Vaughn's, but constant remodels kept it in the "Home Can Be Heaven on Earth" competition. Sister Drake had all her Christmas decorations up. Helen couldn't imagine how even a McMansion had room to squeeze in one more twinkle light, one more ceramic elf cavorting in the Santa village at the foot of the two-story high tree, one more sprig of not-faux holly. The fragrance of Sunday roast reached from floor to ceiling, floating on the pine room freshener that was helping out the tree.

Helen's failings as a homemaker hit her in the face.

And what was Brittany having for dinner tonight after a full day cleaning condos? Definitely not pot roast.

Eve offered Helen an overstuffed chair in the midst of all that perfection. As its sides rose up to envelope her, Helen felt every fiber of her exhaustion and her hunger. And it was only the first day of her calling.

She fell back onto automatic. Before any business, it was important to make some flattering comment about her hostess, the home, something. Difficult, when it made Helen feel so unworthy herself. Would her attempts at Christmas decoration measure her worthiness to see Wizzy again when she died?

Then she saw the blue and white elf. Among all the red, white and green ones, this little fellow stood out like a semaphore—little gal, actually. The elf wore a cheerleader's pleated skirt, although the plastered-on smile was the same as the rest. And was that the BYU fight song Wizzy was trying to remember the words to?

"Oh. You went to BYU, too, Eve?" came out of Helen's mouth. That wasn't exactly a compliment. And the look that crossed Eve's face convinced Helen she'd really misspoken. Fortunately, Eve was ever-gracious. She followed the direction of Helen's gaze and plucked the blue-and-white fantasy creature gently out of the spun glass angel hair on the tree. It still waved a toothpick BYU pennant in each little felt hand.

"Yes," Eve said, cradling the doll. "That first Christmas we were married, this was our only ornament. It's our nineteenth anniversary coming up. Hard to imagine how the time has flown. Once the kids came. And they came fast."

*Only nineteen*, thought Helen from her spot at nearly twenty-five years. Eighteen of them unhappy.

"What year did you graduate?" Helen thought she might find common ground, if not with this woman, then at least with her own BYU alum and distant husband Mark by learning the answer.

Another faux pas, by the look Eve tried to hide by nestling the figure back upon its cloud. "I never graduated," Eve said shortly, the tone warning Helen not to pursue the topic.

Helen was wondering what she could say when Eve changed the topic, to Sarah, of course. "It's her precious dog," Eve said.

*The precious Horehound.* Helen gritted her teeth. She said, as cheerily as she could, "I met Taffy yesterday. At the girls' cute little house on Main Street." A chill always went down her spine whenever she used the word "cute, but it was expected of her, especially now that she was head of a Relief Society. The chill still came.

"Cute" was obviously not a word Eve Drake was willing to use for the little house on Park City's Main Street. She had been trying to find a way to get her daughter out of that house, and now she'd found it. "Sarah will not be returning to Park City. She is not suited to such conditions."

"That's a pity." Helen was fully conscious of the social slap she and hers had just received. Sarah was not suited to such conditions, but Brittany and presumably Brittany's aunt were. Helen knew Brittany couldn't afford the house on her own, not with the job that was beneath her best friend Sarah. Sarah, who could still aspire to the Olympics without either a house in Park City or a job cleaning condos.

All of this went unsaid, except by the two-story high tree and the elves, whose grins seemed to turn smug instead of playful.

"But she does want Taffy back as soon as possible," Eve Drake was saying. "Taffy is a service dog. She can and should accompany my daughter everywhere, into restaurants and stores."

But not on the ski slopes or to work or bars or into the lairs of mountain men.

This woman clearly enjoyed—no, thought it was her duty as a righteous Mormon—to rewrite the laws after her own image. That Horehound was no therapy dog, unless by that you meant that the dog was the one who needed therapy.

Eve, perhaps seeing the look of doubt that Helen was struggling with, insisted, "We have obtained the necessary papers to prove it. Sarah needs her pet as soon as possible to help in her recovery from the trauma she has endured."

A medically approved Horehound.

"Has Sarah told Brittany all of this?" Helen asked. Her niece was going to be heartbroken.

"No. We do not think she needs any more trauma."

"Then have you told Brittany for her?"

"I hoped you would take the responsibility to go

up and bring the dog back. You can tell Brittany all of this when you go to pick up Taffy and restore her to her family."

Helen had her mouth open to say that things weren't all that great between Brittany and herself. That seemed the most self-effacing thing she could say after all this grinding down, essentially blaming Brittany's bad influence for Sarah's misadventure.

Helen felt a physical shove against her years of training in self-effacement. She kept her mouth shut. Wizzy gave a counter jolt of confirmation by striking the chords of "Peace, Peace, Be Still." Helen was a Relief Society president, after all. One who had delivered a yam and sausage casserole to her host's neighbor for her.

In that silence, Helen actually felt a twinge of guilt for having called the Drakes the previous evening with news of Sarah's whereabouts.

Just then, Sarah flounced down the staircase that swept around the Christmas tree.

# Chapter 14

Sarah showed no ill effects from her time spent in the snowy mountains. If there had been any, a scented bath, such as she never got in the little house in Park City, had washed it all away. Her sweats had something written across the rear end, and the highlights in her hair and her makeup belonged on a much older woman.

Indeed. Helen noticed a similar style between mother and daughter fashion. They probably shopped together—something Helen would never do with a daughter. No wonder she hated shopping. Heresy for a Relief Society president.

But who was copying whom?

Sarah flung herself down on the leather couch next to her mother and addressed Helen as if she were a servant. "You *will* go up and get Taffy for me, won't you, Sister Snow?"

The girl's spoiled pout was the last straw. Helen hoped she showed by her rigid body language that this really was too much to ask, even of a Relief Society president.

Sarah kept at it, however. "Mom won't let me leave the house." Did the girl hope that if she said enough about her trumped-up plight, Helen would cave? "And *she* won't leave, either. She won't even let me use a *phone* to call Brittany."

"Your mother wasn't sitting on your phone yesterday when you could have at least called Brittany to ease her worries," Helen said.

"Your niece is not responsible enough to take care of my daughter," Eve interjected.

Helen couldn't speak to a mother passing the buck like this. She focused on Sarah instead. "You left without telling her where you were going."

"But she figured it out," the girl replied. "I wish she hadn't. And I really wish she hadn't called you, Sister Snow."

Helen took the accusation to heart and looked down hopelessly at her hands. She wasn't worthy of the Relief Society. No wonder she hadn't been allowed to raise Wizzy.

"Besides." A little remorse wafted through Sarah's speech like the smell of pot roast. "I couldn't phone. There's no reception at Ben's."

"He didn't kidnap you, did he?" *Fresh courage take*, said the hymn. Helen took it, grasping at straws. "You went of your own free will."

Sarah gave a shrug: a teenager's "Yes."

"Sarah, dear," said Eve Drake, "you *mustn't* say things like this. I know we can trust Sister Snow, but you don't want to say anything that will ruin our chances in court. A conviction of that horrid man is the only way we're going to save your reputation."

"I didn't want to press charges. You made me."

"Dear, you're traumatized." Eve looked at Helen with a pleading smile. "She doesn't know what she's saying."

"That rape kit you made me go through—*that* was like rape, let me tell you!"

Helen hoped the girl didn't really know what rape was like. "You took a rape kit?"

"Sarah, go back up to your room," Eve ordered. "Sister Snow and I need to discuss this in private."

"But it's *my body* you're discussing." Sarah didn't sound like a girl who'd been raped, not like a girl who'd lost all notion that her body was her own.

Helen looked away. Her gaze fell on the blue-and-white elf on his angel hair cloud. Compassion swamped her heart. Not for this entitled young woman before her, but for Eve Drake. For Eve whatever-her-maiden name was. Eve said the children had come fast. Too fast? *Nineteenth* anniversary?

Helen remembered her niece Brittany expressing jealousy for the party Sarah had thrown for her eighteenth birthday. Brittany had wondered, with her parents just called to a mission, whether she'd get anything close. That had been before the girls graduated from high school. It must have been May, when the weather for an outside barbecue had been in question.

But Eve and her husband could have been married at Thanksgiving. They could have been married at Halloween. Or even Labor Day, for that matter. Helen didn't like to count months. But the kids had come fast. No, Eve had said it was "coming up on nineteen years". So the Drakes were newlyweds at that Christmastime, with Sarah, their oldest to be born in May?

Helen checked the shoulders of Eve's red satin blouse for temple garment lines and found them. Nineteen years was plenty of time to repent, to make one's self worthy to raise a daughter, to amass mountains of Chinese-made ornaments to obliterate that school-spirit elf. To repent, but probably not to forget being called before the BYU Honor Code office, that lived above the secular law that made re-victimizing a victim a third-degree felony. Not enough to forget being expelled from school, never to go back to the life she had planned for herself, the shame of a marriage in the Relief Society room at the ward instead of the temple. An off-the-rack dress, no reception, no gifts. The whispers of classmates, of relatives, of two full wards. Okay, maybe it was the mutual consent of two hormonally charged eighteen-year-olds as naïve as Sarah had been when she set off into the storm Saturday night. But it might have been something uglier, and nineteen years is not long enough to forget the "r" word, even if—especially if—you'd been forced to marry it.

Was Eve claiming for her daughter what she never could have for herself as compensation? Had Eve's own lost innocence reinforced her desire not to have important talks with her children?

Did Eve think her body was her own, even now? The body that, even after children, looked like it could lead cheers. And Brother Drake, still and always the football player, even after eighteen years without a touchdown. But as a priesthood holder, the Honor Code wouldn't crash down on him the same way.

What would Karen do? Helen thought of the sister whose shoes she was helplessly trying to fill. Karen would follow the Honor Code office line.

No, Karen probably wouldn't have even noticed the blue-and-white elf, or deduced its meaning. She'd only see the proper amount of pride of home given to the Prince of Peace's birth.

Helen hadn't heard a word that passed between mother and daughter for the last few minutes. Now she blurted out, "Oh, Eve, honey. I am so, so sorry."

Her ill-timed expression came in the middle of Sarah shouting, "That rape kit's going to tell the truth!" The girl burst into tears.

"Perhaps I should go." Helen got to her feet.

Eve attempted to put a comforting arm around her daughter. Sarah shoved it off—twice. It was embarrassing to watch. But Eve must have heard Helen's words over her daughter's. Eve Drake stared at her guest and turned white.

Okay, good Mormon households where parents were honored never reached this pitch. They certainly never let Relief Society presidents see it. That's what the pallor was about, not—

"But somebody has to go get Taffy," Sarah wailed. "Taffy's my only friend!" Such misery surrounded by the opulence of two stories worth of twinkle lights made an image that cut to Helen's heart.

At that, Helen sat back down—on the white leather couch this time, on the other side of the girl. Sarah accepted Helen's arms where she had refused her mother's.

"I'm sorry, Sarah," Helen said. "I'm sorry I called your parents."

"Helen, I'll thank you not to interfere." Eve still stared at Helen over her daughter's highlighted hair.

"I'm afraid I already have—too much."

"Yes," whispered Eve. "Too much."

"Too much?" echoed her daughter mockingly. "For a Relief Society president?"

"Excuse me." Eve got to her feet. "I think the roast is burning." She left for the kitchen, where, Helen knew from previous years, little elves gamboled among the Wüsthof knives. Something akin to horror house clowns, which Helen knew her niece and Sarah Drake had seen at the movies when a misguided Young Women's leader had taken the class to a movie she shouldn't have. One probably cheerleader Eve had never seen. Helen stayed in the living room with Sarah.

"I did call your parents," Helen said, apologizing. "Even though Brittany had asked me not to."

"Brittany's such a good friend," Sarah sobbed. "And now we can't be roommates anymore. My parents said."

Helen wasn't sure this was the best disciplinary plan, but knew it wasn't her place to criticize Eve Drake and her husband. She had been the one to call them with the heads-up about their daughter, after all. She regretted it more and more.

The next Relief Society lesson on "the blessings of being part of a family according to Heavenly Father's plan"—translation, "discipline"—wasn't due until after Christmas. Until then, everyone was shooting from the hip, so to speak. Honor Code. Discipline. Disciplinary council. Mormon code words filled Helen's head as she took another glance at the cheerleader elf. There was no song here. Where, oh where was Wizzy? Heavenly Father had let the Drakes raise their daughter because they righteously didn't abort.

Helen took a tissue out of the depths of her bag, registering that she'd given most of them to Brittany and would have to buy more. Along with new hot pads.

"But you did go to Ben's of your own free will, didn't you?" she asked gently. "He found you in the storm on the mountain and took you in."

Sarah nodded.

"And he probably told you it would be a good idea if you left."

Sarah nodded again. "But I insisted, once the storm stopped. He did show me the quick way down to Dave's condo. It's not too far. He even lent me a headlamp when I said I could spend the night with Dave. That was my plan."

Oh. *Oh.* It took an effort to keep her expression sympathetic, not shocked. "It sounds like this Ben is a very good man."

"Even though he's not a Mormon?" Sarah looked up at Helen wanly.

"I think it can happen. I think Dave was a good man, too."

"Oh, yes, he was, or I never would have—" Sarah cut herself off.

"That would have made a very different rape kit, wouldn't it?" she asked in a small voice. "The results, I mean. If I'd—I'd lost my virginity last night."

Helen took her turn to nod silently. She heard a chorus from a suddenly returned Wizzy:

"Rise my soul! Behold 'tis Jesus ...

All thy sins were laid upon Him,
Jesus bore them on the tree ..."


Not a Mormon hymn, more grace than works. But Ben wasn't Mormon. He had lied to Brittany, saying he was the one who had skied down to the condos, taking Sarah's sins upon him. And now he was suffering in prison for that Christian act.

"Poor Dave," Sarah murmured. "I can't believe he's dead."

"A terrible accident." Helen let the girl cry for a while longer. Then she said, "But he was alive when you left?"

"Yes, of course." Enough indignation filled the girl's tone to convince Helen it was true.

"So those were your tracks on the hillside. Coming and going."

Sarah nodded and continued to sob.

"But when you left Dave, he was quite well, wasn't he?"

Sarah nodded.

"He just didn't want you to stay."

Sarah nodded again, silent in her misery.

"Why was that? Did he say?"

Sarah burst into fresh tears. "He doesn't ... didn't ... like me ... like that."

"Did he say so?"

"N ... no."

"What did he say?"

"He said I should come back. Another day. Just ... just he was busy that night."

"See? I think he did love you. I think he said it himself. He was just busy."

Sarah shuddered in Helen's arms.

Helen let the girl think about things for a while. Then she asked, "What was he doing, that he was so busy?"

"He was in his swim trunks. He looked ... he looked so good."

"In the hot tub?"

"In the hot tub, out of the hot tub. He'd get out, get cold, jump back in."

"Why would he do that?"

"He said they did that in Iceland. Gee, how would it be? To travel to, like, Iceland? In Iceland, they soak in the thermal hot springs. Jump out and roll in the snow. Jump back in."

Helen took a moment to unpack how Sarah's desire to travel the world conflicted with her parents plan to nudge her toward as an acceptable eternal companion, as decided by the Brethren. "Unpack" was not a word that appeared in any hymn Helen knew of, although perhaps it should. This thought conflicted with her own firmly held conviction that a hymn was not something newly minted by a Relief Society sister in Panguitch, Utah; a hymn had to be something you'd heard as a child, when you could still hear with the ears of Heaven. That discounted much of the most recent hymn book, but not classic rock, nor any of the songs Wizzy sang. Nor the now-abhorred "Heavenly Mother" verse that was never, ever sung any more.

Helen heard quite clearly the middle of "God of Our Fathers",

"The tumult and the shouting dies,

The captains and the kings depart.
Still stand the ancient sacrifice,
An humble and a contrite heart."


Sarah was still describing the fatal hot tub. "Dave said it was good therapy, that it got the blood pumping."

"Was anybody with him?" Helen asked.

"Well, yeah."

"Who?"

"All these kids."

"Kids?"

For one moment, Helen thought the worst. Kids playing in a hot tub with a grown man in his swimming trunks? Had it indeed been murder? And was it, perhaps, justified by some horrified, protective parent? Some parent who had not gone to the police?

But that simply did not match Brittany's descriptions of the dead man: vegetarian, eco-friendly Dave Jaramillo.

"He was playing with these kids. He'd sink under the water, the kids would creep close. He'd jump out and say, 'Boo', and they'd run away shrieking. It was a game."

That seemed innocent enough, definitely an image of the good man one wanted as an eternal companion. There were paintings of Joseph Smith rough-and-tumble playing with kids like that. Only the Prophet did have his shirt and old-fashioned suspenders on. And was not above marrying fourteen-year-olds in celestial marriage. The Church had come out recently and admitted it of their sainted founder. The vile suspicion of child abuse did not match Dave

Jaramillo, however much it might apply to Joseph Smith. It did not match Wizzy's soundtrack, which was now The Beach Boys.

Helen considered. "The kids were staying in the next condo?"

"Yeah. I can tell you, I didn't want to have to clean that unit after they left."

"Instead you went skiing, leaving that unit to Brittany."

A little guilt colored Sarah's tone. "Yeah."

Sarah had no idea just how bad the unit had been by Saturday, how frequently and messily sick little kids threw up. Thank heaven her flirtation with Dave had failed. She was not old enough to be a mother, even though she was.

So what had happened? What had gone wrong with the hot tub?

Suddenly, Helen remembered the television on Dave's sideboard. "Sarah, I want you to think very carefully. Was there a television on the deck anywhere?"

"A TV? No. Dave hated TVs. He said they were 'Corporate invasion of your mind.' He always kept the one that came with the condo in the closet out on the deck."

"Not just unplugged in his unit?"

"No. He hated them. I was ... like, trying to be worthy of him ... recently ... I was trying not to watch so much."

Helen thought that the young man had been a good role model, then. She hoped someone would mention that at his funeral. Would there be a funeral? Where? Who would sponsor it? She couldn't think about that now. "But maybe someone from one of the other units brought out the television?" she suggested.

"No. No one else would know it was there. The TVs in the other units are, like, bolted to the walls. I know Pine Enterprises goes and buys TVs by the truckload any time RC Wiley's has a sale. Dave told me so with, like, disgust. Even with the bolts, people steal them. We have to fill out the form and order a new one any time we find one missing when we clean. Or we did. I'll never clean again." Sarah burst into new tears.

Helen nodded. The girl was going to be denied even that portion of adulthood: a horrible job.

Helen asked, "Why would Dave be playing with the kids?"

"He liked kids."

*Don't say that to the cops,* Helen wanted to advise. *Or we'll have another innocent man condemned.*

"Do you know what it's like for a woman when she sees a man playing with kids? I'm like, *that's a good man.*"

Yes, Helen thought she knew. She also understood Sarah's renewed sobs.

"I was going to convert him."

*After sleeping with him. Ah, to be that age.*

"I mean he was, like, almost there," Sarah continued. "So good. So what if he refused to eat funeral ham?"

"But don't folks in the different units usually keep to themselves?" Helen asked. "A family full of kids moves into the unit next door; if I were a young man, I think that, if anything, I'd be annoyed at the noise."

"But Dave liked kids. Like I said."

"What if a bunch of partiers moved in at the other side?" Helen was remembering the bag of marijuana.

"Dave wasn't much of a party guy. Too serious."

"That's why you liked him?"

"Well, I was trying to be serious enough for him. I guess he just thought I was, like—no, he told me not to say 'like' so often. He thought that I was too silly."

"I'm sure he didn't. But I'm still not sure I understand. Yes, maybe Dave liked kids. But why would a mother with all these kids think it was okay for the kids to play with a strange, lone man wearing nothing but swimming trunks, who lived next door? Did you see a parent anywhere around, keeping eyes on things?"

"No. But the lights were on in Unit A."

"The parents?"

"Could have been."

Helen looked over her shoulder at the reassuring safety of the Drake's McMansion. "I mean, look at your mother. Look how concerned she is about you in this world of 'stranger, danger'. And you're older. They must have trusted him."

"Dave was good with kids. What else can I say?"

Helen thought of something. "Did you know any of the kids?"

"No. Why should I? They were probably from out of town."

"Do you think you might recognize any of them if you saw them again?"

"No. It was pretty dark. They had the lights on the deck off. To make it scarier for their game."

"I see."

While Helen puzzled, Sarah came to her own next

topic. "And Ben. Ben was—is—good, too."

"He's innocent—and in jail."

"Yeah. Mom made me."

"Made you press charges?"

Sarah nodded. "Okay, he's a little odd. Likes to live alone in a mine. In the snow. But the mine was real comfortable. They don't call him 'Gentle Ben' for nothing."

"He helped you out."

"Yeah. And mom made me go to the all-night clinic. Made me do the rape kit."

The rape kit perhaps Eve wished she'd had.

"We'll have to see what we can do to help Ben," Helen told Sarah, her niece's best friend. "We can't have an innocent man suffer for our mistakes, can we?" Helen did feel that it was her mistake, too. Brittany had asked her not to call the Drakes, but she'd done it anyway.

"Yeah. He and Dave were real good friends. Dave wouldn't like anyone who was bad. Ben told me—that night—he told me Dave had helped him out so many times. And he was going to help him even more."

"Even more? Did Ben say how?"

"No. Something about Pine Enterprises and ... I don't know."

Eve Drake stepped back into the living room, her lips set in a line that said she wasn't going to do anything rude, although sorely tempted. "Sarah, time to set the table, please. Helen, do you want to stay for dinner?"

Who asked a Relief Society president to stay for dinner? Only someone suggesting she'd outstayed her welcome.

"No, thank you," Helen said.

She struggled with herself, between Wizzy and the Relief Society handbook. *How to handle this?* Sarah was going to need all the help she could get to come around to telling the truth. A glance at the girl's mother told Helen she wasn't likely to get help here. Still, Helen felt she had to encourage doing what was right.

"Eve." She took the other woman by the arm and walked her toward the door. "Are you sure the story Sarah gave the police is true in all its details?"

Eve did not want to come. She removed Helen's hand from her arm. "Are you suggesting my daughter is a liar?"

"Not at all. But she is very young and in a difficult situation. I'm not sure that I would know what to do or say if I were—"

"You're right. You wouldn't know."

The blue-and-white cheerleader was gone; Eve Drake stood in her place, eyes hard. And she had found someone non-Mormon, hence fair game, to pin her own pain on. Because, like those notorious rape verses in Deuteronomy, she when "a maiden" had not cried out. Or she had, but to the wrong people. To readers of Deuteronomy.

"You *don't* know what to do, Helen Snow," Eve said. "I did not raise a girl to go off on her own and spend the night with a strange, crazy man. Drakes do not lie, and Drakes always present the best face to the world."

Did Eve not see the contradictions inherent in those claims? In this mass of materialism heaped upon the humble manger in the stall? "No crib for a bed," as Wizzy might have sung but didn't, because Wizzy was always perfectly charitable. Well, that must be the rope Eve Drake walked, pulled tight and tighter by her daughter's misbehavior.

"Yes." Helen bowed her head. How would she react if someone had suggested something similar about her own daughter? Her own Wizzy? Pretty much the same. Would the priesthood let her ever see Wizzy again?

"I'm sorry," Helen said. "It's getting dark, and I need to get up to Park City."

In response to the unspoken questions in two pairs of Drake women's eyes, she replied, "Well, I have to go get H—Taffy, don't I?" She'd almost said "Horehound" aloud.

Sarah flew across the stretch of living room and threw her arms around Helen's neck. "Thank you!"

"No need to thank me," Helen said. Those famous last Relief Society words.

# Chapter 15

At least getting Horehound and bringing her back to Sarah will keep Brittany from having to care for that beast another night, Helen told herself. Perhaps there's a way, through the dog, to convince Sarah to go against her mother and admit to the authorities that she's charged an innocent man. It's my job, as Relief Society president, to keep confidence. What do the Catholics call it? The Seal of Confession. I will keep confidence. It's Eve Drake's business to move beyond her own past for the sake of her daughter. Can she do it? Perhaps the therapy dog .... Most importantly, for me, it'll be a chance to patch things up with my niece for betraying her trust.

> "Get your motor running,
> Head out on the highway ..."

That was the oven mitt Brownie, still lying in the back seat of Helen's car. He made "brum-brum" noises as the motor revved.

Santa was silent, probably sulking about Helen's threat to replace them.

The radio on Helen's drive up Parley's Canyon

interrupted her thoughts and Wizzy's song with new details in what had become *the* story of the local news cycle: the capture of the fierce, crazed Benjamin T. Ursule for kidnapping and assault, and the freeing of his unnamed beautiful young captive from his mountain lair. The story fed everyone's notions of who were the good guys—those who went to church on Sunday—and who were the bad: those who didn't. The whole community should be thanking her for her deed of blabbing—and destroying Brittany's trust.

Bail, she heard, had been set at five million dollars for Gentle Ben. That sounded like an awful lot. She didn't know how bail worked, but the announcer filled in this much detail: the accused had been unable to pay and so would have to stay in Summit County Jail until his trial. That's the level of threat that he was deemed to pose to the public.

The sun went down behind her as she drove. Helen turned off the radio, turned on her headlights and then called Mark to tell him that, although she had a roast defrosting in the fridge for Sunday dinner, he would have to do something for himself. He had encouraged her to become Relief Society president. This is what being Relief Society president meant: big inroads into Sunday dinners. Also into every other day. She did not tell him that she was nowhere near the ward that was meant to be her stewardship. Brittany, she thought, counted as her stewardship. Brittany came first.

As she drove between them, the steep, snow-covered hillsides turned gray with the twilight. She thought of their wildness. She thought of Ben. "Gentle Ben." She thought of wild things living in their burrows to either side of the busy freeway, minding their own business. She thought of bears. She thought of a beautiful, wild bear, trapped and caged. Unable to post bail. That would make the beast crazy.

The bright lights of Kimball Junction hove into sight. The Factory Outlet stores that Karen enjoyed so much came just before, but they were closed on Sunday evening. Karen had forced Helen to visit this shopping Mecca at least once a month, with the theory that this was just a step down from what the wealthy folks in Park City did. The righteous should emulate the wealthy, since God always blessed the faithful with material goods.

Wizzy had always hated the place, hated trying on "cute" outfits, hated being pushed around the crowded walkways in her stroller. The monthly jaunt had become easier when Helen could just see it as time to spend with her sister. Now the empty parking lot in the deepening darkness had the look of a bombed-out war zone. This guise led Helen to consider the factories, in countries thousands of miles away, where the bargain items Karen exulted over were made. Distracted by that thought, Helen saw too late that the Park City exit to route 224 was upon her.

> "Looking for adventure
> In whatever comes our way."

*The Book of Wizzy* made Helen fail to take the turn.

The Devil made me do it? An oven mitt named Brownie?

Not that Wizzy in life had ever expressed a preference for snarling Steppenwolf electric guitar riffs, or been "born to be wild". Her wheels had been that sturdy pink stroller. Helen had wept when she'd had to give it to the Deseret Industries thrift store. She had wanted to hang around to see what hard-strapped family would buy it so she could go up to them and say, "Have you heard about my daughter?"

But Wizzy had taken all "the world in a love embrace". And Wizzy had shown a marked preference for having Brownie slipped over her little hand. Even though he was the one Santa smacked.

Well, Helen would just have to get off at the next exit and turn around. She did, landing in a jumble of unfamiliar, badly marked roads with no buildings to either side. Her headlights hitting an "I-80 Salt Lake 31 mi." sign washed her with relief. She was probably making an illegal turn to follow that beacon, but no other cars were around.

Then her headlights hit another sign she had not been expecting, but which caught her attention: Summit County Justice Center. The feeling it gave her had a little roughness, wildness, to it; but that very edge whispered to her that this was the way she should take. It was not the easy way, the comfortable way. It was, in fact, the road less traveled ... but that would make all the difference. Once someone in the pulpit had confused Robert Frost with scripture, as they regularly did with Shakespeare and the King James Version.

*The Book of Wizzy* turned to hymn number 29 again: "A Poor Wayfaring Man of Grief."

Helen remembered that this was the hymn the Prophet Joseph Smith had asked the Apostle and prophet John Taylor to sing during the last hours before their martyrdom.

> "In prison I saw him next, condemned
> To meet a traitor's death at noon ...
> My friendship's utmost zeal to try,
> He asked if I for him would die ..."

Curious, Helen thought, how scripture admonished the faithful. "I was in prison and you visited me." Christ had been in prison. St. Paul had been in prison. Joseph Smith, prophet, seer and revelator, had spent even more time in jail. Indeed, the cell where he'd spent his final hours before martyrdom, where President Taylor had sung that song, was now a shrine to be visited by the faithful on pilgrimage in air-conditioned Beehive Tour buses to Nauvoo/Carthage, Illinois.

Yet, Helen had never been to prison. No one she knew had ever been to prison. Never even to visit. Well, there was the bishop in the next ward, who was doing time for playing on the trust old folks had shown in him by investing their money in his Ponzi scheme, but nobody ever talked about that. No one ever visited the fallen man. It was as if it never had happened. Certainly the social security set was not sufficiently warned, for it took no prophet to see that it would happen again, sooner rather than later, in Happy Valley: fraud capital of the world.

The pulpit would scorn her for having anything to do with anyone whose mere appearance of evil landed him in jail. "Be ye therefore perfect" presupposed a world where jails did not even exist. Karen's world. Disneyland had no jails, except in Pirates of the

Caribbean where a dog and a bone offered ready escape. One acquaintance, of seriously sinful cynicism, had once told her that below the park, in the underground city for Disney performers, was a private Disneyland prison.

"Choose the Right." Hymn 239.

"Summit County Justice Center" pointed to a small road going off to the right before she reached the freeway. The hymn meant "choose correctly", of course, but Wizzy wouldn't think literally.

So, though to do so with an early winter's Sunday night creeping in was probably a fool's errand, she made another turn over packed snow obscuring the lines to "Summit County Justice Center".

Thank heavens for four-wheel drive.

Another similar sign.

And another.

No street lights meant that she had only walls of plowed snow to keep her on the straight and narrow, so to speak.

She suspected that she was getting close when a strip mall in chalet style opened up on the left. The operation must have rules regulating signage as well as rooflines in keeping with the faux-chalet theme. A paint store looked pretty much like the spa, and both had signs framed with raw logs. So did "Bail Bonds". There was none of the slightly humorous tone shown by the bail bond signs in the vicinity of the Salt Lake Valley correctional facility, where the elite who came to enjoy the winter sports season occasionally wound up.

Whenever she had ventured far west in that metropolis she had seen those signs: "The Key to Any

Jail", or the winged and mustachioed cartoon Monopoly Man getting out of jail free, or "Bad Girl Bail Bonds. Family owned and operated for thirty-five years", as if ending up in need of a bondsman were just another of the mad things life threw at you or a loved one, nothing to do with your own agency.

Could that ever be how it was?

Hadn't it that way for Gentle Ben?

She pulled into the strip mall parking lot and stared at the rough-hewn "Beehive Bonds" sign playing off the industrious and team-player state logo. Helen idled—another illegal act when inversion threatened—running the heat so the car's exhaust swirled around her in the brake lights like a scene from Dante's Inferno.

The bonds office was closed, but the sign promised 24-hour service by calling a Salt Lake number. Helen thought Beehive Bonds might have been one of the more sober signs she'd seen over on the West Side. Calling the number seemed a better choice than further pursuit of "Justice."

"Umm. I was just wondering ..." she told the bored male voice that answered her ring.

"Hurry up, lady," he told her. "I haven't got all night."

"How would I go about getting a ... a man out of jail on bond?" Things would go much faster, Helen was certain, if she didn't hem and haw so much.

"Who's the man? Husband? Brother? Son? Name?" Now the tone of voice suggested interest. Actual business on a Sunday night.

"Just ... just a man. A stranger, actually."

"Do you know his name? I have to have his name."

"Yes, but I'd rather not say before I make these inquiries. I don't even know how bail works."

Helen heard the sigh through the phone. "Do you at least know what his bond's been posted at?"

She remembered the radio report. "Five million dollars."

The other end of the line went silent. *Oh, my heck,* she thought. *That number probably let him know right off who we're talking about. How often does bail get set at five million?* She had no idea, but had to think it wasn't often.

Before Helen could disconnect, the man on the phone reappeared. He sounded as if he were reading from a law book. "Bail bonds require the defendant— or a friend of the defendant, that would be you—to give the bondsman—that would be me—ten per cent security up front."

Helen paid tithing; she knew how to figure ten percent.

"Or something worth that amount—say, a home— could be offered as collateral," the bondsman went on. "We are talking $500,000, lady."

There was no way Mark was going to put up that kind of money to make things all right with Brittany, even though she was his niece, too. It wasn't even for Brittany, except indirectly. It was for a complete stranger charged with heinous crimes. An innocent stranger named "Gentle Ben".

"Thank you."

By the time she had said this and hung up, Helen was perfectly certain that Mr. Bored Bondsman knew exactly which high-profile local case she'd been asking about. That had piqued his interest. And here she was, avoiding the appearance of evil, for all the good her attempt at anonymity would do her. Bondsmen must have caller ID. The thought made her burn with shame, even alone in an empty parking lot where her idling for heat should have shamed her more. She couldn't make herself head back to face her niece for several more minutes.

Then headlights, out on the road heading towards "Justice"—the first she'd seen since she left the freeway—made her shift out of park. She turned around in the empty parking lot and edged toward the entry onto the street. She set her turn signal to enter nonexistent traffic going the other way, back toward I-80. The car passed, followed by another. Then another. And another. All sheriff's cars, as her headlights revealed. All with passengers in the back.

Helen's car seemed to drive itself. Helen switched the turn signal to the left; at least she could be legal. When she was certain that no more sheriff's cars were coming, she followed them into the unknown.

*****

Past what looked in the dark like condominiums but which were really storage units, the sheriff's vehicles pulled into one end of a well-lit parking lot. Their lights caught a honeycomb of chain link that slid open for them.

Helen parked as far from them as she could, while still in the same lot. She turned off the car and her lights. She didn't dare break the idling law here. This end of the public building seemed more, well, public. It had the dignity of courtrooms, of a one-step-above-trailer, built-on-a-budget sort of structure. It was also completely deserted. Her attention was riveted on the other end of the lot.

Behind chain link, under floodlights, the sheriff cars unloaded. Three of the crowd were moved along by the rest, hands held rigid in front of them, clearly defendants. A fourth was also "herded" not "herder", but he struggled along on crutches.

Helen nearly jumped out of her skin as she realized who the figures might be. That nice young Quinn from condo unit C! Was it? She couldn't tell at this distance, and all the figures quickly vanished into the building.

Then she jumped even higher when sudden light blinded her, and sharp blows from a billy club seemed to be trying to crack her window.

# Chapter 16

"Sister Snow?"

It was Deputy Moody, billy club and flashlight in hand, investigating a strange car on a Sunday night in the Justice Center's lot. Helen didn't know whether to breathe yet or not. And Wizzy seemed to have withdrawn in confusion. Or fear.

Although Helen had accepted a female doctor and a female lawyer, female law enforcement still seemed like something out of mythology. Karen would certainly think so. It was as out-of-place as if a wearer of the flowered print of a Relief Society skirt showed up in the presence of the all-male elders' quorum congratulating itself on the purchase of a new snow mobile, instead of being down the ward house halls chasing a three-year-old. *Even though you've stepped into her shoes, you don't have to think like your sister*, Helen chided herself.

"What are you doing?" the chimera demanded through the pane of glass.

*Don't ask me that. I don't know. Following the guidance of the Holy Ghost? Would you believe that?* Although perfectly legitimate Sunday-School speech, "the Holy Ghost made me do it" was better known as being what nut cases in Utah used, just before they pleaded "Not guilty for reasons of insanity".

Mentioning Wizzy, or *The Book of Wizzy*, was out of the question.

Helen still couldn't breathe. Her eyes refused to blink, wide with confusion, with fear.

Helen's car dated to the years of Wizzy. It was so old it had no paternalistic automatic lock to come into play at ten miles an hour. She rarely felt the need to push the lock button in her daily life. So when Deputy Moody pulled at the latch, the door opened. An inhalation set Helen breathing again. Rapidly.

"Never mind," the deputy said. "Whatever reason, it's good you are here."

Helen gasped. Did that count as the Holy Ghost entering her?

"I have some questions I need to ask," Deputy Moody went on. "But why don't we come on in to my office where it's warm?"

Helen took comfort in this indication that jail cells, even in Summit Country, were warm.

Fluorescents flickered to ghostly life inside the middle portion of the Justice Center between the courts on one side and the chain link on the other.

"Stay there," Deputy Moody ordered as she slipped under a sort of doorframe, circled around behind some electronic equipment to the left of the door, and set some lights to humming.

"Your handbag, any metal, cell phone? That all goes here."

The deputy extended a plastic tray in Helen's direction. This reminded her of security at the airport. She complied with a straight face, not certain whether to be scornful of the state's stupidity to think she—a Relief Society president, no less—could possibly be a terrorist, or secretly proud that the law thought she might be capable of springing Gentle Ben without half a million dollars. And she began to review all the items in that over-kill bag of hers that might be of use. Swiss army knife. Bottled water. Nail file. Li'l Debbie cupcakes: stress food. Nail file in the cupcakes, maybe? In lip-gloss? No, she'd already blown that as a bribe.

More fluorescents came on in an office so narrow it barely accommodated two chairs and a desk no bigger than the computer needed. "This way," Deputy Moody said, and Helen took the chair with her back to the door that remained opened to the darkened offices around them.

"Excuse me just a minute."

The deputy powered up her computer and became engrossed in something she found there.

Helen attempted a few words. "Those people you just ..." she hunted for the word, "brought in? They're not the boys from Pine Enterprises Unit C, are they? The Unit next to the one where Dave Jaramillo was ... was found dead? Those nice young snowboarders from California?"

"Nice?" Deputy Moody grunted. Then she admitted. "You hit the nail on the head. I've got to make sure their photos get up on the website ASAP."

She turned the monitor halfway between their two chairs. Sure enough, fresh mug shots appeared even as they watched. Hunched over his crutches, there was "Quinn Albert Rhodes" trying to smile under his shrub of clown hair. The height lines indicated that he was five nine and a half. Morphine was, however, clearly getting the better of him: the slackness in his face, the serenity in spite of what was happening to him.

Three other young, scrubbed faces that screamed "California" appeared after him. Their alleged crimes, Helen noticed, were all listed as "POSS CON SUB—3F". Whatever that meant. POSS ... possession?

The top of the web page was very careful to warn that "All persons are innocent until proven guilty," but who reads the fine print?

Most of the names below these most recent additions were Spanish, Helen noticed, like Jaramillo. She offered a thought—it might have been a prayer—for Brittany's friend Consuela.

There, too, was Benjamin T. Ursule from barely twenty-four hours before, the same photo that had been playing on all the news shows. He did look like a bear. A lost bear, caught in the headlights. Helen felt sorry for him.

"I understood those boys were going to return home to California tomorrow morning after their week's vacation," Helen offered.

"Well, they didn't move fast enough."

"Don't you find it odd? All these crimes centered on that one condo where young Dave Jaramillo died. Only no one thinks his death was anything but an accident."

"Not odd at all," Deputy Moody said gruffly, as if oddity were an accusation leveled at the sheriff's office rather than at the incident scene itself. "Risky behavior often leads to accidents."

"Sitting in a hot tub is risky behavior?"

"We found marijuana in Jaramillo's sock drawer."

Just plain "Jaramillo" without the endearing "Dave" seemed so harsh to Helen, but she didn't want her softness to be taken as guilt. "Yes, I was there when your colleague found it."

Deputy Moody raised a brow. "I suppose you were."

"It didn't look to me like it had been opened. The bag was full."

The brow went higher. "True. That's what first raised our suspicions. The bag was indeed sealed."

"Dave could not have used any, then."

"There is such a crime as 'possession with intent to sell'. It's a felony, second degree."

"What does that have to do with the young men in Unit C?"

"Perhaps you didn't see, but the sealed bag from Jaramillo's had 'For Medicinal Use' written all over it."

Helen's confusion must have been written all over her own face.

"It was purchased legally, in the state of California, on December first. They have a labeling system that can tell us, yes, when the weed was obtained. In her statement, your niece told us she had seen Jaramillo alive and well when she cleaned his condo on that day last week. Can you confirm that?"

"No. I never met Dave Jaramillo, only heard about him from my niece."

"You don't work cleaning with your niece?"

"No." Helen remembered where she was—

someplace that she'd never been before—in a sheriff's office. "You remember I came later, answering Brittany's call. I gave you lip gloss."

"That's right. I was just thinking how that manager of Pine Enterprises said he always sent his cleaners out in teams. And that second cleaning carry-all."

Helen felt sick. Lying could get her in deep trouble. It would get Brittany in trouble, and Consuela.

Deputy Moody applied lip-gloss and indeed, seemed to forget about the inconsistency in the stories. "Not important. The guests in Unit C, we knew, hailed from the Sunshine state. That was enough to get us a warrant to search Unit C. Where we found two more, larger, bags."

"Purchased legally?"

"One of the young men in C has a pot card. He claims to have purchased that bag and the two larger bags in his home state, and our calls have confirmed it. He suffers, so the card says, from 'depression'."

"College life can be very stressful," Helen said, being sympathetic.

Secretly she thought that the leafy green stuff looking like dried sage. And hadn't the Lord encouraged the use of "every wholesome herb and fruit in the season thereof"? Pot certainly had more to do with scripture than the blue pills of concentrated good mood Helen had been given when Wizzy died. Marijuana had to be more natural than the calm those pills had induced in her, where even in dreams horrible things could happen and she'd just smile and say, like the hymn, "All is well, all is well."

Deputy Moody gave a masculine bark of laughter. "What have Californians to be depressed about, huh? They've got medicinal pot, and Disneyland. It may be legal there, but the minute you carry it across state lines, it's a felony. They should just learn to keep their state in their state, like Utahns should learn to keep things like Prop 8 at home, too."

"Those poor kids," Helen had to exclaim.

"Poor kids, nothing," Deputy Moody said, still a little flushed from her tirade. "Right about now they're all getting their phone call. They'll call Mom and Dad; Mom and Dad will take the next plane into SLC. Or they'll take the corporate jet. Mom and Dad will post bail, buy out the judge to expunge the record. And Summit County will continue to operate in the black, have excellent schools and libraries. Some folks, you know, call us 'Revenue Agents' instead of cops. Summit County, a little bit of California here in the Rockies. Without the ocean, of course."

The deputy sighed deeply.

"I'm glad to hear that," Helen said.

Helen had been thinking that if she couldn't afford to post bail for Gentle Ben, she might have to do it for the young man with the broken leg so that he could get the care that he needed, care the Summit Justice Center was unlikely to offer him. They wouldn't let him chew two morphine tablets at once without water any time he felt like it.

"Glad to hear what? That Utah is supporting a little bit of California in the Back Wasatch? Forget about the border to the South and all the illegals crossing over, we've got enough grief we can't control just between states."

Too close to Consuela for comfort. While Helen was trying to decide what to say next that wouldn't implicate herself, Brittany or the undocumented Consuela, Deputy Moody suddenly mentioned the elephant in the room. "What are you doing here, Sister Snow, if I may ask? At seven o'clock on a Sunday evening?"

"I was just ... I was just ... I took a wrong turn."

Helen added them up. Six wrong turns. Could six wrong turns possibly add up to a right?

Deputy Moody quirked an eyebrow. She might as well be singing along with Wizzy's "no toilet paper here".

Helen was in deep doo-doo.

# Chapter 17

The quirk in Deputy Moody's eyebrow and her silence made Helen decide telling more of the truth would have to happen. A little, anyway. It was the only way she could think of to draw the officer off all the lies that had been told ... all with the best intentions, of course. "I came here because I'm ... I'm a little concerned about Gentle Ben—Ben Ursule, the man who ..."

"I do know who our facility's most infamous inmate is," the deputy said. "And I was there on the mountainside when he was apprehended. Red-handed."

"Yes," Helen offered. "I saw you on the news. But those were Sarah's tacks, not Ben's."

"Jeez, I hate those pictures—" Deputy Moody stopped herself.

People, Helen realized, knew what they looked like and hated to be reminded of it on the morning news. There were other losses that caused pain besides the loss of a loved one. The loved one might be a pudgy child's starlet image of herself—of being fairytale material—before taunting in kindergarten teaches her differently and sends her into even more pudginess.

And a career in law enforcement.

"I worry about Benjamin Ursule, too," the law officer admitted. "He's a man who needs to live alone, since his selfless service to this country in foreign lands. He knows that, and there's no crime in that. He can trust nature so much more than people."

Than Eve Drake. Than Sarah, whom he had granted shelter in the storm. Than herself, who had disregarded *The Book of Wizzy* to make a phone call, listening to fears instead of to the voice of innocence.

"I look at him in that cell," Deputy Moody went on. "He wouldn't hurt a fly, and I feel he's going to die in there, it's hurting him so bad."

"My feeling, too. Why else would people call him 'Gentle Ben'?"

"Why did he have to abduct a young girl, then, if he knows he has to live alone? And why did he have to ski down to the Pine Enterprises condo during the night? We all saw the tracks, plain as day. He's giving us nothing that might help us understand the death at Pine Enterprises, either. He's going to get life for this. And that is surely a death sentence for a man like him."

Surprisingly, Helen felt a weight lift from her shoulders. The law wasn't all that blind. Deputy Moody already felt the truth about Gentle Ben and was groping towards it. A deputy sheriff might nudge the law in the right directions.

"Ben can't explain it," she said, "because those are Sarah's tracks, not his."

"Sarah?"

"Sarah Drake, the girl he—that he's accused of kidnapping. He didn't actually kidnap her." Should

Helen's compassion side with Sarah or with Ben? Brittany's trust was on the line here, too.

"Are you telling me Sarah Drake went up to that mine of her own free will?"

All words froze in Helen's mouth. They froze in her brain as well.

The deputy seemed to take nothing as a positive. "How do you know this? We have her sworn statement."

*Taken when her mother was present, right? Eve Drake means well, but her daughter's reputation is on the line. Her own reputation. I'm sure I'd have done the same, if Wizzy had ever ... but I was blessed; Wizzy never became a teenager.*

"Sarah Drake isn't a minor." Why on earth was Helen saying this? "I remember that big birthday party. It was last summer."

"We're just waiting for the results of the rape kit."

What Sarah had said about that rape kit throbbed in Helen's temples. She said nothing, but the deputy pressed on without her.

"If they were the Drake girl's tracks, that would mean she was free to come and go during the night. If she'd wanted to. You know, I thought there was collusion going on between that mother and daughter. Happens all the time. But we can only go by the statements they sign."

Helen breathed a huge sigh of relief. She hadn't doubled her betrayals. "You can't test the tracks to see whose skis made them?" she suggested.

"No, by the time we found them, the morning sun had been on them, cold though it was. They were ski tracks, they led to Ursule's lair ... where we found the girl." Deputy Moody licked cherry flavor off her lips in her concentration.

"Why would Sarah Drake make a false statement?" Helen thought she knew the reason all too well. She just didn't want to make the statement herself. The Seal of Confession and all that. But she must urge the law in the right direction.

"Because that's the only way she could explain her absence to her parents ..." Good. Deputy Moody was feeling her own way. "... and to future husband material. *Husband* material!" Deputy Moody laughed out loud at her own phrase. "Why on earth would a girl who's worried about husband material ski off to a mountain man's lair?"

"She wasn't interested in Ben. She was interested in Dave."

"Jaramillo?"

"Yes. Ben was his friend. Sarah cleaned for Dave, and she knew about Ben."

"I thought your niece did that. Cleaned for him."

"They did it together."

"So those two carry-alls—there *were* two cleaners."

"Yes, but ..." Helen saw the corner her lies had painted her into. Either Sarah or Consuela or Brittany had to be thrown under the bus. And the wheels went 'round and 'round.

Deputy Moody smiled, not unkindly. "Never mind. I can guess."

Helen figured she might as well come clean—on this thing at least. "Sarah Drake is—was—my niece's roommate. Until night before last."

"What? You mean here in Park City?"

"Yes."

"But she gave her address as ..."

Deputy Moody consulted her computer notes. Just in time, she seemed to recall the fact that she probably shouldn't give out addresses to just anyone. Particularly not to someone she had once accused of being a journalist. Not that the media hadn't already squirreled the details out and weren't already camped on the Drakes' doorstep.

"Some place down in the Valley," the deputy skirted. "East Millcreek somewhere."

"I know exactly where," Helen assured her. "I was just at their house. I took a casserole to a neighbor for her mother."

Here came the good cop smile again. "You *are* the Relief Society president."

"I am. And Sarah and my niece have been best friends since grade school."

Deputy Moody stole a glance to an inner door where, Helen supposed, the prisoners' cells were. "What a screw up," she said. "Maybe not the worst we've ever had, but a first-class screw up nonetheless. How can this have happened?"

"It's probably my fault." The Mormon guilt—which always made a member feel a little self-righteous—kicked in good and hard, so hard the tears came. "Brittany trusted me with the fact that her roommate hadn't been home for a couple of days. And I ... well, I was worried and I ...I guess the hip word is ... I ratted."

"You called Sarah's parents, who then called us."

"They must have called immediately." Helen nervously studied her hands, the tears dropping there unabated. "Am I under arrest?"

*Am I condemned to Outer Darkness?* was the more pressing question: that place where one got sent for denying the Holy Ghost, which Wizzy's voice had been. During long Gospel Doctrine classes Outer Darkness had always appeared in Helen's mind like The Little Prince's planet, a place where you had to sit alone in the middle of dark space for all eternity. A place like his present jail cell must be to Ben.

*Will I never see my angel Wizzy in the next life—or Brittany in this one—again? For my sins.*

The deputy's laughter this time was a Santa Claus sort of chuckle. "Of course not, Sister Snow. I just don't know how we're going to fix this. Not my job, I'm afraid. A job for lawyers, and I've worked here long enough to know you can't trust those guys. Not when the plaintiff lives in East Millcreek and the accused lives in an abandoned mine and will have to go with the public defender—Summit County's public defender."

Helen remembered the news image of Sarah screaming something at the TV camera. Or had it been something at the deputies who'd been manhandling Ben? Maybe she'd been trying to tell him he was innocent. Before Eve came along. Eve and the little blue-and-white elf she couldn't toss out of her store of Christmases past.

"Could Sarah drop charges?" Helen asked the deputy.

"She could, but I can't make her. Well, I tried, when we were taking the statements. I took her aside from her mother. I took the mother aside, too. 'Do you really believe your daughter in this?' I asked her.

'Do you know what trouble false charges can bring?' I asked them both."

"I can't make either of them change their stories for you, either. I'm just the Relief Society. Excuse me. You have to understand, I didn't know anything about even bail bonds until this evening."

"Yes, the girl could drop charges, but then things might not go so well for her. Filing false charges and all."

Yes, Helen really didn't want that to happen to Brittany's friend, who was only trying to please her mother—who was only trying to protect her daughter.

"I don't know how anything you or I can do can force her to testify against her sworn testimony," Deputy Moody said. "I just collect the testimonies and arrest people. I can tell you this, though, she won't be the first person to have given false testimony, and she won't be the last." She shook her head.

What would Wizzy do? "A Poor Wayfaring Man of Grief," hymn number 29, came up again. "I can't afford to post his bail. But could you arrest me and hold me in Ben's place? Let the poor man go?"

Deputy Moody guffawed. "What an idea!"

Helen took a tissue out of her bag and used it herself. Then her head cleared, remembering why she'd driven up the canyon in the first place. "Maybe I have a plan."

"Yes?"

"It will require taking someone hostage."

Helen wished she had a picture of the expression that crossed Deputy Moody's face then.

"I'm sorry, Sister Snow. Are you confessing a plot

to commit a crime? To get me to arrest you? As a woman, you'd get nowhere near Gentle Ben, and you can't trade places with him, if that's your plan. I refuse to arrest you. Now. But I must warn you that anything you say may be used against—"

"Oh, not a person. I don't mean take a person hostage."

"No?" Deputy Moody sounded relieved, confused, and suspicious all at once.

"A dog." And Helen said the name aloud with some glee. "Horehound."

# Chapter 18

Helen took the freeway back one exit and drove through the night to Park City. She tried Brittany's phone once more on the way, breaking the law again.

No answer. Again.

Helen's ring tone on her niece's phone was "Down to the River to Pray". Brittany would know who it was.

Main Street was packed, all the vacationers finishing up their fun-filled week with dinner and drinks at the fancy restaurants and bars. They would fly out in the morning, leaving behind any damage they had generated.

Helen must have passed the mall but missed it in the dark. She had no idea how to negotiate the buses, or even if they were running. She could find no parking, even so far away from Brittany's that she feared that she'd get lost on the walk back. And she was still wearing heels, even if they were sensible ones. In the end, in desperation and hope that no police car would drive by at this inopportune time, she left the car idling in the middle of the narrow street and ran up and over the snowplow's exhaust-begrimed heap.

Next door, the Happy Miner was picking away at the mother lode on his sign with a jaunting rhythm, the squeak of his mechanism drowned by sound, and the building was bursting at its seams. A rowdy cover of "Something Like That" twanged away to the pulse of the neon lights. Young people with beer bottles in their hands were line dancing on the sidewalk outside.

Wizzy had once become car sick to Tom McGraw. Helen wasn't sure how connected the music and event were, except in her own mind; it might just have been the winding mountain road.

The porch light—a bare bulb—was on, welcoming. Lights were also on inside the tiny old miner's house. Helen knocked.

Horehound barked. *You're my next victim,* Helen thought.

The front curtain shifted a little. *Good. At least she screens her visitors.*

Then—nothing.

Helen knocked again.

Horehound was going crazy. Maybe it would burst a blood vessel and Helen's plan would fail.

"Brittany?" Helen called and knocked again.

She began to cry, quietly, but enough that the closest dancers stopped and stared in shock or disapproval, their festival mood broken.

"Brittany, please. I know you're in there. You have every reason to be angry at me, but I've come from Sarah. She wants me to pick up Hore ... I mean, Taffy. She's missing Taffy. I'm supposed to fetch her."

Nothing. Probably Brittany couldn't hear over the noise next door.

Helen knocked. The flimsy plywood on the door threatened to burst. Helen decided to desist, though it made her cry again to do so. Turning to the street, she saw goldenrod lights strobing across snow-packed storefronts and old houses gone to condos. Summit County's finest revenue agents were out in full strength. Not enforcing noise ordinances, if the town had any, but handing out parking violations left and right to keep the coffers flush. You could just mail in the fine from whatever corner of the world you found yourself in on Monday morning.

Helen scurried back over the grimy snow bank and drove away, keeping to the speed limit. She got twisted around negotiating the one-way streets. Suddenly, the parking lights on a black BMW with California plates on her right glowed alive. While she watched in astonishment, the foreign vehicle pulled out of a stall right in front of her. If she didn't take the vacated space, the rental coupe behind her would. She turned hard right and found herself, with only one pull back, snug in a spot. A legal spot. It was a miracle.

She could walk back to Brittany's little house to try again. Or …

"Everybody's Got a Hungry Heart". Was that music thumping out of another bar up the street?

No. This was *The Book of Wizzy.*

When had Wizzy ever heard Springsteen?

Didn't matter. They probably had Springsteen music in heaven. Somebody's heaven.

Helen found herself right in front of a restaurant from which the wonderful smells of burgers and fries warmed the dark street. Twenty-dollar burgers and fries, maybe more at night. What Relief Society president could justify having a Sunday dinner like that?

"Everybody needs a place to rest ..."

*This is really crazy. I've never eaten alone in a restaurant in my life. I should go home to Mark and —*

A young woman with a clipboard wearing only a black T-shirt and jeans in spite of the weather asked for Helen's name. Helen gave it obediently—as if the young woman had been a police officer—and actually started to reach for ID.

"That'll be a forty-five-minute wait," the young woman said.

*I should go home to Mark and ...*

The young woman moved on to the next couple without comment, as if a single woman dressed in panty hose and sensible heels, a rayon-flowered midi skirt, a string of faux pearls and a belted, boiled-wool coat were the most common thing among the large, loud groups, the skinny jeans, après ski apparel and cowboy boots packing her establishment on a Sunday night.

*I look like a Relief Society president. And who could love me but a worthy priesthood holder? But my priesthood holder ...*

The young woman with the clipboard told the young couple, "The wait will be fifty minutes."

The couple jiggled up and down in the cold, but said, "Great."

*I should go home to Mark and ...*

*And what? Eat alone at the other side of the kitchen table?*

In the dark with the crowds spilling out onto the sidewalk, Helen didn't recognize it as the same place where she and Brittany had eaten the day before, not until she recognized the T-shirt on the young woman as sharing some sort of kinship to the one her niece's friend Simon had worn.

At almost the same moment as realization dawned, the young man himself spied her through the front window. He set burgers and fries in front of the couple seated there. The next minute he was talking to the young woman with the clipboard, and she was looking at him with eyes that said, "Anything for you, Simon."

Simon in his tight black T-shirt shouted "A single!" to the restaurant at large and got Sister Helen Snow seated at the bar in ten minutes.

*A Relief Society president at the bar.* It wasn't easy clinging to the perch in heels, even sensible ones. And such an array of bottles glinting in the light. Helen scarcely knew the names of any of them, just the throb of "sin" they threw at her.

*What if ...?* What if somebody tried to pick her up? Like in the movies.

Helen Snow felt herself flush red to the roots of her hair, and then saw her reflection in bar's mirror.

No. No one was going to try to pick her up.

Wizzy would have stared in wonder and delight at the glittering wall.

"Brittany's not speaking to me," Helen told Simon awkwardly as he handed her the menu. Maybe he'd kick her out with this news.

"I know," he said.

"She told you?"

"We skied together looking for Sarah, met old Ben. I helped her move all the stuff out of Dave's condo. We had a couple of good, long talks. And yes, she talked a lot about you."

"She said she never wanted to see me again."

"Something like that."

Helen couldn't meet his eye. Did Simon not want to talk to her any more than Brittany did?

What did the menu in her hand mean? What was she doing in this restaurant so far from home? Helen had lost her appetite.

Simon hurried off to serve another table.

When he returned, they both tried to start talking at once. Simon let her go first.

"I really feel terrible about this," Helen said with new determination not to be driven off, a Wizzy chorus of "Hold to the rod" firming her resolve. "I've been trying to tell her. And I even came just now from the prison. I was trying to see if I could get Ben out. I know he's innocent. Sarah told me herself. But I can't afford half a million dollars' bail. And Brittany won't see me."

Simon nodded curtly and did not say what he had started to say. Instead, he gave his waiter spiel. "Can I get you something to drink? Coffee? Tea?"

"Water," Helen said.

"Lemon?"

"Please." Then, in deference to the weather, "No ice, please."

When he returned—it took him quite a while—he did say, in that BBC voice of his, "Not English, are you?"

She couldn't understand what he meant; the

mirror reflected her blank look. Her mind had been miles away, listening to a *Book of Wizzy* rendition of "Don't You Let Nobody Turn You 'Round". Was he adding insults to his unwillingness to talk to her?

"We don't do ice in the UK," Simon explained. "Too cold." He took out his order pad and pencil. "Now, what will you have?"

Helen hadn't even looked at the menu. She stammered in confusion.

"Same as yesterday?" he tried to help her out.

"Okay. Yes."

Hamburgers two days in a row? Twenty-dollar hamburgers? So be it.

When Simon returned with the order, Helen was ready for him. She'd turned her back to the mirror. How could she bless food before, not the face of God, but the glinting eyes of a hundred liquor bottles? Utah law said a bartender could not perform the lurid task of mixing drinks within view of the innocent eyes of children. What about Relief Society presidents?

"I've got to make Sarah see the error of her ways and retract the statement she gave to the police." Helen looked around; no one in the crowded, noisy restaurant was eavesdropping.

"Good luck with that. Ketchup?"

Helen nodded. When he passed a bottle of the condiment to her, she checked for eavesdroppers again and spoke. "Simon, maybe I shouldn't have told Sarah's parents where their daughter was, but—"

"Oh, no, Mrs. Snow—"

"Call me Helen, please."

"Definitely you did the right thing, Helen." That British reserve was so charming. "Her parents needed to know, even if she is an adult. But everyone after that seems to have turned into right nutters."

Helen stared at Simon. Was he saying what she thought he was saying?

"We Brits have all these jokes about Americans reaching for their guns to solve any problem. How many Americans does it take to change a light bulb?"

"Did someone get shot?" Helen asked in horror. It did seem that had to be the next step.

Simon chuckled good-naturedly. "No, not this time. 'More guns.' The answer to everything is 'more guns'."

The large red-haired man on the stool next to Helen chimed in "Damn right, young man!" and patted the bulge beneath his mohair sport jacket.

Helen felt less comfortable than ever in the crowded conditions in which she found herself. How many movies had she seen where the mirror behind all those liquor bottles was shattered by gunfire? It seemed to her that's what such displays existed for. Nonetheless, Helen thought she got the joke and tried to match her chuckle to Simon's. Simon smiled and walked away to deliver his next order.

Helen reached for the ketchup. She made an effort not to bump the shoulder-holstered man next to her—who, she noticed, happened to be left handed.

The burger was rarer than last time. She should have specified medium well. Ketchup looked an awful lot like blood. Replacing the bun helped, but she still remembered the adage that if you showed a rifle over the mantel in Act I, the gun would have to be fired by the end of Act III. She wondered about the bar's mirror and its array of glass. She should try to get the burger down before the shooting began. The burger had cost twenty dollars, after all.

"That's not what I wanted to say, that joke. I'm sorry."

Simon was back at her elbow, carefully on the side away from the left-handed man. He didn't ask "How's everything?" because the first bite hadn't passed her lips yet. She set the burger back on its square plate and leaned in closer so he didn't have to speak so loudly over the noise to continue.

"We Brits do say, 'Americans are the teenagers of the world,' and that's just what I saw happening. Sarah's parents calling the police, the police calling in a helicopter, the Special Forces and the news. The teenaged, cowboy news. After all of that, what's Sarah supposed to do, with her parents pressing her to be their good, obedient, always-stylish daughter? Say, 'Sorry, I just went out for a little ski to visit a man'? No. 'I was kidnapped.' She's got a reputation—and the reputation of her family—to hold up against all of this."

"You think Sarah's lying?"

"Let's put it this way. I've had my eye on the pair of them since they first walked into the library together. To be honest, I had my eye on Brittany, but I couldn't get her alone to—"

"You were always interested in Brittany and not ...?" Helen realized she had been carrying around the assumption that all the boys were attracted to Sarah and regarded her niece as second best. That was how Brittany had always presented the duo.

"Your niece, Mrs. ... Helen ... is far more serious. The quiet one, but the more intelligent of the pair. A reader. That attracted me. I'm not sure why Sarah ever came into the library, except for that last time, to read the maps and plan her escape. All the other times, it seemed to me, she came to chaperone Brittany, to tell her constantly, 'No, that's not the fellow for you, dearie. Foreign. Not Mormon. Not rich enough. Your parents wouldn't approve. A librarian, for God's sake,' ... whatever her objection was. Or because she wanted first crack at me and would only hand Brittany her cast offs."

He said that bitterly.

"All I can say is that I had no chance with Brittany as long as the pair of them were thick as thieves and Sarah was calling the shots. And I was heartily glad the first time I saw Brittany with someone other than Sarah—that someone being you.

"Oh, and yes, I know Gentle Ben. He'd come in and use the library computers sometimes. I cannot believe he did what he is accused of."

Helen stared. Her jaw might even have dropped open. She continued staring at the same spot even after an irate customer shouted at Simon, "Is it possible to get some service around here?" and the young man, the emotion red in his clear English skin, had to hurry off.

# Chapter 19

Helen was still staring at the same spot in the restaurant—a blur of beautiful, recreating people—when Simon returned to it.

"Something wrong with your burger, ma'am?" he asked.

Her burger had probably congealed, but she took a brave bite and said around the mouthful, "Not at all" in a very rude, American sort of way. Simon grinned that British-toothed grin of his as he waited for her to swallow.

"So Brittany is still defending Sarah?" Helen asked when she could.

"Yes, but at least she's still talking to me. I did drop the subject when I saw it upset her too much."

"I've been to the sheriff's about this."

"Yes?"

"Just now." Helen thought about scenes in movies where the sheriff pushes into the saloon through the swinging doors. The mirror and all the bottles in front of it shatter shortly thereafter, but she kept her focus. "The deputy I spoke to actually believes they're holding an innocent man."

The British reserve broke into an ever-so-slight look of relief.

"But what can they do, given Sarah's sworn statement?" Helen said. "It'll go worse for Sarah and her parents the longer she puts off telling the truth. This is illegal, this lying to the police. When the results of the rape kit come back—negative, she told me they would be negative—how's she going to explain that?"

In an effort to continue to appear busy, Simon reached over and reset the ketchup bottle on the bar. The bottle was identical to the one Helen had at home, nothing gourmet about it.

Simon shrugged. "I hate to say it, 'cause she's a friend of Brittany's, but Sarah is spoiled rotten and as silly as they come. I won't feel too bad when she gets her comeuppance."

Very interesting. Simon was indeed attracted to Brittany after all, not just as a tag-along to the more glittering Sarah. Helen found herself thinking she'd gotten everything she needed out of this twenty-dollar burger, but sensed Simon still had more to say and was only trying to figure out how to go about it.

She attempted a joke of her own. "Is it because of her name?"

"Her name?"

"Do you like her because of her name? Brittany? Britain?"

Simon laughed, and although Helen had the unhappy feeling the joke might be at her own ignorance, he was too good-natured for her to take offense.

"Why do Americans think that?" the young man

asked. "What is with that name?"

Helen felt herself blush.

Simon noticed and tried, clumsily, to overcome the mistake. "Brittany's on the other side of the Channel, a part of France."

"Oh." Helen's blush deepened. Her brother-in-law, who still religiously ordered freedom fries, was going to be really unhappy.

Simon seemed not to notice. "I sort of wish their names were reversed. A Sarah would be better to take home to Mum and Dad than trying to explain 'Brittany' to them."

Mum and Dad? He *was* serious.

"But I suppose the name's her parents' doing."

"It is," Helen assured him.

"I'm learning to like it."

"If you knew my sister and her husband, you wouldn't be surprised for a moment."

"Yes. Brittany's tried to explain them. I guess I'll have to meet them to believe it. What does the Good Book say? 'Faith is the substance of things hoped for'?"

The vision of a young man hoping for something instead of feeling entitled brought moisture to Helen's eyes. She looked away. "And 'the evidence of things not seen,'" she concluded.

"You will put in a good word with your sister for me?" Simon asked.

Helen nodded and tried another bite. All of a sudden, she had recovered her appetite.

"As I was saying," Simon went on, "the only reason I don't want to see Sarah get her comeuppance is if it hurts Brittany."

"Well, I've managed that," said Helen, miserable. "I've hurt Brittany with this business. But it's *not* my business, and it's not yours. We've got to support Brittany in her own decision, that's it."

Simon shrugged those excellent shoulders in their T-shirt and turned to go back to work. Helen caught him by the arm.

"Were you going to see Brittany tonight?" she asked.

"For a little. When I get off here." Simon was trying to assure her that he would not spend the night again.

"Okay, she won't see me, won't talk to me, but she will see you."

"Right. I'll put in a good word for you."

"We'll put good words for each other," Helen said as her waiter left without her getting a chance to even mention the dognapping scheme.

Helen faced the bar mirror and ate her burger. *The Book of Wizzy* played loud and clear, drowning out the thumping Muzak, not deviating from "Don't You Let Nobody Turn You 'Round". It helped her glaze over the horror of seeing herself chewing.

Shortly, Simon returned. Helen made sure to swallow, but they both spoke at once. Amazingly, their words matched except that one phrase was "I've a plan," and the other was "I have a plan".

When they stopped, Helen told Simon, "You first."

"First—I know this doesn't seem to have much to do with Sarah—but I have to know about the other case. What do you think about ... about the hot tub ... and ...?"

"Dave Jaramillo? Definitely murder."

Helen's confidence got the better of her; she must have spoken too loudly. The heat-packing, left-handed, red-headed mountain of mohair next to her swiveled around, his bar stool complaining, and stared. The man carried murder under his arm like deodorant and was shocked by a dowdy woman's use of the word. He threw a large bill on the bar and quickly ushered his lady friend out of the restaurant.

"Thank you for being our guests at this restaurant," Simon called after the retreating couple. When he said "restaurant", Simon left off the final "t", like a Frenchman. Simon moved quickly to wipe down the bar while the bartender bused the dishes—mostly glasses, actually.

Perhaps Helen had just saved the life of one bar mirror and a boatload of liquor. All in a day's work for a Relief Society president.

"Murder," Simon repeated, carefully choosing a lower decibel.

"I'm not sure why you say the two cases are not connected, Sarah's disappearance and the young man's death. They seem closely connected to me." They seemed that way to Wizzy, too, who was singing "ever be one" from Hymn 3.

Simon mopped the wood as if he hoped to take the glossy shine off it and seemed to consider Helen's words. "Brittany believes it was murder as well, and she can't really explain why. It has her quite upset."

"The sheriff is convinced it was an accident." Helen brooded, remembering how alarmed she'd felt to be sitting next to someone who carried a concealed weapon. She hadn't felt safer; quite the contrary. She'd felt as if the man held her—and the bar mirror

—hostage the entire time. And yet... "Do you know," she said slowly, "statistics say police officers in this state shoot more people dead than gang and domestic violence combined."

Simon, being from a strange land where even the "bobbies" went unarmed, stared at her.

"Fun fact." Helen shrugged, feeling more relaxed now that she and Simon were on such good terms. And now that she'd eaten. "That's the only way the peace officers can gain our respect in a nation of rugged individualism and land rights." Why, she'd forgotten she ever had a sense of humor.

"The coppers sound like they're running around on hair triggers, feeling threatened. And who can blame them? They know other people are toting more fire than they are. Funny you should mention land rights, however."

Simon shifted back to her left side, wash cloth still in his hand, so a new couple could take the vacated bar stools. They were, Helen noticed, the same couple who'd been given a wait time of fifty minutes. My, how time flies.

"Tell me your plan for my niece," Helen urged.

"In the short run?" Simon opened his mouth as if to say something else, but it came out "Excuse me." He had to see to a diner who'd been snapping fingers at him.

So there was a long run, too. He had mentioned "Mum and Dad."

Helen ate the last of her fries, twirling them in ketchup on the strange square plate. She tasted nothing, watching the young man scurry here and there under pressure, carrying six meals at once, dealing with the crowded restaurant and irate customers of the sort that could never be satisfied. Then he went into the kitchen again.

"Let's try the plan, then," he said when he returned.

"What plan? You never even told me yours."

Instead of answering, he asked, "Care for some dessert? Another piece of lava cake?"

"No!" Helen said, horrified. "Two days in a row? Without Brittany to help me eat it? I won't fit in anything if I do. We just got through the Thanksgiving leftovers, and now Christmas is coming up."

Simon grinned, but he handed her the dessert menu anyway.

"No, really—"

"I want you to have a look at that."

He had passed her something else, tucked into the menu. She unfolded a single sheet of a yellow legal pad and read the small, neat, block print, written in felt-tip pen, that covered nearly one whole side.

It was a detailed description of plans to turn the whole mountain behind Pine Enterprises into a nature preserve. Right there—on some very valuable real estate next to the famous resort—there was to be no more building of condos, no more grooming the mountainside for ski runs and lifts. The phrasing was at least semi-legalese, as if the writer had been drawing on memories of legal documents, or even referencing ones on a computer screen. It was signed: David S. Jaramillo.

Under the signature, the paper was dated December first, less than a week ago.

Even more intriguing was the "page 2 of 2" at the top of the paper and how it started in the middle of a sentence: " ... the presence of Benjamin Ursule, to whom I grant the right to live ..."

Although the sentence continued enticingly over the next few lines, there must be more to this story running on "page 1 of 2", Helen knew. Much more. Wizzy even hummed Hymn 131 "More holiness give me, more strivings within," in a rather less than holy tempo.

## Chapter 20

"Have you changed your mind about dessert?" Simon asked when he came back.

"No. But where did you get this?" Helen held the paper out to him by one worn corner.

"I helped Brittany clean out the condos this morning."

"Yes. You told me."

"She went through the books and selected a boxful that she would never read to donate to the library."

"She said she often does that. That's how you met."

"Well, I took the box over to the library when I did my one-to-five shift. My colleague Holly did the sorting into 'keepers' and 'book sale', and this was in one of them."

"But there's more. This is only page two."

"I know. I couldn't find page one."

"Which one? What sort of book was it in?"

"Right. Well, to tell the truth, Holly didn't remember," Simon said. "And yes, I asked. She just dumped the lot of bookmarks in the dustbin, and that's where I found this. I went through the whole bin, after that."

Helen murmured condolences at a tedious job. "But I have to commend you for diligence."

"A lot of books we get donated have things in them," Simon said. "People will use anything for a bookmark. Pressed flowers. Old photographs. Empty toothpaste tubes."

"No."

"Really. A lot of receipts, often for the book itself. I can't tell you how often I've seen that someone paid $27.99 for that very book, and by the marker we can see they only got to page thirty-five. We usually toss such mementos, as Holly did, straight away. There's nothing we can do with them. But I always like to see the stories they tell us first. I just picked it out of the bin. It lay on top, and the color of the paper caught my eye. Then I saw the name."

"It probably would have been in a big book. Hardcover."

"How can you tell that?"

"This is a big piece of paper, even folded. It would overwhelm a paperback."

Helen had a sudden image of the titles she'd seen on the sideboard in Dave Jaramillo's condo, of the television shoved among them.

"Could it have been a New Age book?" She felt she hardly needed to ask. It must have been one of the books on that sideboard in Dave's condo. "Something like *Food for a Small Planet* or *The Spontaneous Fulfillment of Desire* or *The Monkey Wrench Gang*."

Something, in other words, church authorities would say demonstrated a condemning lack of proper faith.

"Yes, now that you mention it, there were a number of books in the box like that. But there were other titles, too."

"I'd like to see them." Something about that shelf could stand more scrutiny.

"Unfortunately, the library's closed until tomorrow."

Another patron demanded his attention. While she waited, Helen reread the yellow paper.

What if the incomplete sentence in its entirety was "The only exception to these restrictions of use is to be the presence of Benjamin Ursule to whom I grant the right to live, and to take wood and game as long as he may live and to whom I grant the control of this property in my absence or in the case of my death"? It had to be something like that, didn't it?

A twenty-something young man thinking about his own death. And of his friend, Gentle Ben.

Less than a week ago.

When Simon returned, he brought the bill in a black folder.

"Do you know of any connection between Dave and Sarah Drake except a crush on her part?" Helen asked, indicating the document.

"Some reason that she may have had to wish Dave dead?" Dread saturated Simon's voice.

"Or at least to have Ben arrested and the key thrown away? Are they relatives?"

"Who?"

"Ben and Dave? Dave and Sarah? Sarah and Ben? Any of them?"

Simon raised his brows. "Well, that is convoluted."

Helen couldn't help herself. Relations explained a

lot of what went on under the surface in Utah. She had to tell the old joke. "Put five Utahns in a room, and they'll all be related in half an hour. It's an old saying. It means they'll have figured out how they're related, no matter how distantly, in half an hour, and how intermarried. Also what sort of genetic diseases they're prone to."

*And how we stand in the hierarchy*, she thought. It occurred to her that this was why a lot of her fellow believers did genealogy, to stand their own in these contests.

"That's how we do things around here," she added.

Families, indeed, are forever. Sometimes not a good thing.

"People come into the library all the time looking for ancestors," Simon concurred. "They usually find them. And sometimes they wish they hadn't. But there are always plenty of relatives. Makes someone like me feel a little left out."

Helen felt her head spinning with possibilities. The Family History Library downtown surely contained information that could be of help here. Or perhaps not, since anything after the 1940 census was still off limits by law. But maybe the secular branches of local government would be more revealing.

Helen might have learned to use those genealogical resources, had she needed to see that Wizzy was baptized. But doctrine taught that children with severe mental handicaps, as well as those who died under the age of eight, had no need of the saving ordinance. They flew directly to salvation, so doctrine assured parents.

Helen could learn to use contemporary resources.

With time. With the help of a computer-savvy young person—like Brittany. Was time a thing she had as Relief Society president? Would she ever have Brittany's help again?

Simon gestured at the yellow paper in Helen's hand. "Do you think Ben knew about this—what are we calling it? A will?"

"It's not witnessed or anything. And we've only got page two. I don't know if that it would hold up in a court of law. That's part of why I'd like to know which book it was in, and if there's a chance anybody else knew about this."

"And then thought it was worthwhile to put Dave out of the way, before a legal, binding version could be made."

Helen watched Simon consider. "Maybe Dave was going to change his mind and Ben had to stop him," he said, "to at least delay the land falling into developers' hands."

"Sarah said those ski tracks were hers. But could she have been covering for Ben?"

"Covering for a man she's since accused of rape?"

"Or for someone else? Who?"

Suddenly Helen couldn't wait to be on the doorstep of the Family History Library when it opened in the morning, or the courthouse, or wherever records could be accessed.

She jumbled the restaurant bill and the yellow sheet of legal paper. Her hand would not relinquish the yellow sheet. *The Book of Wizzy* had even turned to Hymn 274 and kept singing the chorus over and over, that chorus only a bloodless General Authority could hear without thinking dirty thoughts: "Hold to the rod ..." A General Authority or Wizzy, for whom nothing was dirty. But really, the hymnal editors should try raising a pair of teenaged boys. Distracted by reminiscences, even once she pulled the papers back out of her purse, Helen found her pen hovering for a moment below the "David S. Jaramillo" instead of the correct heat-sensitive "merchant copy".

"May I keep this?" Helen asked Simon, about the yellow document.

For the first time since the very start of the evening, Simon seemed reticent, less than the perfect waiter, complying with her every desire. "How about you take a photo on your mobile?"

"I don't know that mine can do that. I could make a copy for you at the Family History Library tomorrow."

"Let me see your phone."

She handed it over. He made the camera work in under five seconds. The first attempt didn't come out so well. Against the mirror and liquor bottles, the flash—there was even a flash in that thing?—caused too much glare. They spread it over the bar and got a decent shot on the next try. Using the magnifying feature—who knew?—she could read it all, except one corner of Dave's signature.

Helen would like to see James Bond come up with a niftier gadget for sleuthing than the phone she carried around in her bag all day. Wizzy even played James Bond theme music with throbbing saxes, twanging electric guitar on the lower strings and a swishing brush on the drum kit.

If Helen ever admitted to seeing an R-rated film, that would be the end of her tenure as RS pres. They probably wouldn't even let her go back to playing the Primary piano.

She should take this photo to Deputy Moody. But wouldn't it be better to have clearer information about where it had been found? Perhaps show it to Sarah? But not tonight.

Finally, Helen opened the black plastic bill folder and found, in place of the mints she'd been expecting, a large, old-fashioned key.

"What's this?" she asked.

Simon grinned. "My plan." With a conspiratorial wink, he added, "that's the key to the Park City Library. I often have to open up or close in the evening."

"And you want me to ...?"

"Go in and have a look at the book sale shelves, see if anything looks familiar."

A shiver of excitement ran down Helen's spine at this taste of real sleuthing. She was consoled for the absence of mints.

"I can't get off for another hour or I'd go with you," Simon continued. "But see what you can find. The door this key opens is around the right side, to the back." On a napkin, he drew a map of the way to the room where the book sale would be and then instructions for the few blocks' ride on the bus. "I think we already sold some of the titles Brittany gave us this afternoon as soon as I put them out."

"But it's worth a try." Helen was more excited than ever.

"I'll head to Brittany's once I'm done here, and I'll call you as soon as I soften her heart a bit. If I can soften her heart."

Oh, yes. Helen remembered her own plan, about using Horehound to sway Sarah's testimony, but none of it meant anything if Brittany wouldn't speak to her. She decided to put that off. She caught her departing waiter's arm again instead.

"Tell her 'Wizzy'."

"Excuse me?"

"If Brittany doesn't seem forgiving at first, just mention the name Wizzy."

"Wizzy? What's Wizzy?"

"Never mind. She'll know."

"Wizzy. Brilliant," Simon said, not sounding at all convinced that would be enough.

His reaction made Helen think that perhaps her niece would take this evocation of the dead to be some sort of manipulation.

Not on Simon's tongue, surely.

Helen hadn't even had a chance to mention her dognapping plan yet. If these first schemes worked, then—

# Chapter 21

Brittany, who'd just been thinking about putting down her paperback, having a hot shower and getting in her pajamas, groaned out loud. Yet another knock at the door, sounding over next door's Country Western beat.

Would Aunt Helen never give up?

Brittany had trusted her aunt as long as she could remember. All these years, the woman had listened to her when her mother had been too busy. She had been there for her when Brittany had questions, or just a thought to which her mother's answer had always been, "It's simple. You know such things don't go along with our values," or "You know we always obey the brethren."

"We believe in being honest, true, chaste, benevolent ..." Chased by an elephant.

Aunt Helen's version of these replies had been more like, "You could pray about it. You are entitled to your own inspiration." Or sometimes skipping that step altogether, just, "Well? What do you think? We all make mistakes, but that's how we learn."

Brittany's mother's "brethren" probably included the sheriff. And yes, her mother would have busted

211

Sarah to Brother and Sister Drake as Aunt Helen had done. But Brittany would have known better than to spill the beans to her own mother. She'd thought she could trust Aunt Helen.

Huh! Maybe her mother wouldn't have even believed the story about Sarah in the first place, citing the ninth commandment: "Didn't I teach you not to bear false witness?" Brittany's mother had once borne her testimony before the whole ward, about how God had blessed her that all her children had chosen wisely in their friends, Sarah Drake in particular: "Young people who share our highest values." Brittany's mother probably couldn't name *another* friend of her youngest daughter. Brittany wasn't sure she could, either. She clung to Sarah for that reason. It was a very lonely thing, to be friendless.

Sarah was popular, Sarah was fun. A friend with such press wouldn't do anything dangerous, much less lie. Would she?

That wretched dog was going crazy at the second, maybe third round of knocking. Brittany did have to question Sarah's judgment to pick this dog for no other reason than "Isn't she *cute*?"

Brittany certainly wasn't going to get any more reading done as long as that barking kept up. And something sounded different in the dog's frenzy than the time earlier that evening when her aunt had knocked. Brittany put down her book and went to pull back the sheet at the window for a peek.

It wasn't her aunt. It was Simon.

Her heart flew to her throat, her hand to the door's deadbolt. Simon had said that he was worn out after their ski on Saturday and would probably be too tired after his work at the restaurant to come and see her again Sunday night, but here he was.

She threw the deadbolt and was about to work the handle, too, when a consideration made her stop.

"My aunt Helen's not with you, is she?"

"No. No, she's not."

Something in his voice caused Brittany to leave the handle and look out again. Simon certainly seemed to be alone, rocking from foot to foot in the cold. His breath wreathed his head and glowed like Christmas lights as the Happy Miner next door neoned strike after strike at his mother lode.

"Are you here because she told you to come?" Brittany demanded.

"I brought you some leftovers from the restaurant." It was delightful, the way he said 'restauran'", without the t.

But the idea of cold fries—Simon would call them "chips"—following the chips—Simon would call them "crisps"—she'd just had with the last of the clam dip didn't seem worth the trouble. Besides, much as she enjoyed Simon's company, it felt unfaithful to Sarah, who'd never liked him. Not rich enough.

"Aunt Helen's behind this, isn't she?"

Brittany couldn't trust Aunt Helen, she couldn't trust Simon, and it made her miserable. Sarah was the one Brittany had to cling to. Even though Sarah's parents wouldn't let her talk or text or anything.

"Aunt Helen told you to come," she repeated when Simon said nothing to justify himself.

"Alright, she did come to the restaurant. We had a good long talk."

"About me, right?"

"About you and Sarah and Dave Jaramillo and Gentle Ben and how we only want to see you safe. We want the best for you."

*The best for you.* Deadly words. The "best" didn't make her happy.

On the sidewalk, smokers from the Happy Miner had turned their heads toward her front porch to watch.

"I'd rather not have this conversation through a plywood door, Brittany. Could you—?"

"Go home, Simon. I'd rather not have this conversation, period."

One song from the bar ended. In the blessed silence, Brittany heard her own heartbeat, felt tears sliding down her cheeks she hadn't felt before. The smokers on the frozen sidewalk dropped their butts to sputter to death in the ice. Another song started.

Through the crack in the sheet-curtain, Simon seemed poised to go, shaking his head in failure. Then he shouted, "Wizzy."

"What did you say?" Brittany demanded at the crack in the door. She couldn't have heard right.

"Wizzy. Your aunt told me to say Wizzy. She said you would know what it meant."

Elizabeth. Wizzy. The little cousin almost her age Brittany couldn't even remember ever knowing. Only once in all those years of aunt-niece dialogue had Aunt Helen even mentioned her dead daughter. Always, Brittany realized with shame, it had been "me, me, me" from Brittany herself. Aunt Helen always assured her she didn't mind, that listening to Brittany made her feel better, but that one time ....

Brittany hadn't forgotten, not the conversation, not the look on her aunt's face as she talked about her daughter. And afterwards, when that same look would come across Aunt Helen's face, it would hit Brittany: *She's thinking about Elizabeth.*

"But Aunt Helen, Mom told me Elizabeth—Wizzy—was ... what's the word? Handicapped?"

"Handicapped?" Aunt Helen had laughed, as if the notion surprised her. "Is that what your mother called it?"

No. Brittany's mother had used the r-word. But Brittany couldn't say that.

"Did she say Wizzy's birth was because of our sins? Your uncle Mark's and mine?" Aunt Helen had asked, quietly.

Brittany had grown quieter still, feeling the fear her mother had instilled in her that if she didn't "keep herself pure" she, too, might be cursed with something like that, a retarded, damaged child. Brittany had thought about how she couldn't really depend on her mother for support, not in the way she could with Aunt Helen; maybe Aunt Helen had hoped for support from her sister, with no better success.

Aunt Helen had recovered from that exchange faster than Brittany had. Aunt Helen had given a little chuckle and sung, as she often did, a brief snatch of hymn. It had sounded like "There is Sunshine in My Soul Today, only it sounded like she said, "For Wizzy is my light."

"No more handicapped than any of the rest of us, I've always thought," Aunt Helen had said. "Wizzy's was more obvious, that's all. But when it comes to being selfless, patient, loving, living every minute in joy, pure joy ..."

Aunt Helen had stopped there, fighting tears, although her lips smiled.

Handicapped? Everyone? Even Sarah, who had everything going for her? So much so that she had to lie at the first indication that it might be otherwise? It had never, ever occurred to Brittany to think of Sarah as handicapped, as her mother as handicapped.

When she'd been able to speak again, Aunt Helen had said, "And doesn't the *Book of Mormon* say 'Man is that ...' No. Let's translate this correctly, as women: '*Woman* is that she might have joy.' "

Joy? What, exactly, was joy? Although they quoted that scripture often enough, they didn't explain it very well in Church, if you didn't count the rather bitter, self-deprecating joke her spinster Young Adult leader Sister Joy had repeated nearly every week: "Man is that he might have—*me!*"

"Joy to the World."

When had Brittany ever had joy? Joy was not fun, which had always been Sarah's reason for doing anything. Brittany bet the word "fun" didn't exist in the whole quad combination of LDS scripture, but that was what was offered as a substitute, like "Let them eat cake". And drink Kool-Aid.

With Sarah, that best, testimony-sanctioned friend of hers—"such a fun girl" had been Brittany's mother's exact phrase—when had Brittany ever had joy? Sarah, who'd always tied Brittany up in knots because she wasn't wearing the proper clothes. Concerning any young man Brittany dared to mention an interest in, it was either, "I won't be seen with you if you go out with such a geek," or "Mine." Sarah, who always copied Brittany's notes, her quizzes even. Whose study sessions were gab sessions, whose parents were at school bullying teachers to raise her grade "because our daughter is born to do well."

Brittany realized it was reasonable for her friend to behave like the people who raised her. Sometimes shopping with Sarah, Sarah would laugh with the salesclerks if Brittany put an item back saying, "I can't afford it." "It's ugly," was better, but not if Sarah had already declared it "cute". When Brittany had to move up to the size-twelve rack while Sarah stayed at eight or even six, there had been more laughter. Brittany remembered how she'd left her studies for the ski slopes because Sarah had mocked her interest in biology as "gross".

"You know, they do have surgery that can fix those ears of yours," Sarah had said on more than one occasion.

Was such behavior bullying? Sunday school lessons talked about the virtuous child stepping down from her God-sanctioned world to protect the bullied. The reward was a grateful conversion by the bullied to Mormonism, which the protector could add to her slate of good deeds. The bullied child then ceased to be a bully-target, through whatever alchemical mystery. A girl living the Gospel couldn't possibly be bullied. Lessons were never about the virtuous being bullied by their fellows.

Sarah sometimes carried her behavior over to Facebook, where all their friends could see, then she'd write afterwards "Brittany: my BFF". Sarah would invoke the gospel behind her bullying, saying with tones she must have heard from her mother, "But you have your free agency, Brittany, and if you

don't use it right, Heavenly Father won't be happy."
*And I won't be your BFF.*

Sarah, Brittany thought, was responsible for this confounded dog, yet she'd abandoned it. Sarah Drake thought she could marry and convert wealthy Dave Jaramillo, who really wasn't interested but could be charmed or forced to change his mind, as it suited Sarah. It had been Sarah's plan to live on their own in this terrible place and work, although she'd forget to show up with the first flake of falling snow.

How was that for free agency?

Wizzy.

Joy.

Brittany found herself leaning hard with one hand against the paint-peeling doorframe. A song had wormed its way into her ear, an old one she'd seen once on YouTube and watched over and over until Sarah had told her to "stop being a dork." A sixteen-year-old Janis Ian backed by a wailing organ nothing like a church organ: "Baby, I'm only Society's Child."

Was that Sarah? Was that Brittany herself?

Wizzy was the one free of society. And Aunt Helen would fight for anybody's child to be herself. She would fight for the safety of body and soul, not for appearances, just as she had done for Wizzy.

"When we're older things may change." Brittany remembered that line from the song.

Did one lose joy in the waiting and in the substitution of fun?

Through the crack in the sheet before the window, Brittany saw Simon turn to step off the porch. Simon, who wasn't wealthy, but who had ambition and could work hard.

She threw open the door.

"Wait!"

And the wretched dog took a chunk out of Simon's trousers.

*****

The library where Simon worked, to which Helen held the key, was housed now in the old Park City High school building; she remembered when it had been in the old Miners' Hospital. Just as Simon's napkin map promised, her walk over dark, shoveled walks, with ice forming from the day's melt, brought her to a door where the key fit and turned easily. She fumbled for and found a light switch.

Polished balustrades and dignified hardwood floors gleamed in the sudden light, much more conducive to scholarship than the modern building that had replaced this for grades nine through twelve on the other side of town. The smell of beeswax and old books delighted her senses. She jumped as the old building creaked in the silence.

An absurd fear of ghosts wrapped itself around her thudding heart. A lot of places in Park City were supposed to be haunted. No one in history had come to Park City to get poor. Most had abandoned family and civil society for mining silver or for the easy picking of tourists, a quick fix to their problems. Such aspirations sometimes lead to quick death: shoot outs, or suicides after poker games; or the slower death of miners' black lung.

Women in Helen's family had been told in whispers how her great grandmother had one day put on her Sunday-go-to-meeting hat, left hearth, home and thirteen children to take the train alone —back in the days when there was a train—up to Park City. She went to consult one of the ladies of easy virtue who served the men too hot with desire to strike it rich to jump through the hoops necessary to support wives. The whispered question had been, "How do I keep from having a fourteenth child?" So maybe unborn spirit children haunted the town, too.

Had Karen ever told Brittany that story? Somehow, Helen doubted it. Maybe Helen should, relate to the next generation this step beyond Mormon bounds in desperate times. If she ever got to speak to her niece again. She felt like a ghost herself, unable to communicate with the living: dead to her niece, the murder weapon a cell phone.

And then there was a lonely condo hot tub. Plenty of ways to make ghosts.

Helen took another deep breath of library smell and told herself that if the place was haunted, these were friendly spirits who also liked to read. The creaking was just them welcoming her.

Or maybe David Jaramillo, urging her to find clues to put his sheet of yellow paper in context.

*The Book of Wizzy,* though no copy of it existed in the Park City Library, began to insist on having its say. Her daughter bombarded Helen's quiet time with "Choose the Right", the pounding 4/4 time of Hymn 239. Helen didn't know any way to tell Wizzy the hymn had been entirely too commercialized, what with the CTR rings that made a girl feel less-than-holy if she got a less-than gold copy to wear in her eighth year at baptism.

In any case, the song didn't seem likely to help her find the first page of the yellow document, nor the book that it might have been stored in. The "Book Sale" shelves were where Simon had said they'd be. *The Spontaneous Fulfillment of Desire* was even there; Helen recognized it as the one from Dave Jaramillo's shelves. No one had had a spontaneous desire to fulfill by buying that book yet. She shook it out. She shook out everything else on the shelf. Nothing.

A book—hardly more than a pamphlet, really—on the same shelf caught Helen's attention and held it for some time. Could be a donation from the same condo, right? She slid it from between the two larger books that dominated it and opened it carefully. In this autographed, self-published pamphlet, the founder of Pine Enterprises got to toot his own horn for thirty-four pages. James Costain was his name, and the man grinned out from the frontispiece in shirt and tie (no vest, vests being pretentious in Mormon haute couture) as if he and his success were God's gift to the world.

*You're a lesser mortal if you can't go and do likewise,* the photo in the pamphlet seemed to say. *Just follow my same simple plan.* He was like a modern version of the Hofmann Jesus hanging over a bishop's desk: exhorting and inspirational, and only subliminally reproachful.

His plan no doubt included "the will of Heavenly Father" hammered out in smokeless back rooms, and blind obedience on the outside. Helen noticed that Sister Costain, his "sweet eternal companion", rated mention only as she might appear on a genealogical sheet, full first, middle and last names, the maiden name emphasized because it was the name of a Prophet and a whole, powerful clan James Costain had had the good business sense to marry into.

In spite of herself, Helen started working out the genealogy, the relations, the hierarchy. Perhaps some serious ranch land near a ski resort had come with that maiden name of the "sweet eternal companion" as a dowry, the not-so-subtle bribe for taking a daughter off her father's hands.

Perhaps Helen could skip the Family History Library.

But how did a name like Jaramillo work into the picture?

Sister Costain earned only a quarter page photo in her wedding gown, standing in front the Temple. That had been a long time and many, many loads of laundry ago. All those loads of laundry, ironed shirts, and suppers kept warm had nothing whatsoever to do with James Costain's success? There was no acknowledgement of them.

The quarter-page photo of an only daughter, also from some time ago and grainy, would not be enough to get the man elected to public office, not in this state where at least six happy children, their spouses, and grandchildren, all in matching red-white-and-blue outfits, would be required for the campaign literature.

The frustration Helen felt emanating from these few pages was enough to choke her. However much James Costain had accomplished, it hadn't been enough, despite all his efforts at self-aggrandizement. *Ambition.*

The library didn't want this pamphlet. More frustration banked up behind the happy smiling face on the frontispiece. The pamphlet was on the discount sale shelf, not with the prized collectibles and signed first editions that were sold on line. The sign said "all paperbacks 50 cents". She left a dollar in the space she'd taken the pamphlet from and slipped the slim volume into her bag next to the phone with the photo of the yellow legal sheet on it.

Her phone beeped with Simon's message. "The coast is clear." Even his texting had a British accent.

Helen would confess to what she'd done the moment she saw him and returned the key. The moment she saw him—and dear, dear Brittany.

And that would be ...

She heard a noise coming from the space between her and the exit. She turned cautiously.

"Hands up!"

The yell made Helen jump out of her skin just as she turned into the hallway that led to the back door and turned off the library lights, plunging herself into darkness in the face of a well-aimed service revolver.

# Chapter 22

The thin floor in Brittany's little cottage bounced with the beat from the bar next door. The furnace banged and clanked in counterpoint. The place still smelled of mildew; the toilet still sank when you sat on it. But it was better than going back to the Summit County Justice Center in handcuffs. Which, for half a dozen heartbeats, it had seemed would be Helen's fate after her break-in at the Park City Library.

"You!" Helen and Deputy Moody had said together when the lights had come back on. Helen hadn't turned them on. She'd been too afraid to move. There were those statistics: more Utahns died at the hands of law enforcement ...

"We had a report of a break-in at the library," the deputy had presently said.

"It wasn't a break-in. See? I have the key."

And the pamphlet in her bag. She'd paid for it and would come clean to Simon.

It still took several verses of a setting of Psalm 23, escape from "The valley and shadow of death", from *The Book of Wizzy* to set her heart on an even keel again, and for Moody to holster her weapon.

Facing down a gun twice in one day. This was real

sleuthing.

When Helen showed the photo of the yellow legal-pad paper from her phone to Deputy Moody and explained the search, things got even better between them. Did the officer now think the hot tub might indeed have been a murder weapon? The cherry lip gloss remained closed on the subject, but the eyes above ....

The sheriff gave Helen a ride to Brittany's house, stopping at the Seven-Eleven they passed to buy doggy treats. This dog-napping, Helen mused, was going to be something like *The Ransom of Red Chief*; she and her co-conspirators were going to end up having to pay Sarah to take the little monster out of their lives.

The overflow of bar patrons on the sidewalk scurried for cover at the approach of the distinctive police car. Helen thought that if Simon hadn't declared the coast clear, Moody and her hardware-weighted hips might have broken through the cheap door quite nicely.

Fortunately, that wasn't necessary. Unfortunately, Helen caught a glimpse of Simon in a pair of very snug boxers with a Union Jack and "God Save the Queen" printed on them.

"Sorry," Brittany explained, addressing her aunt's horrified expression, not the officer's speculative one. "The dog tore a hole in Simon's trousers." She used the English word, trousers, instead of pants. "He doesn't have so many pairs this side of the pond. I was just mending them for him."

"Uh-huh," Deputy Moody said, stepping further into the tiny room after Helen.

Brittany tossed the "trousers" across the living room. Simon leapt in the air like a "footballer" going for a "header" to catch them, which did nothing to steer the eyes away from his fine physique. After a perfect catch, he dove for the sanctity of the bedroom to put them on.

Unfortunately, the exit was not as slick as the catch.

Horehound had been in a frenzy from the moment the sheriff's car pulled up and Helen stepped onto the walk. Now the little dog menaced the intruders, yapping and snarling. Deputy Moody's answer to this was to take a stance, hands on hips and hardware, and say, "You want to spend the night in the slammer, buster, to cool off?"

The dog froze for a moment, gave one little whine, then scurried for cover, faster than her claws could gather purchase on the battered wood floor. Horehound hit the bedroom threshold at the same instant Simon pushed the door shut. A wrinkly behind with the stub of a wriggling tail was momentarily trapped between jamb and door before the dog forced herself the rest of the way through. There was a yelp, a slam, a snarl of redoubled ferocity, a high-pitched Simon scream, and a tear of fabric.

"Oooh." Brittany winced.

"I will take that monster in, if you want," Deputy Moody offered.

Brittany took a moment to consider before she said, "No, I guess. Not tonight."

This gave Helen hope for her dog-napping scheme. Then Brittany welcomed her into a teary embrace, each of them asking forgiveness.

"Thank you, Wizzy," Helen whispered.

Simon, trousered, slipped out of the bedroom, slamming the door. The dog's frenzy—blessedly on the other side of the door—added to the bar's cacophony. In fact, Helen expected the deputy to get a call on her radio from the Happy Miner owner, complaining about the disturbance to the peace.

Deputy Moody, taking the hands-hips-hardware stance again, demanded to see the yellow legal pad paper, "this will of David Sebastiano Jaramillo."

Simon turned greyer still in the throbbing neon from next door. Simon, it turned out, didn't have the paper with him. "I stopped to clean up at my apartment on the way over, and left it there," he said, but he seemed ready to comply with the order to go with the deputy to pick it up straight away.

Deputy Moody took an assessing look around the apartment, probably finding a dozen violations of code in one eyeful.

Nevertheless, she nodded, got Simon to help Helen forward the photo to her via the cellphone—007 strikes again—and said, "Well, I'll leave you all to it for tonight. It's late. I'll come and pick the original from you at the library tomorrow, if I may? Library opens at nine?"

"Ten," Simon said with a note of relief that he wouldn't have to be at the desk an hour earlier.

"I'll be there," the deputy said, and bade them good-night.

"A Poor Wayfaring Man of Grief" out of *The Book of Wizzy* made Helen look at Simon and wonder. Not all illegals—undocumented persons—had brown faces.

A restaurant, no doubt, but would a library of bees-waxed balustrades hire illegally? Maybe, in a town where so little research or reading went on.

There were more dangerous criminals abroad, however.

"About Hore—Taffy—" Helen said.

All three of them turned to stare at the bedroom door. They turned to look at each other. All three shook their heads in unison. Horehound was going to have to claw her way through the door to get out again. Although it would probably take the creature ten minutes, tops.

"I saw Sarah today," Helen said.

"How is she?" Brittany had them sit around the kitchen table, where, Helen noticed, there was now a rather nice wooden stool. Simon held out a seat for each of the ladies, then perched next to Brittany.

After "Fine" and "Her parents are very concerned" and "keeping her guarded" and "her parents have been really upset", Helen said, "Sarah asked me to bring Taffy back to her."

"Oh, that would be great!" Brittany said, with obvious relief. "Taffy misses her, and," Brittany sighed with the admission, "I'd kind of like to ... to not have a dog. When I have to be gone so much, I mean."

"I don't blame you," Helen said.

"Especially that dog," Simon added.

"So you can pack Taffy up right now." Brittany even got to her feet.

The thought of the long drive down the canyon in the dark with that dog loose in the car—and then all night long—made Wizzy hum "The Eye of the Tiger."

"What I'm going to ask you to do will require Taffy to stay here a day or two longer," Helen said.

She explained her dog-napping idea. "The dog really won't be in any danger."

"Although I may be," Simon grumbled.

"Sarah told me herself that she only claimed that Ben had kidnapped her because she couldn't think how else to explain things to her parents. They simply couldn't, wouldn't believe she'd do what she did."

"I met Ben up on that mountain," Brittany agreed. "He's a bit gruff, but he's not a dangerous man. Except," she went on thoughtfully, "maybe if he has to spend too much time caged up."

"Sarah thinks that sticking to her lie will hurt her parents less and keep her from more trouble, but the sheriff—Deputy Moody, who was just here—already suspects she's lying. When the rape kit comes back, she'll be in even more trouble. She has to do the grown-up thing and come clean. Deputy Moody said that if Sarah does tell the truth, she'll do everything she legally can to see things go easy for Sarah. But not if the case goes to trial. Can you imagine how bad a high-profile case would be for Sarah's reputation? For her life, forever."

Brittany had a very clear notion. Helen saw her grow pale and reach a hand to Simon for comfort.

"I tried to talk her into it, but who am I? The Relief Society president. Her mother won't believe her. So I thought a little encouragement might help. I thought if Sarah had something *she's* responsible for threatened, kidnapped, she would see how adults have to make decisions and consider others."

All three at the kitchen table slid a glance toward

the bedroom door. Horehound hadn't made her jail break yet, but it was only a matter of time.

"So this is how I thought it should be done," Helen concluded.

She produced scissors and a glue stick from her bag. She also provided a blank piece of paper torn from her notebook, although the thought did cross her mind that such evidence would be very easy for the police to trace. They could incriminate her, a new-made Relief Society president.

But it wasn't going to come to that, was it? Sarah was going to see the error of her ways, see what it felt like to have a dependent held for ransom. If she came clean about her trumped up confession, Ben would go free, back to his cave, his mountain, and the rich, natural heritage Dave Jaramillo had left him—if what must pass as David's will was upheld in a court of law.

They began to cut and paste letters, their actions rocking the rickety aluminum chair legs.

Simon pronounced it "aluMINium". They all laughed about that and tried to change accents with mixed success.

"You don't remember Sarah ever saying anything more about why she got so deeply involved with Dave, do you, Brittany?" Helen asked.

"I've known Sarah for practically all my life," Brittany replied. "Well, yes, she did sometimes say she was adopted."

"She was adopted?" This was a strange, new trail to follow, with many interesting possibilities.

"Aunt Helen, I think she only said that when she was angry with her parents. Doesn't she look just like her mom?"

"Well, that may just be the same makeup and the same hairdresser."

What Mormon household ever had children who got so angry at their parents' authority that they dreamed of being adopted? Non-Mormon children, perhaps, but Mormon kids knew they had lived righteously in the Pre-Existence, to have been selected to be born into perfect households "of goodly parents".

"You said the same thing yourself once or twice that I remember, Brittany."

"Well, with me, it seems more likely, doesn't it?"

"If I didn't know better, I'd have to say yes." Sarah's statement then was probably a teenager's false alarm. "Still, I'll want to check that out," Helen concluded.

"Can we come at it from the other direction?" Simon asked. "What do you know about Dave's family?"

Helen thought of the pamphlet in her bag: James Costain's memoir about his founding of the company. Was it still owned by the family?

"Everybody knows everybody's family here," Simon commented.

"That's because we do genealogy and seal eternal families together in our temples. It's important," Brittany explained.

Helen didn't want to go to a place where she would have to examine whether she wanted to endure Mark for all eternity, not just endure him to the end. But she didn't even have to go there to know her answer. No, not unless he got a new character, as they had promised her Wizzy would—and Helen didn't know if she would love Wizzy if she wasn't Wizzy.

Brittany. That was a different matter. Helen did want to be with her niece forever. But surely it couldn't be heaven if you had to accept the crazy family members along with the good ones.

"We also have Relief Society," Brittany said. "It's the Relief Society's business to know who's died, who's born, who needs a casserole." She bestowed a sympathetic gaze on Helen, then went on. "Dave had no brothers or sisters. I talked to his mother today." Brittany went on to tell as much as she could of that encounter, the sorrow of the unmarried mother with no other family in this life or the next. She also mentioned the photos in the trash.

"Anyone you recognized?" Helen asked about the photos.

Brittany went and fished the pictures out of her backpack. They shoved mounds of magazines out of the way and spread the photos out.

"A pudgy older girl. But not a sister," Helen mused. "And a not-very Latino man." He looked vaguely familiar, but ....

"Put him in a suit and tie, and he could be anybody's stake president," Brittany agreed. "I didn't recognize them."

"What's a steak president?" Simon wanted to know.

"A church thing."

"Your church has blokes presiding over slabs of beef on the grill? Where do I join up?"

Brittany had to disappoint him. She explained about stakes—districts formed of six or seven wards—

holding up the tent of the gospel.

"So by 'stake president' you just mean a dowdy businessman?" Simon's disappointment was palpable.

"See?" Brittany pulled the picture closer between them. "Dowdy businessman on vacation with his kids."

Helen didn't listen much. She'd known what a stake was before she'd had teeth to eat the lay kind, not that she'd ever got to; in her working-class family steak had been the prerogative of the male priesthood alone, along with blessing babies and pulling the carts of folding chairs out from under the stage in the cultural hall to set up for a funeral luncheon. Women and children got "weenies" in those innocent days before that word elicited a blush.

Helen's confusion had been in the other direction: Why would you eat all the good folk of the stake unless the church had secrets deeper and darker than Avenging Angels, polygamy, racism, the mark of Cain and Mountain Meadows all combined? Something Donneresque?

The "suit and tie" was what stuck in her mind. She almost went and pulled her own show-and-tell, the Pine Enterprises pamphlet, out of her bag. There was a businessman. A stake president, too, perhaps.

Instead she asked her niece for confirmation in another direction. "You don't recognize these people?"

"Except Dave, no."

"But Diana Jaramillo did?"

"Probably. I don't think she liked them. She threw the pictures away, even though they had her dead son in them."

"So there's family you get sealed to and family you don't," Simon suggested. "Does the kind you don't get sealed to get material benefits in this life? I assume benefits in the hereafter are out, but how does that work in a court of law?"

"Diana Jaramillo seemed to be well taken care of," Brittany said, "for a single mom who arrived in this country to clean houses."

"And Dave claims the whole mountain as his own in his document." Simon pointed at Helen's pocket where her cell phone resided, referring to the yellow legal sheet.

Something to be looked into, they all agreed, but not on Sunday night.

They tried to sing carols for a while, but the music from next door was too overwhelming. Brittany and Simon ended up singing along, when they knew the words, which was more often than Helen would have thought possible. Helen heard nothing from Wizzy at all after that attempt at "Silent Night", and somehow didn't mind.

With the three of them working, it didn't take long for the message to take its final shape on Helen's notebook paper. In letters cut from the magazines, the message read:

TAFFY HELD FOR RANSOM

Helen had cut out an H, an O and an R before she remembered the dog's correct name. During that short time, Horehound took three nips out of her shins.

FRIENDS OF GENTLE BEN INSIST

TELL THE TRUTH

OR YOU WILL NEVER SEE YOUR DOG AGAIN

Simon considered his torn trousers, Brittany her bedroom door. None of the criminals wanted to have to make good on their threat and keep Taffy from Sarah a single minute longer than necessary.

# Chapter 23

There was still plenty of glossy paper left by the time they were done, depicting anorexic starlets in seasonal dresses no real person could actually squeeze into, much less afford. The three conspirators had scissors, they had glue. They began to make Christmas chains from the rest of Sarah's reading material.

"We'd do this to decorate the schoolrooms at Christmas," Simon said with a touch of nostalgia. "Even though a good half of my classmates in old Bradford were Muslim, the Church of England still carried the day. Or maybe chains were as non-sectarian as we could get."

"We did it, too," Helen said, "but at home."

Thinking of crafts made Helen remember Janis Evans, who was in charge of the upcoming Super Saturday for the sisters of the ward. It was not an optional event. She would have to attend and assist in making crafts of the season or be branded a heretic. Some young mothers, Helen knew, would take advantage of the free daycare provided to play hooky and make a Christmas shopping run to get what they really needed; Helen had done it herself in the early days. And then there would be a luncheon that many of those same women would have spent half of another day preparing for, lest their contribution be found as wanting as the biblical talents of the "Unprofitable" servant.

Helen excused herself, had a look at her phone and, sure enough, as promised, Janis had texted her the list of crafts she had on offer to her membership along with the cost to a sister who wanted to make each item:

1- "Bloom Where Your Planted" wooden signs—$16.33

2- Pine Cone ornaments with glitter and ribbon—$5.85

3- Glass Block Temples—real lights embedded in the blocks—$45

4- Nativity Sets made from clothes pins—$13.99

5- Photo Books—$16.95

6- Living Christ photo mats—$11.80

7- Pictorial Family Trees—$40—bring your own high-resolution family photos on a CD

8- Coasters out of tile—$29.99

9- Boutonnieres and corsages from the flowers dried during the summer—bring your own flowers—ribbon and lace offered free

10- The standard "gifts in a jar"—barley soup $5 per jar if you bring your own quart jars and lids. Chocolate-chip cookies, $4 and $6.

11- Sister Gail F. will lead aerobics in the Primary room to whittle away those holiday pounds—free

"Carols played and holiday snacks throughout.

Should be something for everyone," Janis concluded.

*Except for me, the president, who will have to go anyway*, Helen thought.

No "Magazine chains on offer, free. Bring your own magazines." Helen began typing to suggest it, then stopped. If ever there was an inspired church calling, it was Janis Evans as Super Saturday leader. Helen knew better than to rock that boat.

Helen still remembered playing with bobbins at her mother's feet under the quilt frame on a Wednesday morning, as the stay-at-home sisters pieced and hand-stitched a quilt for each girl of the Ward who got married. This is what quilting bees and corn huskings had devolved to. It didn't seem fair—it didn't seem holy—that the tasks that had once filled women's days—cooking, needlework, gardening—now were devalued to "hobbies". These women worked in office cubicles in order to pay for supplies so that, once every two months, they could spend Saturday slapping pre-mixed acrylic craft paint and pre-chewed sentiments onto blocks of wood carved by slaves in China and purchased in bulk at box stores. The same sentiment for every house on the block.

Yiddish had a word for such things—*tchotchkeys*. Mormons needed the same word, but the Janis Evanses of the faith took them too seriously for Yiddish's tongue-in-cheek. Their faith rose or fell on Super Saturdays.

In Helen's mind, the translation of tchotchkey was "clutter".

Wizzy herself was humming:

I'd like to build the world a house

And furnish it with love ...

Wizzy didn't do irony, but Helen did. The Church didn't allow Coke—or kombucha—but Jesus at $11.80 was okay.

Instead of knotting a cord with her craft skills and cleansing the temple, Helen sighed, and texted back "That's great, Janis. Let's go with it."

See? Being Relief Society president wasn't so hard, as long as you threw serious thought of personal time, economics, globalization and cultural integrity —and sleuthing—out the window. Helen wondered what would happen if she instructed Janis, instead, to divide the Ward sisters into two large Mormon mobiles. She could drive one load to Walmart for tinsel and the other to trendy Gardner Village to shops with names that translated to Spoiled Rotten, Spoiled Rotten Babies, and Shopaholics. That would make a Super Saturday to remember.

Helen returned to the chain making, loving it, reminiscing. "My mother said there was always one of the eight kids home sick at any given time during the holidays. This is what she'd give us to keep us quiet and busy during those long days."

Brittany dangled *Vogue* high-fashion cut-out earrings from her ears and turned to Simon to gauge the effect. "I remember doing it at your house, Aunt Helen."

"Sometime I'd bring the glue over to your house, too, if you were sick."

"I remember."

The smile Brittany gave her warmed Helen's insides like the hot cocoa her niece had made, heating the water for the abandoned instant packets in her only pan, a battered old aluminum skillet. Aluminum wasn't supposed to be healthy to ingest. Now Helen knew what she could get Brittany for Christmas.

In the meantime, undertaking the mass production of colored strips of paper for the two young people to paste, chipped mug at her elbow, Helen approached the subject of the titles Brittany had decided to keep from the condo clean-out. Helen was glad to see that *Diet for a Small Planet* had made the cut, that her niece was looking for healthy recipes—when she could afford the ingredients. The latest Young Adult fantasy novel—"from Unit A"—had likewise made the cut. Unit C had produced no reading material at all, even with one tenant laid up all week with a broken leg. Helen hoped that young Quinn Rhodes had had an e-reader.

This was useful information, however, only for the process of elimination. The title of the book that had produced the yellow legal document—well, half of a document—remained elusive.

"Of course, Dave's mother wouldn't have liked to see his wealth go to someone else, either," Helen mused. "If she found the document—or half a document—while she was cleaning up, she would have tossed it."

"She would have burned it," Simon agreed. "No sign of a fire this morning, Brittany?"

"No." Brittany gave a little laugh at the idea, then sobered. "I liked his mom. I feel sorry for her. I don't like to think ..."

Brittany got up, entered the bathroom, releasing a

waft of mildew into the kitchen.

"I just wonder that I didn't see that paper sticking out of a book when I boxed them up." Brittany carried a fresh armload of magazines from the bathroom and dumped them on the kitchen Formica, shutting the door and the smell behind her.

"And what about the television?" Helen asked.

"Television?" Simon hadn't been informed of this detail.

"I remember seeing it shoved there among Dave's little library. Unplugged."

"Unplugged and with its brains completely burned out," Brittany said. "Dave had had it taken off his wall and stored in the closet out on the deck because he didn't want a television in his life. Tom—my boss—said he'd have the maintenance man come and put in a new one, and I could have the old one. But we tried it there in the condo while I was cleaning up. Jerry the maintenance man said it was all blown out inside."

"Dave must really have hated televisions," Simon said.

"So I put it out in the dumpster with the rest of the trash."

"I guess it's just as well," Helen said with a smile, wondering if that was where her Relief Society sisters' kids' time for making Christmas chains had gone, into watching shows on black boxes. "This house—this home—doesn't really seem to want a late model television."

"No, just books." Simon and Brittany exchanged the secret look of couples on the same track in home decoration.

Then they gave each other magazine earrings five loops long.

"You know, all those times we made chains, Aunt Helen, Mother would never hang them. They were not perfect enough."

Yes, "tacky" was a word Karen might have used.

Brittany reached across the table and squeezed Helen's hand. "Thanks for that, Aunt Helen."

"It was always my pleasure."

"I mean thanks for tonight, too."

Helen sat back—carefully on the rickety aluminum —and admired their handiwork. She glanced at her watch. It was after eleven. This was crazy ...

Standing on the sturdier stool, Simon draped magazine chains across every living room wall, crossed them in the center and made a floor-to-ceiling triangle that sort of sketched a pine-tree shape in the corner by the skis.

Stepping back to admire the effect, all three of them looked toward the closed bedroom door. Cautiously, Brittany opened it. Horehound had given up and fallen asleep in the warmest corner. The creature was almost decent like that. Only twitches in the little paws showed that an angry pursuit of something haunted her dreams. Otherwise, she seemed to enjoy being a hostage. It required no change of venue at all.

"Not a creature was stirring ..." offered Wizzy.

Now Simon and Brittany were line dancing together in the middle of the floor to the music from next door. That was easier when there was no furniture: an argument against Ikea for the first five years of a relationship, anyway. In a little while, they progressed from line dancing to swing, a dance where couples touched and danced together.

They even tried some dips. To do this, Simon had to establish himself firmly on both feet while Brittany arced backwards over both of his bent knees, the muscles in his black restaurant T-shirt straining but holding, holding, her loose brown hair brushing the raw wood planks of the floor. Her left knee went up in the air, her highest point; her right foot barely touched the ground. How she had to trust him to hold her! How he had to be trustworthy, there under the decorations they'd created together with such joy in this tumble-down house.

Helen ignored two calls from Mark and a text from Sarah wondering when she'd show up with Taffy. She ignored another three calls from people she didn't know, but whose exchange numbers let her know they must be in the ward. Something for the Relief Society president, which she decided she wasn't, not at that moment. Not in the midst of this homemaking she was getting a rare share of tonight.

At last she managed to pull herself away. She gathered up her craft supplies, found her coat and mittens and headed for the door.

"I'll walk you back to your car," Simon sang out, "when this tune ends."

But he couldn't take his hands off Brittany, even when the music ended.

"Never mind," Helen said. "There are plenty of people out on the streets right now, richer people than me, if somebody's interested in robbery. All they'd get from me would be a pair of scissors, a used glue stick and a notebook with a page torn out. And the ransom note."

She was thinking that she ought to have bought a package of condoms to add to her emergency bag. She could have left it behind the cracked mirror of the medicine cabinet for her niece. Better safe than sorry.

What sort of Relief Society president was she?

"Are you sure?" Simon was dragging Brittany with him to the kitchen to get another beer.

It was only his second. He'd been dancing hard, and the fridge was full, after all. Brittany selected a 7-Up to chase down her cocoa.

Helen stopped in her tracks. In the darkened kitchen, the refrigerator light lit up the interior like a stage. Among the beer and the pops were three or four bottles that didn't fit in at all.

She stepped back into the room to stand alongside her niece and her niece's boyfriend. "What's that?"

Brittany picked up a bottle. "This? Kombucha."

The name sent a shudder through Helen's spine. A bit of slimy mold twisted through the amber liquid in the refrigerator light.

Kombarfya.

"A product made from tea," said Simon with the nonchalance of one coming from a country where tea was the national beverage.

"Supposed to be healthy for you," Brittany said.

"I might try some," Simon suggested. "For breakfast. Not Earl Grey, but worth a try. This house doesn't have anything else."

"We tend to give the tea and coffee that we find in the units to the Hispanic girls," Brittany explained. "I don't suppose you can make tempura batter out of it, like you can with beer to get rid of the alcohol."

"Don't drink it!" Helen exclaimed. What were the chances?

"Aunt Helen? What?"

Helen swallowed, calming herself. "They're all sealed, right? The ones you brought home?" Her niece hadn't been that cautious with the clam dip.

"Yes. Aunt Helen, what is it?"

"Yes, I'm Relief Society president." Helen laughed anxiously at herself. "I'd want you to get rid of the alcohol and the caffeine and the mold." Helen considered. "And the ..." She stopped herself before she said mood enhancers.

Brittany laughed, too, a little apologetically to Simon for her crazy aunt.

"I hadn't quite decided what to do with it," she admitted. "Maybe one of those health cookbooks from Dave's condo will have a suggestion."

"You found the kombucha in Dave's apartment?" Helen tried not very successfully to hide the panic in her voice.

"No, actually. In unit A."

"In unit A,' Helen repeated, her terror confirmed.

"I don't suppose the kids liked it much."

"Unit A was the one with the family? The kids? The sick little girl?"

"That's right. Five kids. An older boy who likes World of Warcraft. A girl with perpetual earbuds."

The video game, a retreat into headphones, and a sick three-year-old were as common as dirt, as Helen's father might have said. "But not kombucha," Helen said aloud.

"Only one bottle was open, half drunk, and I—"

"You poured that away?"

"Yes, Aunt Helen. I poured that away."

After that, Helen couldn't get back to her car and down into the valley fast enough.

# Chapter 24

"Up in Park City with Brittany, okay?" Helen defended herself from Mark's questioning on Monday morning. He'd been asleep when she'd come in the night before, and she hadn't wanted to wake him.

He was awake now, putting on his tie in the bathroom mirror for his accounting job just down the street from their home, on Highland Drive.

"The new duties you've taken on are not in Park City," he pointed out.

And who made me take on these new duties? she wanted to ask. "Yes, I know it's not Relief Society business. Not for this ward. But isn't compassion for all God's children part of my job?"

"The Bishop's Storehouse of food and goods is only open to those who get a note from their bishop." Mark flipped the red, white and blue striped silk over and pulled it through the knot. "We take care of our own first."

"Not my sister's keeper but my sister's daughter's? That's too far removed?"

"I think there's something more than Brittany going on here. Brittany never kept you out 'til midnight on a Sunday before."

"Brittany has never been just-turned eighteen before, with her parents off to Anaheim on a mission."

"Brittany's not the sort of girl to need this sort of attention."

*Shows what you know,* Helen thought, and reminded herself to add condoms to her bag.

Karen would die. The bishop would never speak to Helen again.

Helen realized that she hadn't even told Mark about Dave Jaramillo's body in the hot tub, which had started this whole quest. He may have heard about the death on the TV news, but he would never guess that his niece had been the one to come upon the young man, or what distress it had caused her. And if Helen suggested she might be playing sleuth? She'd never hear the end of it.

She didn't tell him. Why start sharing anything after fifteen years of silence?

"You're right. It's not about Brittany. It's about me."

"You are Relief Society president. It's about your immortal soul."

"Being Relief Society president is what you want me to do. You and the bishop."

"And our elder brother Jesus Christ."

The Hoffmann Jesus flashed before her mind. She tried to see Wizzy's eyes in there instead.

"A lot of women do a lot of other things besides Relief Society," Helen said. "Some have a bunch of kids. Some have jobs *and* kids."

"But you haven't been doing anything. Not for fifteen years."

"Keeping house for you and the boys is nothing?"

Helen studied his reflection in the mirror, the bald spot quite big now. The gray. A different man from the one she'd married. One who'd had constant sorrow for eighteen years and yet who'd gone to work every day at that soul-numbing job, so she could do what? Sit home and grieve their lost child.

She saw the look come over him, the look that said he was shutting down again and wouldn't come out. Until what? His next disapproving lecture? The next time Ethan or Nathan was allowed to call home from the mission field?

"I can't tell you what this is like for me. This ... this new thing I'm doing. Just a little something with Brittany."

She wouldn't say "sleuthing". She'd just keep it vague, and Mark would put anything she did with a female teenager in the box of "I don't need to think about this." She saw him do that now, behind his sheltered eyes.

"I will carry out my Relief Society duties," she promised. "I'll delegate authority if I have to." Then she found she couldn't keep it all to herself. "But this thing with Brittany ... I feel like I go into a phone booth. I go into a phone booth and change from a mild-mannered Primary pianist into ... into Superwoman with a cape and tights and a giant S on my T-shirt. I feel like I'm ..."

She couldn't say "channeling". She couldn't say "receiving inspiration".

Yes, there was Mark not listening to her, shrugging into his suit jacket. So what she said didn't matter. She said, "I'm getting in touch with my daughter again."

But he was listening. The look on his face in the mirror nearly broke her heart.

"Our daughter," she whispered. She sought for "I'm sorry" and couldn't find it.

She ran from the mirror, locked herself in the laundry room and put in a load of whites until Mark's car had pulled out of the driveway.

*****

Helen was still crying after she got the laundry load in the dryer. She said a prayer, heard a few strains of "What a Friend We Have in Wizzy" and unlocked the laundry room door. She put a bagel in the toaster—she'd fed Mark, she had not had her own breakfast—washed her face at the kitchen sink and then sat down at the table. A cursory look through Mark's abandoned newspaper stopped her short at the obits, that shadowy, pointillist Most Wanted list she used to compose at the *Trib*.

My, those Catholics moved fast. David Sebastiano Jaramillo was already there. The body in the hot tub. Twenty-one years old. "A tragic accident ... *Te quiero, m'ijo.*"

The newspaper now let friends of the family post comments on line. Helen looked and saw they were all in Spanish.

The funeral, Helen noted, was set for Tuesday, tomorrow noon, at St. Joseph the Worker church, clear over on Redwood Road, on the west side. She carefully cut out the obituary to give to Brittany.

Then she went online to the Summit County Justice Center and looked at the pictures of the inmates again. There they all were, miserable mug shots. Including a young man named Cesar Jaramillo whose booking time was just ten minutes off of Quinn Rhodes'. The cousin mentioned in the obit, native of southern California.

You'd give a bag of pot to your long-lost cousin if you came from California, wouldn't you?

Only as a third task did she turn to check her phone. The thing hadn't stopped binging and bonging with messages since she'd been set apart in her calling.

Once assured nothing had Brittany's ring tone of "Winter Wonderland", Helen assumed Simon had stayed longer and that all was well—except that once again she found herself mentally adding condoms to her shopping list, which made her blush, but also think insanely that she should probably suggest that at the next leadership meeting.

She started through the other electronic leavings—and stopped dead at one of sobbing more intense than hers had been just moments before. She couldn't do anything about her own tears, but she could play this one again.

"Sister Snow, the bishop told me I should call you. Brushed me off is what he did. This is Jen—"

Then came the real descent into sorrow, muffled by a turn away from the phone—perhaps to monitor the squeals? shrieks?—of children that Helen heard in the background.

The number was restricted; Helen couldn't merely press "redial". She didn't recognize the voice. Tears could account for that. Plus the fact that Helen had probably not exchanged more than a "Good Morning" to half the sisters in the ward. There'd been a lot of anonymity behind the Primary piano keyboard. The name, what she'd heard of it, didn't ring any bells either. Jin? Jen?

Helen turned to the ward roster. She was supposed to have it in her phone for autodial. She couldn't get the app to work. A person needed the proper software to be saved these days.

She looked through the paper version instead, bound to be dated. Counting Jennifers, Jennys, Jennis and Jenns, the ward had seven, all from that thirties to forties age group when the name had been so popular. Even a third replay did not help her decipher the last name out of the intro. Cutting out those who were listed with no children only narrowed the search to five. Her sleuthing got her nowhere.

Well, there was nothing for it. She would have to contact all five, but she wanted to be dressed and showered before she began what looked like a day on the phone.

Half an hour later, returning in plain navy blue sweats to the kitchen table that was already as cluttered as Karen's had ever been, Helen opened the roster to begin at the As. She never got to the first Jennifer. In the A's, the name Virginia Allred jumped out at her to the tune of "The Battle Hymn of the Republic".

Allred. The purple fingernails pounding on the Relief Society piano with an anger—or was it a fear?— rarely seen within church walls. Virginia. Ginger. Ginny. Not Jen; Ginn.

Three kids.

No Brother Allred.

Helen reminded herself to buy condoms for her bag, and wondered about parents who would call a girl Virginia in a world where "Virgin" was rarely whispered.

"Onward, Christian Soldiers."

Helen replayed the message. This time that she knew what she was listening for, it seemed pretty clear: Ginn Allred.

Helen tried the number listed.

"This number has been changed or is no longer in service."

The roster was at least six months old. Changed phone numbers could mean nothing. Or they could spell an erratic life, leaping from phone plan to phone plan. The address was one of the cheaper apartments on busy 33rd South.

Helen looked over the kids' names. Cody, Dakota and Kali. For the Hindu goddess of death? Helen knew with a burning in her bosom that she was on the right track.

She shuffled through the mountain of official papers she'd been handed by the bishop, many of them with her sister's handwriting on them. She found a file calling itself "Family Needs Visit Reports". This was supposed to be an app, too, but Helen couldn't get that to work, either. So paper it was.

The file contained a number of blank forms with titles such as Food, Clothing, Health, and Job Capabilities running down the left-hand side. There were also a number of the forms filled out in her sister's hand. A good third of these had the name "Ginger Allred Household" on them. On most of these, Karen had written "Instructed Jenn in the principles of self-reliance and obedience to attain self-respect and dignity". Phrases straight out of the *Bishop's Handbook*. On several were notes that managed to look exasperated even through her sister's best hand-writing. Apparently, not one but two visiting teachers had asked to be released. They didn't like visiting the Allred home. It was hard on their clothes and harder on their nerves.

Helen wouldn't have been surprised had Wizzy jumped out with some rap song right then. Wizzy in blond dreadlocks and strutting with a temporary Little Mermaid tattoo on her arm singing a song neither of them had ever heard that went something like:

> "Self-reliance
> Yo, obedience
> Dumb as an ox
> Yo, paradox"
>
> "Badda boom."

Logic had never been one of Wizzy's strong suits. Neither, it would seem, was it Karen's. How could one be self-reliant while at the same time rendering blind obedience? Karen liked to just wind up those Small World dolls and get them going.

Six words whispered in Helen's mind. She knew the aphorism wasn't very Mormon. It wasn't even very Catholic. In fact, the third century church father Tertullian to whom it was attributed had died in heresy and was not a Saint. The phrase came to Helen's head anyway: "I believe because it is absurd."

The tension between self-reliance and obedience was a tight rope everyone had to walk. Helen knew the peril.

She added her parka, a scarf and mittens to her sweats. She stuffed her oversized purse with forms, Pet Smart poop bags, an old stuffed bear of Wizzy's and the doggie ransom note. No condoms yet. She could always kill three birds with one stone, which, Karen liked to say, was a Relief Society president's calling. She put an ecstatic Jinx on his leash and headed out for a walk.

*****

The valley smog inversion had settled in hard since the storm Friday night. When Helen and Jinx crossed the east-west grid roads under street lights just dimming, they could only see ghosts of the Wasatch Range. She and her dog could have walked that distance in half an hour, if they didn't want to destroy their lungs. So much for the Mormon doctrine of Eternal Progression, which taught that everything only gets better for the blessed.

> O Ye Mountains High
> Where the clear blue sky ...

No, Hymn Number 34 didn't suit. To the rhythm of her strides, Helen jumbled that one with 338 "For purple mountain majesties"—how they'd been in the clear, cold winter mornings of her youth—and the concluding words Elder Richard L. Evans used to pronounce in comfort at the end of Tabernacle Choir broadcasts "Again we leave you from within the shadows of the everlasting hills ..." Every man in the highest levels of leadership, and every man who aspired to such greatness, tried for that same tone with mixed success. All those white male voices sat like an inversion.

Thinking seven AM might be early for a visit, she took their path into the next ward boundaries for starters. A van with an outdoor-light-trimming service and a handful of media cars still parked in front of the Drake's home prevented Helen from delivering the ransom note. She wanted an empty casserole dish in hand. Besides, it would never do to deliver a threat of dire things happening to a beloved dog with her own happy, healthy dog on the leash with her.

Helen went the few houses down to the Vaughns' to see about the casserole and met the woman who must be the mother of the family on her front step. The woman was a woman Brittany would call an "x-ray", disturbingly thin. In fact, the T-shirt she wore over special thermal jogging gear announced "You can't be too rich or too thin." The woman was performing leg stretches against her garage wall. She could touch her nose to her knee. This all made Helen very anxious about her own body image.

"Onward, Christian Soldiers."

Helen suppressed her humming and her own feelings.

"Good morning. Sister Vaughn?" Now Helen was self-conscious of the stains on her old parka.

"Yes?" Sister Vaughn did not stop limbering up. She did it with the compulsion of following an exercise gospel. Her chilled breath left her body as if it were her soul made visible.

"My name's Helen Snow. I'm Relief Society president in the west ward. I wondered how your daughter is doing."

"Fine, thanks. She's out of danger. We got to bring her home last night."

Very close-lipped. Helen remembered overhearing, in almost this exact spot, Brother Vaughn's conversation on the phone. Well, if you were responsible for the drugs your child had overdosed on, you'd be pretty quiet about it, wouldn't you?

"I'm glad to hear it."

The chill in the air, which came as much from the woman as the inversion, should have driven Helen back to Jinx and their stroll. Instead she said, "I brought a casserole over from Eve Drake."

"You'd think, poor woman, with what she's been through with that daughter of hers, Eve Drake would be the one whose kitchen is full of strange dishes, everyone's worst, what they can afford to lose."

"Indeed, yes. I visited her yesterday." Helen tried for lightness. "There are enough casseroles to go around."

"Some people don't know how to raise children." That stretch would have torn a tendon in a lesser being.

Helen had to pretend that the gasp she stifled was just because the air was so bad. And some perfect family like this was going to get to raise her Wizzy in the afterlife if she didn't get her holiness act together?

"I don't think Sarah and her mother are to blame," Helen said. "But I just wondered, if you'd finished with the yam casserole dish ..." The frigid silence stretched. "No matter if it hasn't been washed yet."

"My son doesn't like yams."

Or kombucha.

"And sausage is too fattening for the rest of us. My husband ate some, but we won't finish it for several nights."

"Very well. I'll call back then."

"Now, if you'll excuse me, I have a schedule to meet. My husband has to leave in an hour for work and he is watching the little ones for me now."

Off she ran, at a pace Helen knew she could never keep up with.

Fortunately, Sister Vaughn didn't see Jinx do his business on the dirty snow of her parking strip. Helen carefully scooped it up and dropped it in the first dumpster she met upon reaching the strip malls lining 33rd South.

Jinx loved snuffling around the backs of closed strip malls. While he did, Helen rehearsed how to present the doggie ransom note to Sarah Lance.

# Chapter 25

Apartment 113 was in the basement, one of those that are dank and impossible to heat, especially for little ones crawling on the floor. Helen couldn't believe this call was more important than her pursuit of what had happened in Unit B at Pine Enterprises, but her calling description said she should be here. More importantly, Wizzy seemed to be going along with the decision.

Helen tied Jinx up to a wobbly handrail. She clung to the same handrail on her way down north-facing steps that must always be in shadow. The steps had been poorly shoveled. Little ovals of ice, like skating rinks for dolls, lingered. In summer, free of snow, she had no doubt the cement of those steps, eaten by the snow, must be worn down to the crumbly pebbles of their rotten insides. She worried she might tear the handrail up by its roots.

Once on solid ground, she considered. It wasn't quite eight. Was it too early? Or, if Virginia Allred had a job, was it too late?

It wasn't too early. The shrieks of little kids rattled through the thin panes of the aluminum siding window and the bed-sheet curtains.

The bell hung by a corroded wire. Electrocution being on her mind, Helen didn't like to press it. She knocked three times before a woman, her eyes puffy with crying and a wailing baby in her arms, answered the door.

"Hello? Ginn Allred? I'm your new ..."

"The new Relief Society president. Yes." Ginn looked tentatively over her shoulder, into the room where two older children were screaming. "It's not a good time to—"

"I hope to make it a better time for you."

Half an hour later, after seeing an empty Fruit Loops box on the floor, a bottle of milk, past its expiration date and quite unpourable with curds, on the table and only an almost-empty bottle of ketchup in the fridge, Helen had given Ginn all the money she had on her. She had also emptied her bag of Li'l Debbie cakes.

Ginn, newly dressed but carless, had taken the snow-filled, ripped-seat stroller parked beside her door down to the local Dan's Market. Unfortunately, Helen didn't think the seventy-three dollars she had would do much more than fill the stroller, but it would be a start and go a long way to quiet the children.

"Remember fruits and vegetables," she tried to preach, but knew that convenience foods offered more bang for the buck for hungry tummies.

She didn't think Ginn could hear her over the din of a cartoon on the crummy TV.

Helen turned off the TV as soon as the door was closed. The kids stared at her as if she'd just turned off the world.

Helen decided not to bring out the teddy bear, first because she couldn't cut the bear into pieces like the cupcakes, and second, she decided she couldn't part with this piece of Wizzy. Not yet.

Instead, she played "Swing Low, Sweet Chariot" with the kids, each of whom probably had a different father, none in evidence, by the skin tones they represented. Her back didn't last as long with these three as it had with air-light Wizzy. Besides, Helen was fifteen years older, these kids were stoked on the cupcake sugar rush, and that middle kid was just about ready to play line back for the Packers.

Helen had to give up on the swinging and tried "Joshua Fit the Battle." The boys had never heard of Joshua before, but toilet-paper-roll trumpets were just the thing. The garbage hadn't been taken out in so long that there were empties for everyone. Also, someone in the household had a new hobby: unrolling toilet paper rolls and trailing the tissue in toilet water.

Helen hoped all the neighbors were already off to work; the walls did seem very close to "a-tumblin' down".

Helen was out of breath. She wanted something quieter. They could make magazine Christmas chains. Helen found no magazines except for a *People* so recent Ginn probably still hoped to get something out of it. No glue. Christmas in this house, she got the feeling, would be enriched only by Primary school drawings of lots of jagged green pines trees and red-blob Santas stuck in the window, and no passerby could see the basement-level artwork.

Instead, Helen brought in Jinx, who had infinite patience. "Doggie, doggie" filled the living room, with its stained shag carpet from the seventies. This seemed much better than the collection of really depressing, broken plastic things no self-respecting child could grow attached to, corporate soullessness oozing out of each toy. Jinx, bless him, had the fortitude of a saint. He should be Relief Society president. Or at least be assured of a place in the Celestial Kingdom. Soon Cody and Dakota were preoccupied with a living, breathing alternative to the plastic mockeries.

Holding baby Kali (maybe an incarnation of the Hindu goddess of death, with her clinginess and her runny nose pressed against the top of her pacifier), Helen sat down with her phone to attack the biggest crisis of all.

While putting on her coat and spike-heeled boots to go to the store, Ginn had said, as if just passing time, "Kali's father left us this apartment, the scumbag, when he walked out. I managed to keep it for a few months, but ..."

The upshot was that Ginn's rent was due. Overdue. If she didn't have a check to the landlord by five this evening, he would evict them. Into the snow. Three weeks before Christmas. Talk about Ebenezer Scrooge!

Helen called the bishop, who was already in her speed dial. He was a young father. He was at work, a lawyer, in court with a big case all day. The two counselors, having done their duties by installing a Relief Society president, had gone on golf vacations to St. George.

Helen called Barney the clerk. She got him. He was retired from his day job. He'd been clerk forever. Long enough, certainly, to have perfected the sigh that preceded his statement of denial. "The Bishop holds the purse strings. I just count the beans."

Always the bean counter, never the bishop.

With a twinge of longing, Helen thought of the days of her great-grandmother: the days of *The Women's Exponent* when Mormon women had their own publication and their own funds, days before the money to help was subsumed under the priesthood budget so a Relief Society president had to go through "proper channels" and curb her values to bureaucracy.

Ginn Allred and her children were the oversight in the oversight.

Helen would have to ascend farther up the ladder. She rifled through her papers, which had been Karen's papers, and found a list of the stake hierarchy and their phone numbers. It looked well used. Food stains colored it and one corner was torn, so the last fellow's number was half gone, and he was off the hook. But who knew how old the roster was?

Mustering all her courage—this was for the children—she left a message for the stake president himself, the son of a man currently serving among the Seventies, judging by his name and the "III" after it. That's how church government worked, this faith-based scientific gene theory. The president was, his voice mail announced, "Unavailable."

So were his counselors. Religion was seeming like a weekend-only thing for the priesthood.

The High Priests' leader, Helen knew, was in for a hernia operation, and casseroles were due to the family by five pm.

The Elder's Quorum president answered on the

second ring with the bark of his last name "Hanson here" as if he were Donald Trump. Wow, what a difference from the pink-faced, round-faced man who shook her hand every Sunday.

Helen got no more than half a sentence out before the man replied, "Look, Sister, I knew Virginia Allred in high school. She was a tramp then and she's a tramp now, and the Church is not in the business of underwriting behavior like that."

"But the children—none of this is their fault. None of them are over eight and ready for baptism."

"They all made bad choices in the Pre-Existence to be born to such a woman."

Elder Hanson hung up. So much for not casting the first stone. No self-righteous guy like a young self-righteous guy, hoping to climb to the top of the holy tree by hook or by crook.

Helen felt a moment of despair for the direction in which the huge tanker of Mormon charity was sailing. One Relief Society president couldn't swing it around by herself.

Okay, so there was the government, the secular government; but all Helen knew about that process was that it was heartily frowned upon in this reddest of red states. Oh, and also that it took a long time; Ginn didn't have time. If she hadn't latched on to WIC or food stamps or whatever by now, she would probably have to be walked through it, which meant Helen would have to be walked through it. The steep learning curve had her panting already.

And all this while, any clues as to who might have murdered Dave Jaramillo were disappearing fast.

What other options did Helen have? That seventy-three dollars she had given Ginn was pretty much all the Snow family had until Mark's next paycheck on Friday. Her card was maxed out, and the bank account. That's what came of paying for two sons' missions and getting Christmas shopping done early. Virtue was rarely its own reward.

She considered inviting the little family in to her home, her two empty bedrooms, until something else could be worked out. That would be the most Christian thing to do, wouldn't it? Were these two boys old enough to sleep in her twins' bunk beds? That seemed like a concussion waiting to happen. And another little girl in Wizzy's crib? Wizzy wouldn't mind sharing.

Helen had just had her carpet cleaned with the holiday special. She'd un-child-proofed her home years ago.

No, Wizzy wouldn't mind, but there would be the phone call to Mark. It was his fault she was in this calling, but still ....

Okay. That left the twelve members of the quorum of the high council in alphabetical order. Eleven, not counting Brother Lucky at the end of the alphabet.

Helen was about to start with Anderson when her eye caught on the second name down. A little note she hadn't seen before indicated that he was over her ward in particular.

And the name. James K. Costain. Pine Industries. The pamphlet in the Park City Library. She still had it in her bag.

There couldn't be two of them in the city, could there?

She caught the man at home. He had a quaver in

his voice, as if very, very old.

Little Kali was threatening to start crying. Helen began jiggling her. She spoke her spiel as fast as she could.

"Good morning. My name's Helen Snow. I've just been called as Relief Society president in the west Shadowcreek Ward, taking over from my sister, Karen Bingham."

"Oh, yes, the Binghams," Elder Costain said in the sober drone of General Conference talks. "A fine family. I know them well. They're representing the stake in the mission field now, aren't they?"

Karen would run in such circles.

Helen could hardly contain herself. "I have a young family of four here in dire need. If they do not get their rent paid by this evening at five o'clock, they will be evicted into the snow. Please don't tell me to preach self-reliance to her. And obedience? She is the Relief Society pianist and does her best. This is a single mother and her three small children—"

"A single mother?" the soporific voice asked.

Helen had expected instant condemnation. To her surprise, she thought she heard some compassion in the question.

Kali began to cry, and Helen's cellphone went dead from overuse, just from that morning. The two older kids began another fight. Helen wanted to scream.

"Cody, please," she asked instead, "can you help me? Do you know where your little sister's diapers are?" A box of Pampers could hide the way a basket full of clean cloth diapers could not.

The five-year-old looked at her as if she were speaking Chinese ("Mandarin", her Ethan would have corrected her).

Fortunately, just at that moment, the pinched squeak of stiletto-heeled boots on hard, cold snow came from outside the door. Ginn appeared, her young face much prettier for the exercise.

The two women worked together to get the children settled again, diapers changed (Dakota, although probably old enough to be potty trained, was not) and food handed out. Helen rejoiced at the orange net of clementines that appeared from the plastic grocery bags. The two boys wanted to peel their own and, though Dakota made a bit of a mess, the sweet little sections went down like candy.

The problem came when the allure of working with real food became so compelling that they wanted to open a new one before the last one was finished. By then, Ginn had the rest of her haul out in plain view. Fruit Loops and Pop-Tarts lured the boys away from the healthy snack. Clementine peels and sections were abandoned and soon ground into the carpet. Jinx sniffed at but rejected them.

In the meantime, as they worked, Helen asked, "I noticed that you selected some interesting hymns to play yesterday."

"Yeah?"

"'Battle Hymn of the Republic' and 'Onward, Christian Soldiers'."

"I play keyboard in a band."

"Really? What sort of music?"

"Country. We're trying to make it big. I gave up my job at Hooters to devote to my career, but ..."

No job but this, making music like in The Happy Miner, with its late-night hours. Three little ones and the name Ginn.

"We don't get much call for Christmas carols in our gigs, so I wasn't real confident about 'O Little Town of Bethlehem.' Besides, 'Battle Hymn of the Republic' is how I felt."

Helen sensed that playing for the Relief Society while someone else played for the Primary was cheap daycare for Ginn Allred. Helen also imagined that, if Ginn had had a gig Saturday night, she may have imbibed something at the venue and played with a hangover. Helen had never had such a thing, but she could imagine.

Now that she saw the boy, Helen realized she was already familiar with Cody Allred's presence among the under-twelves. He liked to render the old hymn "Zion is Growing" as "Giant is Growing" and direct threatening giant gestures at the smaller kids.

A creative, imaginative boy.

"I was angry. I was promised gigs but they fell through, so I couldn't pay the rent. I have that hanging over my head. I was trying to make myself feel strong, like I could make something happen. The bishop said if I fulfilled my calling he'd take care of me, but he always seemed to forget the proper paperwork. And that Sister Bingham would only talk and talk."

Helen didn't say Karen was her own sister, now in Southern California.

As soon as she felt she could do so, she left Ginn on her own. "I have some sort of lead," she said. "I hope to be back with a check made out to your landlord."

Helen didn't want to say that was because the

Church authorities didn't want the money spent on anything else, not even condoms. From the look on the younger woman's face, she understood.

"That'd be so great," Ginn said, tears starting to he eyes again.

Helen trotted Jinx home, the din of kids begging for a dog of their own ringing in her ears. *That's the last thing that girl needs,* Helen thought as she put Jinx inside the house. The faithful dog went straight to his bed in the corner. The morning had already worn him out. Helen began to hunt for the phone cord.

Then she decided it might be better to continue her plea to Elder Costain in person. She could pick up the check then and there, and get it to the landlord as quickly as possible. She offered a prayer as she slid in behind the steering wheel. She was taking a whole bunch on faith here: that Costain would come up with the cash, that Ginn would be okay by the end of the day, and yes, that somehow this would lead to information about what had happened in that Pine Enterprises condo.

But the only tune *The Book of Wizzy* was humming was "Shall the Youth of Zion Falter?" Number 254. That bit about clinging to the iron rod reminded Helen of the handrail in front of Ginn's apartment ... and that didn't seem very secure.

# Chapter 26

A Latina housemaid in a pink Pine Enterprises smock answered the door to the large and gracious Costain home far up the foothills. She hesitated to let Helen in.

"I will see if he will come," she said, in response to Helen's self-introduction and request. "He is *muy mal,* very sick."

"I'm sorry to hear that," Helen said to the departing pink smock. "I could come back later—"

No, she couldn't come back later. Ginn needed the church welfare check now.

Fortunately, the housemaid had already moved beyond the range of her voice. She found herself alone in a study with the paned-glass double doors to the rest of the house closed against her.

Helen worked to get her bearings in this stranger's room. It wasn't very hard. Like the bishop's office, it was all straight-forward, all meant for show, each item meant exactly what it said with no nuance. The books were church volumes: Multiple copies of *Mormon Doctrine*—so outdated the church-owned Deseret Books no longer published it. All twenty-six volumes of *The Complete Journal of Discourses* by

Brigham Young—who had had more wives than double the number of volumes—and other nineteenth-century leaders. Also no longer church-published. Ghost-written memoirs of still-living church leaders, coffee-table books on Nauvoo, on the westward trek, up-to-date bound volumes of the *Ensign Magazine*. All church-published. Their fine leather spines in coordinating Moroccan red seemed never to have been cracked.

Sitting on a chair covered with dusty rose-colored needlepoint, Helen felt herself stepping away from a doctrine so mutable that an old man trying to cling to the faith of his fathers struck her as pathetic. As a young man he must have gone through contortions of justification to deny Negroes the priesthood in accordance with the revelations expounded in the *Mormon Doctrine*; now he took the sacrament from the hand of a scrub-faced, nappy-haired, pink-palmed twelve-year-old, and there was an African-American in the White House of a country possessed (Helen thought of demons) of a "divinely inspired constitution". And yet this Elder Costain stood every Sunday to declare witness to the "literal truth of the gospel". What twists and turns of conscience was he asking his flock to make today that tomorrow would also change by divine edict?

Helen thought of the original Grimm's fairytale version of Cinderella, where the stepsisters chopped off pieces of their feet to fit in the straight and narrow slipper, and the cockerel in the yard that crowed out "Blood in the shoe, blood in the shoe!" to warn off a duped prince—the story before Disney tidied it up. Where was a rooster when you needed one? Helen imagined her sister welcoming blonde-haired, blue-gowned Cinderellas to sacrament meeting in Anaheim, California. The Prince Charmings would all be members of the priesthood, of course. No need for any rooster's warning, just some help from the talking rodents who also did housework, and straight on to the perfect ending.

The art in the study showed a similar taste in the same kitchy realism style as epic paintings from the Soviet Union or Mao's China of happy workers waving red flags and declaring, "Now we can control gas." Here Joseph Smith frolicked with half a dozen pioneer-era boys, showing what a down-home guy the Prophet was. There was a painting of the spires of the Salt Lake temple. And there was the Hoffmann Jesus.

Two genealogical charts flanked a large desk. Helen rose to study them. One outlined the descent of Elder Costain's Melchezedek Priesthood from his father, his father's father, back through to Joseph Smith himself, who received it from the ancient apostles Peter, James and John who, of course, received it directly from Jesus Christ. She tended to disbelieve those who claimed the blood of Jesus in their veins as well as his priesthood oiling their heads.

The finely calligraphied family tree on the other side of the desk depicted the more conventional sort of descent, and included women. Ten generations were here portrayed, which was all the paper had room for. Helen herself could go back to the eleventh-century Domesday Book on some of her lines. Yes, it looked like she and Brother Costain shared an ancestor or two in the lush forest of Mormon genealogy, rooted in the thick swamp of polygamy.

Only one child teetered under Elder Costain and his wife to inherit all that heavy load of forebears. Not even a son. A single daughter, Margaret Ann. A husband had been written in for her by a different, clumsier hand. Helen paused thoughtfully over the name that had swallowed the old Costain name whole.

Straight-forward photographs rounded out the display. The requisite wedding photo on the steps of the temple in bleached-out color from the sixties. A pudgy teenaged girl: Margaret Ann. Numerous grandchildren; although they wouldn't be Costains, would they?

Odd, wasn't it, that the song in Helen's head was not in the hymn book, but a great favorite with ward choirs that aspired to Tabernacle level: "God So Loved the World"?

> God so loved the world
> That he gave His only begotten Son …
> For God sent not His Son into the world
>   to condemn the world,
> God sent not His Son into the world
>   to condemn the world,
> But that the world …

The sound of the study door swinging open, followed by a thump and a squeak, drove Helen away from the family tree and back to the needlepoint chair. She felt her cheeks flush as she looked up to meet elfin blue eyes behind thick glasses.

Elder Costain used a walker. The shrunken frailty of his body contrasted oddly with a face and neck that seemed puffy. Even his eyelids were puffy.

Helen jumped to her feet again and ran to hold the door.

"Brother Costain ... Elder Costain. I'm ... I'm so sorry to hear you're ill." She realized this was probably the only reason she'd been able to reach him on a Monday morning.

"It happens to us all. It is God's plan of salvation."

"I'm sorry to bother you. I really ..." No. She had to stay and do this. For Ginn.

"No, dear Sister. A man, even at my stage, likes to be of some use."

As he moved slowly toward the deep leather chair behind the desk, he said, "Do you know how I got this disease?"

It was obviously front and center in his mind. Well, why wouldn't it be? And people would always look for reasons, things they should have done better, or things they should have left undone, things that had consequences.

Sin.

"I'm sure"—*Wizzy*—"God loves you," she said sympathetically.

"Indeed He does, and blesses me every day." Elder Costain swallowed with the effort of negotiating the corner. "You know, I worked in church printing for several years, before and after my mission to England. Before I went into business for myself."

England had been—was still—a plum assignment, reserved for the sons of the wealthy and the general authorities. No one who'd been so called would miss a chance to drop that in conversation.

"I was proud to spread the Gospel through the printed word," Elder Costain continued. "I am still proud that God chose to use me that way. There were, however, chemicals used in the process that ... well, many who worked there got leukemia."

Oh yes. Helen remembered the scandal. Those chemicals had been outlawed by the FDA years before the church got around to weeding them out, only to ship them to a corroded landfill where they bubbled up, causing another scandal. What did that say about prophecy as interpreted by corporations? And the treatments for leukemia could cause infertility. One daughter.

"Over the years, from my position in stake leadership, I was asked to speak at many of their funerals."

Elder Costain choked on the word "funeral". But he had also fallen hard into his seat on that word, so maybe it was just coincidence. People at the end of their lives liked to justify those lives to anyone who'd listen. Unfortunately for them, few would stop to listen. Helen had always listened before. Just listened. That's all she thought she could do, with her issues with words.

But she did have a deadline of five o'clock today. She opened her mouth, "Sir—"

Elder Costain, still panting, beat her to it. "Now. How may I be of service?"

She almost heard the descriptive "Christ-like" in front of that final noun.

"I'm Helen Snow. I called you a little while ago concerning a family—"

"Oh, yes. The single mother." His voice seemed to have lost some of the compassion she had heard over the phone.

"Not me. A woman under my care."

"Of course."

"Yes. As I started to tell you before my phone ... well, I'm afraid its charge ran out."

"A Relief Society president should always see that her phone is charged."

"I understand that ... now. This is only my second day on the job."

"Your sister—you said she married a Bingham, yes? Your sister would know about phones."

"Yes, well, my sister is in Anaheim, and all you've got here is me. Ginn ... Virginia Allred and her three children will be cast out into the snow this very evening and have no home for Christmas..." *you old Scrooge* "if we don't ..."

"Allred. That's a good Mormon name. Is she connected to the Iron County Allreds?"

"I don't know about the Iron County Allreds. All I know is—"

"I'm sorry these trials have come. We all must learn to obey and endure to the end. A blight to your ward at this season of the year."

"Yes, I'd like to say that those apartments are a blight, and if I knew who the landlord was—"

"Sister Snow, I'm a landlord myself, and I know the headaches involved."

*I don't suppose you got this home, this perfect life of yours, renting out the likes of accommodations on 33rd South. But a young man did die over the weekend in your hot tub, Mr. Pine Enterprises. Was that negligent maintenance on an upper-crust scale?*

"Did you preach self-reliance and obedience to this sister?" Elder Costain was preaching. The

General-Conference voice threatened to put Helen to sleep. She had been out late last night. Dancing ... well, watching the dancing ... at—well, next to—a bar.

"She could use a copy of *Mormon Doctrine*. I always keep an extra copy ..."

He struggled to reach up to the shelf behind him. Once it might have been within easy grasp. Not now. Helen didn't get up to help him.

"Elder Costain, I don't know what 'sins' she may have committed to find herself in this situation, but I will not throw the first stone. Or the hundred-and-fiftieth stone, since it seems she's already had plenty lobbed at her."

"Are you confessing to sin, Sister Snow?"

Helen opened her mouth, then shut it again. Speechless.

Elder Costain stopped trying to reach. "The thing is, there are so many of these cases. You prop them up, and they fall over this way. You prop them here, they fall that way. The woman has sinned and she will no doubt sin again."

"No doubt," Helen whispered.

"Sometimes we need hard love to teach us life's lessons. We in the church abhor communism."

*Although the United Order was preached in those twenty-six volumes of discourses behind you.*

"There is a reason God caused the Berlin Wall to fall for its sins."

*And the fittest to remain standing. In 'Zion in the Rockies'. Faith-based Darwinism.*

Taking a deep breath, Helen stopped looking down at her hands under the blows of his sermon. She looked him in the eye. "Elder Costain, this is a single mother and her children, and if you think as Relief Society president, as a human being, I'm going to sit by and—"

His eyes, she suddenly saw, were full of tears magnified by the thick lenses. They slid down his puffed face.

"A single mother," he repeated. The compassion had returned—like a flood.

A miracle.

"A-llelujah, A-llelujah," sang Wizzy at the top of her little lungs. The squinty little eyes blinked down from the Hoffmann Jesus.

"I'm so sorry, Elder Costain." The guilt of having brought a man to tears overwhelmed her. "I didn't realize until I got here that you are so ill, and I ... I should have gone to someone else."

"It's not the leukemia. It's not the three months the doctors have given me to live. I've lived a good life. Or maybe I should say, life's been good to me. It's time for me to go. It's just that ... a ... a death... a death ... close to me."

"I am so sorry."

"My son ... my only son."

*O Absalom, would God I had died for thee.* King David lamenting his first-born son, punishment for his sin.

Although Mormons didn't do this, especially not to high councilmen, Helen put her arm around the bony shoulders. She felt the shudder.

Elder Costain grew rigid. Like Mark, he did not know how to take comfort.

She couldn't help but look around the room again. There was no picture of a young man, not on the family tree, not anywhere. Only the girl, Margaret Ann.

"I was punished. I wasn't allowed to raise him. And now ... now he dies before me."

A strange sense of déjà vu came over her. That voice... the Hoffman Jesus... the fog of mood enhancers that blurred one's perceptions .... *Oh.*

From this position instead of in her chair, Helen could see through the panes of glass to the rest of the high councilman's home. A trim woman of between seventy and eighty years, with what Karen used to call "the Relief Society Special" bluish-grey from the hair salon, had just entered the home. Sister Janet Costain.

But Sister Costain definitely did not look like a woman who had just lost her only son, nor like one with a husband with three months to live. She entered with bags from a shopping trip to the best City Creek shops. The housemaid took them off her hands. The women spoke to each other.

Helen, belatedly, removed her arm from the old man's shoulders. It would never do for Sister Costain to look through the glass door in the study and see ....

Elder Costain could not claim this grief before his eternal companion. Did Janet Costain even know?

But before she moved away she had felt Elder Costain beginning to try to pull himself together. He pulled out a check book. That always focused a man's thoughts.

"Well, let's see that Family Needs form," he choked.

Helen had forgotten the form. She hadn't filled it out. She had, in fact, forgotten her bag altogether.

She was driving without a license. Her palms grew sweaty.

Elder Costain wrote out and signed a check for twenty-two hundred dollars, leaving the payee blank for the landlord's name.

Helen took it, pressed his hand and said, "You are in my prayers during the time of your sorrow."

She did not say, as Elder Costain had said when she'd sat in his office once before, long ago, infant Wizzy on her lap, "You must have sinned, or she must have, in the Pre-Existence." Although it did look pretty obvious that Bishop Costain *had* sinned. His sin had been active, even as she'd sat there and he'd said that, but under wraps. Back then he'd been writing checks for another single mother, the mother of his son he could never acknowledge.

The importance of the begats, that most boring section of Genesis, became clear to Helen.

"As man is, God once was. As God is, man may become." There was a aphorism from *Mormon Doctrine* that Mormons didn't use much anymore. Is this what makes us God-like? That we must lose our children?

*O my son.*

Only this time, the *son's* name was David, not the father's. That death had been the punishment for taking sloe-eyed Bathsheba. Had she been bathing on the roof? Or simply cleaning the tubs?

"You are in my prayers, Elder Costain," Helen said. "Don't bother to get up."

*Neither do I condemn thee.*

Wizzy wouldn't have.

*****

"Of course you must go to your nephew's funeral tomorrow, Consuela," Sister Costain was saying to the maid. "Of course you can have the time off."

Helen, passing through the living room on her way to the front door, turned and stared at the pink cleaning smock with the simple black braid down its back.

How many Consuelas in Pine Enterprises smocks could there be in the world?

# Chapter 27

Please turn in your hymnals to Number 229, "Today, While the Sun Shines".

Actually, the sun was hidden behind the inversion, although it was smiling up the canyon on Brittany where, she reported by text message, it was ten degrees warmer than it was down in the valley.

Work with a will ...
All your duties fulfill.

Ginn Allred had gotten her check to the landlord by noon.

It was time for Helen to deliver the doggie ransom note. Texts from both Brittany and Sarah Drake underscored the need. Brittany even called, just to make sure the message had gotten through.

"And there's something I want you to see, Aunt Helen."

"What's that?"

"A photograph."

"Did Simon find it in another book?"

"I found it. In the *Book of Mormon* in the

nightstand of Unit A when I made sure I didn't have to replace it—we check every Monday."

So Elder Costain had aspirations to be a Marriott. "Yes?"

"It's the same photo as the one Diana Jaramillo tossed from Dave's mantel. The one with the man and the girl with Dave on the river trip."

Helen remembered the photo. "You didn't mean Unit B, did you? *The Book of Mormon* in Unit B?"

But she already knew the answer. She wouldn't be surprised if Elder Costain had had the same photo in one of the drawers in his desk. Or maybe he'd given his daughter, his legitimate daughter, his copy. Maybe she'd said she wanted to make things right with her half-brother. Or maybe she'd just stolen it. And Elder Costain had found it missing when he'd learned of the tragedy. He'd gone looking for comfort and found ...

"No. Unit A."

Helen answered the annoyance in her niece's voice. "I believe you, dear. I think I can even explain it. But first, tell me. Do you remember the name of the mother of all those kids? When she was packing up and her daughter was sick and leaving in a hurry? Did her husband call her something?"

"No ... oh, yes. Wait ... Peggy. I think he called her Peggy. I remember because I heard 'piggy' first, and I thought that was the last name a woman with anorexia should be called."

Margaret Ann. Margaret. Peggy. The same name Helen had heard distraught Brother Vaughn scolding into the phone to his wife watching over their sick three-year-old in the hospital. Margaret Ann Costain

Vaughn. Helen had a pretty good idea now, too, what Code 5 meant on the Pine Industries accounts screen. Both Unit A and Unit B paid for by Code 5. They hadn't paid at all, the same man covering for both. The father of both tenants.

And two of the grandkids in Elder Costain's office, Helen realized, she recognized: young Brother Vaughn, the boy thumbing the World of Warcraft joystick as he told the Relief Society president he hated yams and wished she would go away, and the ten-year-old with the earbuds tangled with her earrings.

"Do you know what this means, Aunt Helen?"

"I think so, but I want to check on a few things first. I'll tell you as soon as I know for sure."

"Here's another weird thing."

"Yes?"

"Just the page that photo marked in the *Book of Mormon*. Near the front. The fourth chapter of First Nephi."

"I know it. The death of Laban. Where the Spirit tells our hero 'Slay him, for the Lord hath delivered him into thy hands. Behold the Lord slayeth the wicked to bring forth His righteous purposes. It is better that one man should perish than that a nation should dwindle in unbelief.' "

"Aunt Helen, you have it memorized. That's kind of creepy."

"Personal struggles. Your mother and I had a great-aunt, Aunt Ivy, faithful member all her life, who never read the *Book of Mormon*. She couldn't get past that verse."

"Still faithful, though."

Helen thought it interesting that the Bible had passages where God ordered whole cities wiped out, and nobody seemed to blink at that. It was this one death, this sawing off the head of drunken Laban, one person killed by one person, that seemed to give pause. The death of Laban had sent plenty into apostasy, not just Aunt Ivy.

So why had Peggy Vaughn stopped reading there? Disgusted and doubting? Or comforted? *Inspired?*

"How's Simon coming with that autobiography of James Costain, head of Pine Enterprises?" Helen asked her niece instead.

"Not so well. Put him right to sleep. But he works so hard ..."

Here Helen listened to a long adulation of her niece's beau's excellent points, to which she only had to say "Uh-huh" and "That's nice."

She listened until her phone was rejuiced before saying, "I'd better go get Taffy ransomed 'Today While the Sun Shines'."

Brittany agreed and rang off. She had three more rooms to clean in the other triplex across the way.

*****

As she approached, Helen saw the X-ray driving off in her SUV with three children's heads and a car seat visible. Gymnastic lessons she guessed. Helen would not miss this chance. She knocked on the door.

Only the oldest boy, Evan, was home. "Yeah," he said in response to her question, "the empty dish is here."

It was, spotless on the spotless marble counter. Helen saw him glance towards the disposal, and

Helen understood how the dish had been emptied so quickly. And the scrubbing? The Drake name on the bottom of the clean bowl had been scrubbed right away.

"I'm surprised," Helen attempted, "that you're not playing World of Warcraft, with everyone gone to gymnastics."

"It's ballet."

It would be ballet, with the strain towards elegance in this household. The music of *Swan Lake* sounded in Helen's head. "My sons loved World of Warcraft before their missions."

Evan wouldn't meet her eyes as he recited. "World of Warcraft doesn't meet our family's values. It makes us violent. Besides, I got homework."

Right. "It's too bad your vacation got cut short because your little sister got sick. Do you want to tell me what happened Friday evening?"

The young man looked up. He didn't ask how she knew. He was just so relieved someone of the nurturing, Relief Society brand knew, and hadn't condemned him.

Helen encouraged the hope she saw spark in those eyes. "So you were playing with your brothers and sisters around the hot tub?"

"Yeah, with Uncle Boo."

"Uncle Boo?"

"He's not really our uncle, Mom says. Dad says some sort of relation, but distant."

"He's a young man?"

"Yeah, lots of fun. He lives in the condo next to where we stayed."

*Lives.* Evan still thought his uncle was alive.

"His name is Dave. It's strange, I got the feeling Mom didn't go up there to ski at all. The vacation meant nothing to her. She went to see Dave. Don't know why. I don't like to think ..."

"I promise you, Evan, your mother was not being unfaithful to your father."

The young man blushed to the roots of his hair, but he seemed to ease a little, too. Yes, he was old enough to wonder what went on behind the facades of perfection. No wonder he liked World of Warcraft, where things were what they seemed—once you understood the magic.

"So the kids were playing with Dave Jaramillo. He was in the hot tub, right?"

"Yeah. Dad and Mom were arguing in the condo, and I wanted to get away, so I played, too. Just silly kid stuff. Dancing in the steam and the snow. Him hiding under the water, then jumping out and saying, 'Boo.' Trying to splash us. Stuff like that. Mom wouldn't let us get in, but we did get wet. That made her mad."

"Then what happened?"

"Well, this young lady came on the deck. She came on skis from the mountain."

"Did you know her, Evan?"

"Well, she looked like my friend Boston's big sister."

The boy pointed through his house wall to the Drakes' house. So that part of Sarah's story was true. The night visitor had not been Ben. All the more reason to get Ben out of jail now.

"Boston Drake?"

"Yeah. But I don't know her very well. Sarah, I

think her name is. She's pretty old."

All of eighteen, yes. "She came to see Dave, though, not you or your parents."

"That's right."

"What did she say to Uncle Boo?"

Evan shrugged. "Uncle Boo said, 'What are you doing here?' And then he stopped playing, got out of the tub and put on a robe. He wouldn't invite her in, even though she kept asking. He kept trying to get her to leave, which I didn't think was very nice. I heard her wail, 'But I love you' and then a lot of quiet stuff. It was so quiet, Mom noticed. She stopped her fighting with Dad, 'cause I bet she didn't want us to hear. She came and said it was time for us all to go to bed."

"And then?"

"Well, she had these bottles of kombucha ..."

"Kombarfya?"

A little smile played at the corners of the boy's mouth. "Yeah."

"None of us were going to drink it, but she had one bottle already opened and she told me to take it out to Dave, that he would like it."

"And did you?"

"Yeah."

"Was Sarah—the girl who looked like Sarah—was she still there?"

"She was just skiing off again. I think she was crying. I think Dave was glad to see her go."

"You gave Dave the kombucha?"

"Yes."

"Did he seem to like it?"

"He said, 'Thanks,' but then he asked if I liked to

play World of Warcraft."

"And you said ...?"

"I said yes, only Mom didn't like it much. He seemed to think anything my mom didn't like was okay by him."

"Including kombucha."

"Including kombucha. Only he didn't drink it. He was having a hot chocolate instead."

"I bet it was cold with all that snow."

"Yeah. Anyway, Dave said how he'd like it if I'd teach him something about the game. I said Mom wouldn't let me use the condo TV. And then he said he had this TV—only it was kind of weird. He didn't have it in his condo—and Mom didn't want us going in his condo anyway—He had this TV—"

"In the closet there on the hot tub deck."

"Yeah, right there. So we got the TV down and set it up on this bench. You know, from the deck. With slats and holes in it so water and snow won't settle. It was kinda wobbly."

"Right," Helen said.

"So I went and got the game box I'd smuggled in in my suitcase, and we played. Dave wasn't very good. He couldn't get over my Pyroclast Barrage." Evan's voice was tinged with the condescension the competent feel toward the clueless.

Helen nodded as if she, too, wondered how anyone could play in such a state of ignorance.

"We played until ..."

"Until?"

"Until the other kids were asleep and Mom came looking for me. She went ballistic when she saw what we were doing." Evan hung his head.

"Does she do that often?" Helen asked.

"What?"

"Go ballistic? Your mother seems like such a controlled woman." *She can touch her nose to her knee. She passed over the ward-gathering punch and cookies until she made herself an x-ray.*

"Compared to what?"

Yes, compared to what? What did a boy know of the levels of explosions in other houses? Only the happy, smiling faces in church on Sunday.

"I could tell she wanted to hit me. She wanted to hit Dave. I just grabbed my game box and ran."

"Back into the condo?"

"Yeah."

"Did you hear or see anything else after that?"

"Mom stayed out there. She talked to Dave a long time, very quiet, so I couldn't hear. But I knew she was really, really mad. I'm ... I'm sorry I made her so mad."

"Maybe she wasn't so mad at you. Maybe she was madder at Dave."

"But he wasn't even a very good player."

"Maybe it didn't have anything to do with World of Warcraft."

Evan took a hopeful glance at the big screen TV in the family room, then at the kitchen clock, trying to gauge how much time he had before ballet class was over. "She doesn't know him very well, I don't think."

"Long enough to talk a long time, that night."

"Yeah. I was almost asleep."

"When what?"

"There was this fizzle and a pop and the power went out."

"What then?"

"Dad came into the room I was sharing with my brothers and said I should come with him into the garage to flip the circuit. I heard Mom crying in their room."

"Not out on the deck still?"

"No. In the room."

"And?"

"And Dad and I went down with a flashlight to flip the switch. Then he went out on the deck."

"What did he do there?"

"I don't know. He was gone quite a long time, and I did fall asleep. I thought I heard him actually going into Dave's condo."

To put away the wet, blown out television, Helen thought.

"I heard Dad shoveling snow," Evan continued. "A lot of snow, out on the deck."

To get rid of his wife's tracks.

"Then I really did fall asleep, although hearing my mom cry made it kinda hard. And in the morning I saw the kombucha bottle on the coffee table in our condo, so I guess he brought that in, too."

"Did it look like Dave had drunk any?"

"Not much, if any. My little sister Gretel drank most of it, though how she could stand the taste, I don't know. She gets up early, wandering around like she does. Hungry. Only Mom was up early, too, and trying to get us ready to leave. 'Nobody out on the deck,' she kept saying. We had to pack as fast as we could. We weren't very fast, 'cause we'd thought we were going to stay another day and hadn't done any packing the night before."

"So the decision to leave in a hurry came before Gretel got sick, not after."

Evan thought about this for a while. "Yeah. I guess that's right. While Mom and Dad were busy with the packing, they weren't watching too closely and Gretel drank the kombucha. And then she got sick. And then we really had to hurry."

"I'm glad your little sister is going to be okay."

"Yeah, me too."

"You're a great big brother, to protect her as well as you do. And it's very grown up of you to do your homework first and take care of your chores or scout responsibilities before you get to play your video game. You're a fine young man, Evan."

He blushed and scuffed the spotless tile kitchen floor. He even scrubbed at one eye that was offending him with tears.

"Thanks for the clean casserole dish. And I will support you with my prayers."

# Chapter 28

The exterior decorator and his crew were just piling into their van to hurry on to the next job. The Drake yard was drenched with fairy lights as if trying to compete with Temple Square. On the surface, then, all was ready for the Christmas season in the Drake household. The media, however, were still vulturing in their vans.

Helen waved the casserole dish at people with microphones and cameras and ran the gauntlet to gain entrance.

"The Vaughns said they enjoyed it very much," she lied to Eve Drake.

"And Taffy?" Eve demanded, taking the empty dish.

"I'm afraid I have some very bad news."

"Bad news? What? What's happened to Taffy?"

"I think I'd better say this directly to Sarah. Is she available?"

When she came downstairs, her niece's friend was wearing Christmas-themed sweats.

"Will you please leave us alone for just a minute, Sister Drake?" Helen asked. She didn't know if her relationship with Eve Drake would survive the affront of sharing secrets with her daughter; clearly, Eve had no intention of leaving the two alone. But Eve Drake was not in Helen's Relief Society, and Helen's conscience wouldn't survive Gentle Ben Ursule spending one more night in jail, despite warm cells and square meals. She stood her ground adamantly.

When they were finally alone, Helen pulled the note out of her handbag and passed it silently to Sarah.

Sarah was not silent. She gasped at the sight of the patched message and burst into tears.

Helen hoped that Eve wouldn't hear and rush in. "Sarah," she said gently, "are you ready to let your mother know the truth?

"This isn't about me! Poor kidnapped Taffy! I will get these people! Who—?"

"Think about what your parents must have felt when they learned *you* were kidnapped—you, their daughter, not just their dog."

"But I couldn't just tell them ..."

"That you skied into Ben's cave on your own? And then down to Dave's condo?"

"I couldn't." Sarah's voice had gone down to a choked whisper. "I *can't*. I mean, look at this place. How can my mother have the kind of perfect Christmas she wants if she knows she has a daughter who ...?"

They were sitting under that amazing two-story high tree with not one bulb blinking out of sync. Helen felt the weight of it, the perfection this girl had to live up to.

"A daughter who makes mistakes but takes

responsibility for them? Who doesn't put innocent men, men who were kind to her, in jail? Aren't the media trucks on your doorstep a bad enough blotch on your holiday? You can't go in or out without passing them, reminding you."

"I haven't left the house since I got home. The cabin fever I've got, just knowing that there's all that snow that I haven't skied on yet, is driving me crazy!"

"Yes, you can't live the rest of your life like this."

"Oh, Taffy." Sarah fanned herself helplessly with the ransom note. "But if I tell the truth, I'll be in such trouble."

"Certainly more trouble than if you'd just told the truth from the beginning. Giving a false report of kidnapping is a five-year jail sentence." Helen had looked it up.

"Five? I'll be twenty-three!" Sarah wailed.

That did sound like the end of the world. "And how will your parents enjoy Christmas then?"

"What returned missionary will have me then?" She sniffled, but then stuck out her chin defiantly. "I won't throw Taffy under the bus, I won't abandon her. I've got to go to the police and show them this." Sarah waved the note frantically.

Under a bus sounded like just the right place for the dog. Helen didn't say so, however. "I'm not sure the police will go chasing after dog-nappers when they have a case to make against a man accused of holding a young woman hostage and raping her. It's a very grown-up decision you have to make."

Helen herself was feeling the struggle. They never became easy, did they? It was her having told too much that had put Sarah in the spot where she'd felt she had to concoct her lie, which put an innocent man in jail. Helen herself could tell what she now knew, but with what consequences? In spite of all the harm that had flowed from that call to Sarah's parents, she still was certain that parents had a right to know what their children had done and run the risk of judging their children too harshly. God the Father was always supposed to know what we had done ... and to love us still.

More often, it seemed God didn't love us; He either didn't care, or He was the stern Judge of the Old Testament, raining plagues and war down upon the innocent than and those who deserved it alike.

Wizzy caused no harm and simply loved.

Wizzy was unnaturally silent at this moment.

No, it was better if Sarah made this call.

Helen watched and agonized with her young friend.

Until the doorbell rang.

Eve Drake knocked on the living room door. Helen handed Sarah a tissue from her bag so she could mop away her tears and be suitable for parental presentation before she called out, "Yes?"

Eve opened the door. "It's the police again."

"Sheriff," Deputy Moody corrected as she strode into the room.

She turned back to Eve. "Excuse me, Mrs. Drake. I'd like to talk to your daughter alone."

"I think that's against the law," Eve Drake replied, although clearly intimidated by the hardware draped like Christmas decorations around the deputy's hips.

"Sister Snow will be with her," Deputy Moody promised.

"What? Why Helen Snow and not her own mother?"

"Just for a moment."

Helen had been half on her feet. She looked back at Sarah and saw that she, with some hesitation, had stuffed the ransom note under her seat. Sarah nodded. Helen sat back down and took the girl's hand. It was not refused.

Hurt and confused, Sarah's mother hovered in the doorway.

"It will be all right, Eve," Helen promised, and was relieved when Eve left the room. Oh dear, another lie.

"Deputy Moody, won't you sit down?" Helen went on to say next. It wasn't her home. With that perfect tree and those perfect cavorting elves, it was nothing like her home. Still, someone had to do the honors, and Sarah wasn't saying anything, only shifting uneasily in her Christmas sweats, sitting on top of the letters cut from her own glossy magazines.

She hoped her lower standards would help her children, like allowing human immune systems to fight off bugs in their own God-given way, which might have saved Wizzy, who probably wasn't meant to be saved, but to do the saving.

Deputy Moody, it seemed, would rather stand. She pulled a piece of paper from a well-worn leather case and waved in her hand. "The rape kit results," she announced, "have come back."

For a long moment nobody said anything. Helen felt she had to speak up. "That ... that was fast. I thought ... I thought there was a backlog. Didn't you think there was a backlog, Sarah?"

Sarah looked down at her clenched hands. She felt

miserable. She had never thought, even while taking the test, that this reckoning would really come.

She was so very, very young.

She would be older by the end of the day.

"The test is negative," said the deputy. "According to the examiner, you are even, Miss Drake, still a virgin."

"Well." Helen tried for the wide-eyed Relief Society stare of "It's a Small World" dolls, even though doing it made the flesh creep down her back. "That is good news, Sarah, isn't it?"

It was a stupid thing to say. Oh, where was Wizzy when her mother needed her?

"Filing a false kidnapping report is a felony offense, Miss Drake."

Once again, Helen felt the weight of having to fill the silence. She opened her mouth, but—

"I know," Sarah said. "Sister Snow was just telling me. Five years." The girl swallowed then squeaked. "It's true. I did lie."

A slight smile twitched Deputy Moody's usually stern mouth. She exchanged a glance with Helen and then took a seat.

"This," she said, producing another paper from her file, "is your statement. Do you want to read it over?"

"No! No!" Sarah snatched for it.

Deputy Moody pulled it away.

Sarah groaned in misery.

Deputy Moody slowly tore the paper. "I am willing to do this," she said, making another tear. "If you will make a statement to the press—I see they're out there waiting—exonerating Mr. Ursule."

Helen made a show of consulting her cell phone.

"And this ..." Helen reached under the young woman's seat and withdrew the ransom note. "I'll tear up."

"Taffy?" Sarah asked, her voice trembling between fear and hope.

Helen tore. "Is safe and sound with Brittany. I just got a text."

Another lie. She'd put her phone on mute before entering the Drake home.

Helen and the deputy tore in unison until confetti added to the perfect Christmas décor.

# Chapter 29

"Just some paperwork to go over," Deputy Moody told Helen as they stood on the Drake's perfectly shoveled sidewalk. "Gentle Ben should be free to return to his cave this evening."

"He might need a casserole," Helen mused, and felt guilty that she didn't know how she could manage to bring one up to him. "I wonder if he likes yams. I wonder where I'd get venison."

"It looks like he will own his cave on the mountain."

"Dave's handwritten will."

The deputy, hands on her hips, stared at Helen. "Exactly." She applied lipgloss, then said, "As it was, it barely qualified as a legal document. Anyone with a counter interest could have challenged it and had a strong chance of overturning it. But once we had the original, the next of kin was contacted." She gave Helen a measuring look. "A legally binding version was composed with remarkable swiftness, I was informed." Another look. "You seem to know an awful lot about this whole business."

Helen shrugged. "I'm a—"

"I know. You're a... "

Together they said, "Relief Society president."

They smiled, but didn't laugh.

"You know," Helen spoke slowly, looking down the street at the Vaughn home, "about this David Jaramillo business ..."

"What else are you going to tell me? That the funeral is tomorrow?"

"On Redwood Road, yes."

"Oh. So you know that, too?"

"Yes. I thought I'd go."

"You'll see me there. I have to go. Part of my job."

"I'd pay attention to who's not there. I'd look at the folks in 3408 down the road there."

"What do they have to do with Jaramillo's death? Don't tell me you think it was murder?"

Helen hated to tell. She'd seen what happened when she had told Sarah's parents against her niece's better judgment, and Wizzy's.

"No, I think it was an accident." But was that a lie? She didn't know for sure. "I am sure there was a lot of anger there. A lot of anger going back a lot of years. Anger in a young woman who couldn't be perfect enough because she was a girl instead of a boy. Because her mother wasn't the love of her father's life, yet they all had to keep up appearances, for his life, for her marriage prospects, for her children. Anger that made her change from a pudgy teenager to an anorexic woman addicted to mood enhancers and running. Besides, the old man is on his death bed. He shouldn't have to lose a daughter, too, to prison, after he's lost his son to death. And those kids shouldn't lose their mother, either. It's all very sad."

"It sounds that way, but I'm not sure I follow you."

"Well, look at the folks in 3408, if you ever get curious. They were the folks in Unit A."

Deputy Moody stared, first at the McMansion Helen pointed at, then at Helen herself.

"Maybe I'll see you at the funeral," Helen said, turning to go. "A Relief Society president has to go to a lot of funerals, even Catholic ones. And I like funerals better than weddings. Weddings are so hopeful. They don't need me. Funerals, on the other hand, have the whole story, or as much of the story as there will be. You can learn lessons at a funeral, whereas a wedding—well, there all the hard lessons are yet to learn."

"Sheriffs don't often go to weddings," Deputy Moody had to agree. "And ... and thanks, Sister Snow."

"Not at all."

*****

Brittany's text said she was already on her way down the canyon with Simon and the ransomed Taffy.

"I'll make you dinner," Helen texted back.

She put four yams in the oven to warm up the old kitchen, a thing she hadn't done since October, when the boys had left on their mission. She breaded a microwave-defrosted chicken and set it to join the yams. She checked to see that she had frozen peas, pre-washed lettuce and a selection of salad dressing. Sarah Lee and sliced strawberries would have to do for dessert.

A Relief Society president was a provident housekeeper.

Then, just before turning to her phone—plugged in

so as not to repeat that morning's expiration—to see what the next emergency of her calling might be, she pulled a shoe box of photos off the bottom-most living room book shelf, the box that enclosed Wizzy's short life. The pictures of Helen, very large, on her way to the hospital, the first birth picture of the scrunched, red little face. Of "Blessing Day", the same day that that long-ago bishop had said they should put her away. Wizzy leaning against the piano. She smiled at the photo held in her hand. Yes, she'd make a scrapbook, maybe decorate the cover with one of the few remaining treasured pictures made by Wizzy herself. It would be practice for the one she'd make for Mark of the boys. Mark had loved photography all his life, the pictures he'd taken deserved better than old shoe boxes.

And Helen's favorite ... wait, where was her favorite? The one taken shortly before the little girl got sick. Wizzy's wonderful smile and the pink bow in her wispy hair? Where ...?

There was only one answer. Mark must have taken it. He knew it was her favorite. He wanted her to forget about their daughter. He—

But the front door was opening. Brittany knew she always had a right to enter.

"Taffy's delivered," she called. "Sarah said she wouldn't go to Dave's funeral tomorrow morning, and I can't. I have to work."

"I'll be going to his funeral tomorrow," Helen replied. "Relief Society presidents go to lots of funerals."

"Mom never did," Brittany said. "Especially not Catholic ones. She hates funerals. She always sent one of her counselors."

Helen wondered about the differences in families, the differences in belief, all within the same church. "Well, I guess I'm a different sort of Relief Society president," she concluded.

*****

"How about we go to Temple Square to see the lights?" Mark suggested, as they finished the strawberry shortcake. "Monday night, Family Home Evening. Show our English visitor some of the sights."

Helen had forgotten what her husband's voice sounded like, at least in such a mode. With a plan. Excited. They hadn't done Family Home Evening since the twins had left on their missions.

"I have to work tomorrow," Simon and Brittany said together.

"We'll take the train and go fast," Helen said. "We won't have to fuss with parking."

They did. Simon and Brittany were young and walked arm and arm, mingling frosted breath. The sight wrenched Helen to the heart.

Old, naked trees rendered brilliant by a million tiny lights. A Disneyland of sights and sounds. Recorded MoTab songs: "O little Town of Bethlehem" and "O Come, All Ye Faithful", to which Wizzy hummed along. On many lawns were poised the seasonal white life-sized figures of wise men and shepherds in search of the nativity trio.

Mark took Simon to himself for a little stretch, as he had always done with the twins, leaving Helen standing among the frozen fireworks alone. "Guy talk", he liked to say.

Simon was a good sport.

"I always think ..."

Brittany was at Helen's side. This time she wasn't alone.

The girl continued to stare at the pair, past the manger between them. Surely she wasn't thinking of ... herself and Simon? Had things progressed so far?

"I mean, a birth," the girl went on. "Any birth, and this birth is the epitome of them all. 'This time,' we always think. 'This time we will get it right.'"

This time it will be a boy. Or, this time it will be a girl. Or this time it will not have a handicap. Or this time I will never yell at him or her. Everyone has a "this time", every time.

"I'm thinking of giving up my lease in Park City," Brittany went on, thinking aloud, "and starting school again next semester. Biology. And I was wondering ...?"

"If you could stay with us? Of course you can, baby."

They embraced, then Helen asked, worried, "What about Simon?"

Brittany looked down and Helen caught her arm as they walked on through the crowd, so full of happy children, each of which, at one moment, had been "right this time".

"If it's right this time, it'll work out."

Helen nodded. "If you're going to study Biology, I hope you don't leave that house on Main Street without gathering samples."

*****

Helen dressed for David Jaramillo's funeral to the tune of Number 85: "How Firm a Foundation, Ye Saints of the Lord", which required two organists and all stops open in the MoTab version. She usually only thought of this one when it was time to think about new bras.

This time, Wizzy sent her mind farther into the verses: "What more can he say than to you he has said?" It was actually in the pre-1985 version, before the ever-careful Brethren had nipped the fun part in the bud: "You who unto Jesus for refuge have fled" repeated over and over so it became "Yoo-hoo, Jesus ... Yoo-hoo", louder with each repetition. "Yoo-hoo, Jesus."

She hoped she didn't look too Mormon, but that was going to be hard to pull off. Once she started into her go-to-church wardrobe, there weren't many options.

St. Joseph the Worker was a round, modern, cement construction. The small, aging priest attempted words of comfort in Spanish with an Irish accent. Helen thought about how it would be to have a calling in a church where you never had children, always lived alone, where you only thought of God and your flock. Then she thought of her Relief Society sisters.

She recognized Deputy Moody across the diameter of the church. Out of uniform, she seemed more presentable: curvaceous, not as awkward as regulation garb and gear made her. They nodded at each other, but didn't speak.

The congregation prayed. "... hallowed be Your

name." You could tell the Mormons, the few. They said "Thy name".

Afterwards, as the crowd mingled, she overheard the priest say, "Sure and I'd rather have ten funerals than one wedding. The mass tells us what to do, gives us comfort. The deceased doesn't care; he is God's. Weddings—you've got the mother-in-law. You've got the mother of the bride. You've got the bride. You've got her attendants—and you wonder why I've gone bald, with all these years of tearing my hair out by the roots."

Helen found her way to the grieving mother, the dark, water-filled Madonna eyes, the black veil. "I am so sorry for your loss, Ms. Jaramillo," she said, taking both of the woman's hands in hers. She had wanted to say "Sister Jaramillo", but resisted. "I, too, lost a child." Form dictated that she say "You'll get over it," but Helen knew better. Instead she said, "David will be with you, every day. For the rest of your life. I will pray for you. Please pray for me."

They both cried, holding hands, and no one told them not to. Helen knew the woman was wondering where they knew each other from, but Helen couldn't bring herself to say more.

Instead, Diana Jaramillo turned to the woman beside her, not wearing a pink smock today. "This is my sister-in-law, Rosa."

Only it wasn't Rosa. It was Consuela—but of course, Consuela would be a name she assumed to take a job, with her undocumented status.

Diana Jaramillo continued, "Rosa and her son Cesar. He's in college at SCU. He and David were friends, very close."

Helen moved on to shake those hands. She did not say, "I'm so glad to see you're out of jail." Ms. Jaramillo, in time, might turn the love she'd had for her lost son to this young man, as Helen had turned to Brittany.

Then Helen went out and breathed the stale valley air. She thought about the Catholics and their original sin. "We believe that men shall be punished for their own sins and not for Adam's transgression," said one of the thirteen Mormon Articles of Faith. But the innocent suffered all the time, for no reason. Maybe the Catholics had a point.

The air was surprisingly warm, a southern wind blowing. Melting snow was sending rivulets across the parking lot. Another storm was heading their way. Thank God; it would clean out the smog.

*Maybe this time we'll get it right.*

*But not until I drive home in my polluting car,* Helen thought.

*****

Elder Costain arranged for Ginn Allred and her children to move into the condo vacated upon his son's death and live there rent-free.

*He's going to have to redo that place after they move out,* Helen thought. *And I hope that hot tub doesn't claim another young life anytime soon.*

Ginn was thrilled. "It's the nicest place I've ever lived," she said.

And there was The Happy Miner nearby; Helen told her about that, and that they employed live bands.

Tears sprang again to Ginn's eyes as she gave her

soon-to-be-ex Relief Society president a hug. "I hear they tip real well in Summit County."

The question of how she'd get there, or even to the grocery store, without a car had not yet been addressed. But it was Christmas. Maybe this time Ginn Allred would get it right. Miracles happen.

*****

On Christmas Day, after the brief calls allowed from each of the twins by their mission presidents, and with Simon and Brittany expected for dinner, Helen and Mark sat opposite one another, going through the outward forms of a temple marriage exchange of gifts.

Mark offered her a flopping package—something cloth—wrapped inexpertly in a scrap of last year's paper.

Helen knew Relief Society presidents who would counsel against allowing such gifts under one's tree. They would detract from the perfection that one wanted to present for the holidays: a perfect presentation to represent the "reason for the season", the birth of the only perfect man.

But what would Mark think of her gift, imperfect as it was? For three nights she'd stayed up late, selecting photos of their children—all three, not just the twins—arranging them, remembering, and fixing them in a handsome new scrapbook, its cover the same color as *The Book of Mormon*. She'd chosen all his favorites: fishing trips with the boys, ceremonies, barbecues, graduation. Under most of the photos she had written down the date, or the place, or the event they commemorated. More than once she'd had to wipe off a tear that had fallen before it warped an image.

Helen pressed her eyes for strength. How much was this going to hurt? After eighteen years of neglect, how could it not hurt?

She slipped her fingers between paper and tape and freed a pink cotton knit. A T-shirt. She tried to steal her face to say "thanks". This, after all the jewelry and trips to Paris she'd overheard the rest of the priesthood had in mind for their wives. After eighteen years of unspeakable pain.

She picked the garment up by its shoulders—sleeves plenty long to cover the temple garments, she noticed—and a piece of paper tumbled out. A photo. It was the missing photo of Wizzy: squinty eyes made squintier by her lop-sided, gappy, baby-toothed smile, the wispy blonde hair caught in a pink bow on the top of her head.

As the T-shirt, in exactly Helen's new, larger size, unfurled, she saw that the same photo had been custom printed on the front. She gasped.

Mark spoke awkwardly. "You said you felt like you went into a phone booth and changed ..."

In a darker pink, a large capital W floated over the picture.

"I don't know when I'd wear it," Helen said. "I can't wear it to Relief Society."

"I thought—maybe—when you solve mysteries."

Helen nodded. Mark reached over and laid his hand over hers where it rested on the pink cotton.

"Our Wizzy." He gave her hand a squeeze.

"It's perfect," said Helen, through her tears. "Merry Christmas, Lorenzo Mark Snow."

It was his name; he was stuck with it. Might as well make the best of it.

"And Happy New Year."

*This time, we'll get it right.*

# THE END

# About the Author

Photo by Kathleen Dougherty

## Ann Chamberlin

Born and raised in Salt Lake City of Mormon polygamist pioneer stock, Ann Chamberlin has ancestors who preceded Brigham Young into the Valley to dig the irrigation ditches. Her mother still lives in the house her great-grandmother bought as two rooms of adobe when she was widowed with thirteen children. On the other hand, Ann's grandfather was forced out of Brigham Young University in 1911 for teaching evolution. There is some tension here.

Ann Chamberlin is the author of twenty books, including

international bestsellers set in the Ottoman Empire of the Middle East, where she can deal with patriarchs and prophets with more impunity. Her plays have been produced in venues from New York, NY to Bogota, Colombia. JIHAD won *The Off-Off Broadway Review's* award for best new play of the year in 1996.

*The Book of Wizzy* is her first contemporary murder mystery.

# If You Enjoyed This Book,

## Please Visit

PENMORE PRESS
www.penmorepress.com

All Penmore Press books are available directly through our website, amazon.com, Barnes and Noble and Nook, Sony Reader, Apple iTunes, Kobo books and via leading bookshops across the United States, Canada, the UK, Australia and Europe.

www.penmorepress.com

# THE MAN IN THE SPIDER WEB COAT
## BY
## PHILIP ACKMAN

Titus Buchanan, a professor who runs a think tank at Williams College, believes he's figured out how to stage a successful revolution. When the United Nations adopts a historic vote spelling the end of colonialism, Buchanan seizes the opportunity to test his theory. His laboratory will be the Splendid Islands, a collection of palm-fringed cays scattered across three quarters of a million square miles of the South Pacific. Its inhabitants will be his lab rats.

But complications arise. The Splendids belong to New Zealand, and New Zealand has no intention of giving them up. The United States has its own secret "space age" agenda for the islands. The Queen of England is bound to support New Zealand, but she doesn't want Britain to fall out with the Americans, who favor independence. Meanwhile, the islanders, gripped with revolutionary fever, have ideas about self-rule. Reverend Geoffrey Brown, originally recruited by Buchanan to run the revolution, joins forces with an unlikely crew of locals and sets out to match wits with powerful opponents.

PENMORE PRESS
www.penmorepress.com

# JAKE FOR MAYOR
### BY

# LOU AGUILAR

Ken Miller is having a bad run of luck. After torpedoing his career as a campaign manager, he drives through tiny Erie, Colorado, when a homeless beagle named Jake causes a series of mishaps that lands him in jail. Ken is granted bail on two conditions: that he not leave town before his trial in three weeks and—much to his chagrin—that he not let Jake out of his sight until then. Stuck in Erie as it prepares for a mayoral election, he's drawn into the local politics by a waitress who vehemently opposes incumbent Charles Dunbar, the only candidate on the ticket.

Unable to resist political adventure, Ken gets a brainstorm. If he can exploit the dog's popularity among the townspeople and get them to elect Jake as a protest candidate, the publicity will put him back on top. But things don't go exactly as planned. Ken warms to the dog, falls for the waitress, and employs her teenage son and his gang as campaign aides in a madcap battle with Mayor Dunbar ... who has no intention of losing to a dog.

PENMORE PRESS
www.penmorepress.com

# THE EMPRESS EMERALD

## BY

## JANE HARLOND

**Stolen: A child, a priceless jewel, and an identity**

Abandoned as a child in a Bombay orphanage, Leo Kazan's life takes an unanticipated turn when he becomes the protégé of Sir Lionel Pinecoffin, the city's District Political Officer in Bombay. Under Pinecoffin's tutelage, the boy, adept at learning languages and theft, is trained as a spy and becomes immersed in international espionage, revolutionary politics, and diamond smuggling. In 1918, during a visit to London, he has a brief but memorable affair with a young English woman Davina Dymond in London before leaving for Russia.

Separated, their lives take different turns. As he matures Leo begins to question his family history, seeking to uncover the truth about his parents. A pregnant Davina is married off and exiled to Spain, where she gives birth to Leo's daughter. They are fated to meet again in Gibraltar in 1936, their love rekindled. But a new war plunges Europe into crisis, the Spanish Civil War tearing them apart, leaving, Leo and Davina in a fight to reclaim their lives and their love amid the violent storms of war.

PENMORE PRESS
www.penmorepress.com

www.ingramcontent.com/pod-product-compliance
Lightning Source LLC
Chambersburg PA
CBHW070756190726
48292CB00002B/558